# Scarlett Springs

# Scarlett Springs

A NOVEL

Danielle McCrory

*To my husband, Ryan McCrory.*
*And to our son, Jackson,*
*who will be making his debut one*
*month after this book's publication.*

# Katelyn

# Chapter 1

The arrow continued its slow and steady ascent up the winding blue line, following the oncoming curves with ease. The line veered to the right, and Katelyn Chambers felt her body gently shift as the Ford Escape followed the bend in the road. She glanced up from her iPhone, her stomach tightening as momentum pulled her to the side.

Outside, a mixture of pine and aspen trees zipped past her window in a blur of green, white, and gold. Sunlight twinkled playfully between their amber leaves, and indiscernible shadows stretched out from their depths and danced across the oncoming blacktop. The Ford paid the shadows no mind, sucking them beneath its chrome bumper as if the vehicle was a voracious and insatiable vacuum.

She returned her attention to the phone's screen, using her fingers to zoom out on Google Maps so she could see more of the road ahead. "Still quite a few twists and turns coming up," she said, her eyes following the blue line that led to their destination. "This place is really in the middle of nowhere, huh?" She set the phone down in her lap, where a storm of shadows and sunlight were competing for a chance to claim the exposed skin of her thighs.

"Sure looks like it," Noah agreed. His arm was casually draped over the steering wheel, the winding road giving him no grief. He dipped his hand to the left, sending the Ford gracefully around another curve. "Travis does like to find some pretty unique places for these little excursions. Last time we got together it was this crazy bungalow on the beach. Damn place didn't even have running water." He chuckled. "We had to go out to this bamboo hut on the side of the house whenever nature called."

Katelyn groaned. "Oh God, please tell me this place has running water. And a bathroom. I'm not very good at being a nature girl." She looked out at the sea of trees surrounding the car. A few golden rays of light had managed to filter through the canopy to the forest floor below, but most of the landscape was thickly covered in shadows. *How could it be so dark in there in the middle of the day?*

Katelyn felt the first stirrings of unease tighten inside her chest as she peered into the dusky wilderness. She was trying to appear as casual and easygoing as she could muster, but the thought of squatting in the woods—a dark-even-during-the-day woods—to do her business sounded downright awful. Maybe if Noah and her had been together for longer than four months she could speak more freely, but she was still very much wanting to impress him. And to not come off as high-maintenance. *Anything but that.* Her mother had always been high-maintenance, and even though her father never spoke an ill word about it in Katelyn's presence, she often caught the glimmer of annoyance in his eyes when her mother's maintenance level was at its peak. And Katelyn did *not* want to be annoying. Not with Noah. Not ever.

Katelyn stole a glance at the man seated beside her—her not-quite-new but definitely not-longtime boyfriend, Noah Hayden. The last four months with him had been so wonderful, and despite her brain's insistence that she take things slow, she found herself more and more often imagining how months could turn into years, and how years could turn into a lifetime. Katelyn had always been something of a hopeless romantic—which unfortunately led to many broken hearts in the past—and this time she was going to try her best to not look too far into the future. Something that was becoming more and more challenging with each passing day since things with Noah had been absolutely perfect so far. The 'we have a future' kind of perfect.

A few weeks ago, Noah had timidly asked her to accompany him for a weekend getaway with his brother and sister-in-law. He assured her it would just be a fun, low-key hangout, nothing to stress out about, and when Katelyn agreed she had tried not to sound too eager. Not clingy-eager anyway—although she would have been beyond thrilled to accept his invitation whether it was low-key, high-key, or any one of the keys in the middle. This would be her first time meeting Noah's family, and Katelyn felt this trip could be a pivotal moment in their budding relationship. As long as she didn't mess it up.

Noah sent the Ford around another bend. Sunlight briefly splashed across the silver hood and then was gone again, the heavy boughs of the surrounding trees reclaiming the light for themselves. "Don't worry, I already checked," he said. "This place has all the fixings. Running water, fireplace. Hell, it even has a roof this time!"

Katelyn gaped at him, her stomach churning. *Not having a roof was a possibility?* she thought. She gnawed on her lower lip. *Don't act high-maintenance. Don't act high-maintenance.*

Noah glanced from the road to the passenger seat, and let out a hearty laugh when he saw her expression. "I'm kidding, Kate. He's never picked out a place that didn't have a roof." He reached over and squeezed her hand.

Katelyn squeezed back, grateful for the comforting effect that always accompanied Noah's touch. She didn't want to let go, but she also didn't want him driving on this crazy-ass road with only one hand, so she released her grip and gently pushed his arm back toward the steering wheel.

"Travis has never picked out a place that was utter crap," Noah went on. "He just likes to find places that are different. Unique. We only get together once or twice a year, and he wants the places we stay at to be memorable."

"And they're always Airbnbs?"

"For the most part, yeah. Hotels tend to be pretty generic, or in Travis-speak, *boring*. Airbnbs are all different, so there's a lot more potential to find something fun and interesting."

"Didn't you guys even stay on a houseboat one time?"

Noah smiled, his eyes focused on a memory instead of the road. *Focus on the road, Noah. The road. The road!* Katelyn took a deep breath. *Don't be high-maintenance. Don't be high-maintenance.*

"Yeah, we sure did," he said, oblivious to Katelyn's internal battle of maintaining an acceptable maintenance level of a four-month girlfriend. "Weather wasn't great and the damn thing ended up rocking back and forth all day and night. That was before Travis married Brooke, though. That boat was pretty small, definitely not comfortable for the likes of three people. Not for the likes of two people, actually."

Katelyn looked down at her phone. The winding blue line continued on through the mountains, its determination to reach the finish line clearly visible as the approaching bends and curves heightened in frequency and severity. A small checkered flag had appeared at the top of the screen: their destination. Google said they still had 7.8 miles to go. Hopefully she didn't vomit before then, her quease factor increasing along with the hazard level of the road.

"And this place we're going to is going to be comfortable for the likes of four people?" she asked, refocusing on the highway. Continuously looking at her phone screen was like an open invitation for car sickness, a third wheel she did not want on her first trip with Noah. Not to mention, a vomit-splattered T-shirt was not an ideal first impression for potential future in-laws.

"Yeah, Travis said this place is pretty special. Way off the grid, *obviously*. And a super cool house. Multiple levels, *and* multiple bathrooms. Lots of outdoor space. He said there's even a private park."

"Wow, that does sound pretty nice." Katelyn felt a wave of relief wash over her. Maybe this would be a fun weekend, after all. And if she did make a good first impression with Travis, maybe there would be more family introductions in the months to come. It was October now, and with the holidays only a couple months away, maybe she would get to meet Noah's parents before the year was up.

Katelyn looked out the window with newfound hope. The forest now appeared beautiful in the scant splashes of October sunshine, instead of suffocating and dark. Her lips curled into a small smile. *I wonder how long it will take for Noah to realize just what a nervous Nellie I am,* she thought with a shake of her head. Then added, *He probably already knows.*

The trees blurred together as they shot past the window, moving by too quickly for her eyes to focus on just one. The transitioning colors, highlights, and shadows were almost hypnotizing, and before long her mind began to drift, her thoughts finally settling on the coffee shop where she met Noah four blissful months ago. *Beautiful Beans* it was called. Tacky name, but good coffee. Katelyn often went there at lunch time for a caffeine fix since the stuff in the vet's office where she worked was more like liquid hell than coffee. She saw Noah there from time to time, and had assumed he worked in the area. Maybe at the university, which was only a ten minute walk away. He was tall and lean, with a captivating smile and dirty blond hair that fell across his forehead in a way that was as endearing as it was handsome.

The sixth time she saw him at *Beautiful Beans*, he finally approached her, dropping the infamous line: "You come here often?" She giggled and nodded, responding to his question with, "You use that line often?" Cheesy, but they both laughed, and the conversation that followed had been engaging and effortless. He asked for her number, and she was delighted when he texted her the very same day, asking if she would like to go to dinner. *And the rest is history,* she thought, smiling as she looked out at the lush forest.

Katelyn had always been a pretty girl—long, wavy blonde hair and a petite frame—but her shy and timid nature always seemed to scare the boys away. Guys like confidence, and that was something she was sorely lacking. The fact that someone as handsome and confident as Noah had chosen her to be his girlfriend still boggled her mind sometimes. But the months kept going by, and his interest in her only seemed to grow. Sometimes she liked to imagine what it would be like for him to tell her that he loved her, but so far those three special little words were yet to be spoken. She wondered if she was ready to say them back, and suspected that she was and she would—but only if he said them first.

The Ford continued along the highway, unabated by the steepening grade and quickening curves. They sat in comfortable silence, letting the trees roll by. Noah rolled down his window, and Katelyn followed suit, sticking her hand out and then yanking it back inside. "Yikes. Kinda chilly out there, huh?"

Noah nodded. "We've been going nothing but up for the past hour. It's a relief after all the summer heat, right? I'm definitely ready for some cooler weather."

"Me too," Katelyn agreed, although she wasn't sure if Noah's definition of *cool* was her definition of *cold*. Or *freezing*.

Katelyn may have met Noah in Boston, but she was originally from Tucson. As in Arizona. As in triple-digit, "it's a dry heat". There were more flip-flops in her closet than boots, and even though her cousin, who she moved in with back in April, kept insisting she needed to go winter clothes shopping, she still had that errand lingering on her to-do list. This would be her first winter on the east coast—her first real winter at all, actually—and she wasn't quite sure what to expect. Except that people wouldn't be sitting on their patios and sipping wine in the middle of January, like they do back at home.

"What's the weather supposed to be like again?" she asked.

"Fifties during the day, I think. And maybe upper thirties at night. Did you pack enough warm clothes?"

Katelyn looked down at her cut-off shorts. Maybe that was a mistake. She felt fine getting into the car back in Boston, but that was two states ago. And at sea level. She was going to need to readjust her mindset of what October weather felt like—more hoodies, less sandals. "Yeah, I think so," she said, although she wasn't entirely sure. "Pants, sweaters, scarves. I think I'm good."

Noah's eyes moved down her frame, stopping on her bare legs. He quirked a brow. "Okay, just making sure." He ran a finger down her exposed thigh, his touch featherlight. "As much as I adore these legs, I don't want my little desert rat getting cold."

"Desert rat? Ugh. That isn't flattering at all. If you must refer to me in that manner, I prefer desert *mouse*." Katelyn gave his arm a playful smack. "And keep your eyes on the road, mister."

"Okay, my petite squeak, you shall be a desert mouse instead."

Katelyn giggled. "Petite squeak? God, you're such a nerd." She rolled her eyes, but was unable to control the grin that was spreading across her face.

"A nerd that only has eyes for you," Noah countered.

The Ford continued on, the crisp wind cutting through the open windows and ruffling through their hair. Katelyn shivered when a particularly chilly gust swept through the vehicle, and she pressed the button on the car's door to raise the window, leaving only a few inches open. Her pants were in her suitcase, way back in the trunk. And so was her jacket. *Dumb dumb dumb. This is Vermont, not Tucson. C'mon, Katy. You need to plan better.*

Noah's words pulled her attention. "How much longer now, Kate? I feel like I've been going up this road for forever."

Katelyn looked down at her iPhone. Instead of seeing the winding blue line of the Google navigator, she saw a white screen with a spinning circle. "Oh, shoot. The map stopped working." She picked up the phone and hit the refresh button. Nothing. She hit it again. Still nothing. She looked up at the top right corner, and saw an "X" going through the bars of reception. "I think I lost the signal," she said, the worry in her voice causing her cheeks to flush. Why did she always have to sound so damn nervous all the time? What a turnoff.

"It's okay," Noah said. "Travis said that might happen. Check the glove compartment."

Katelyn glanced at Noah, her eyebrows raised, but he was busy concentrating on the road, which had started to cut left and right at a much more rapid pace. The queasiness returned to her stomach. *Almost there,* she thought. *Don't get sick now.*

Katelyn popped open the glove box and reached inside. A jumbled stack of papers was there, along with a wrench, a screwdriver, and a tire pressure gauge. "What did you sneak in here?" she asked.

"A treasure map." Noah grinned.

"A what?" Katelyn looked at him incredulously.

"A map to the house. Travis emailed it over in case we lost reception. I guess it can happen in the mountains around here."

Katelyn returned her attention to the glove compartment. "Lose reception? I didn't even know that was possible anymore," she joked, trying to mask the wave of anxiety that had just joined the queasiness in her stomach. She pulled out a recently printed piece of paper and unfolded it. It was a screenshot of Google Maps. The bold line of the winding road looked very similar to the map that had just disappeared from her iPhone screen. "I think I got it," she said.

At the bottom of the page were step-by-step directions. Katelyn scanned the list and found they were nearing the end of step four, which consisted of 18.2 winding miles on a rural state highway. Number five was to turn left onto Scarlett Springs Road. The only issue was she wasn't sure how many more miles were left until Scarlett Springs Road. Last she checked on her phone it was a little over four miles away. But now, who knows?

"We're supposed to turn left onto Scarlett Springs," she said. "It might be around two or three miles away, but I'm not sure."

"Roger that. I'll keep an eye out."

"Can't we call him? Maybe he would tell us a landmark to look out for."

"Uh…" Noah trailed off.

Katelyn watched as lines of worry etched across Noah's otherwise flawless skin. "Am I missing something?" she asked, the queasiness and anxiety in her stomach now feeding off each other, threatening to crawl up from her stomach and into her throat.

"If there's no reception, that usually means no phone calls either," he said, and gave her a nervous, apologetic grin.

"Oh, duh. God, how dumb am I?" Katelyn sighed, now embarrassed as well as anxious.

"You're not dumb!" Noah exclaimed. He reached over and rubbed her leg. "Anxious, yes. But dumb, no." He groaned. "I'm sorry, Kate. I knew the phone thing would bug you, but I was just so worried you wouldn't come. And I really want you to meet Travis. And for him to meet you."

"Yeah, I—I want to meet him, too," Katelyn said. "I just wish you told me we'd be basically cut off from everything and everyone up here. I told my mom I'd call her to let her know how things were going. Now she's gonna worry."

"Like mother, like daughter?" he joked, adding a hopeful laugh to ease the tension.

"Not funny." Katelyn looked out the window, the trees once again feeling more suffocating than beautiful. The shadows seemed to reach out from the foliage, trying to grab her and pull her into the darkness of the forest.

Noah wrapped a hand around her forearm, the Ford wiggling disconcertingly for a moment before righting itself. Katelyn looked out at the road, startled, then over at Noah.

"Katelyn, I'm so sorry," he said. "I was being selfish. I wanted so much for you to come out here and meet my brother. And I was worried you wouldn't want to come. I should have told you about the cell service ahead of time. I was kind of hoping that maybe he was exaggerating and we'd end up having reception, after all. But I guess not."

Katelyn looked at Noah, his eyes almost pleading. Captivating hazel eyes that should be focused on the road and not on her. He appeared to be genuinely concerned.

*So he does already know about my anxiety issues then,* she thought. *And he still cares about me and wants me to meet his family.* She sighed, deciding to let it go. If she didn't, she would definitely fall into the dreaded high-maintenance category. *Can't spend a weekend at a beautiful mountain retreat because of phone reception? Who would want to be with someone like that?*

"It's okay," she said, and forced a weak smile. "It's really not that big of a deal. I just worry about someone getting hurt and then we can't call for help. Or if someone gets sick or something."

"Well, when was the last time we for sure had reception?"

"Um… I think it was around seven miles away from the destination."

"Okay, perfect. So if something happens—which it won't—we only have to drive seven miles down the road and then we can call for help. Which, by the way, we are not going to have to do. Travis may pick some wacky locations, but we've never had a safety issue. We're gonna be just fine, my petite squeak." He gave her arm a final squeeze and returned both hands to the steering wheel.

"Okay, if you say so. We really should be watching the left-hand side now, though. It should be coming up pretty soon."

They leaned forward in unison, both keeping their eyes on the road ahead. Pine trees pressed up against the shoulder of the highway, thick and heavy. Shrubs and undergrowth clung to their trunks, making it almost impossible to see more than a few feet into the forest. The filtering sunlight had vanished, no longer able to penetrate the trees. Minutes ticked by, the only sound being their breathing and the brush of wind wisping through the open windows.

"There," Katelyn said, and pointed up ahead, right before the road disappeared around another bend. "That looks like a turnoff, doesn't it?"

"Yeah, it does." Noah slowed the Ford as they approached the break in the trees. A green road sign appeared, barely sticking out from the dense foliage. "Scarlett Springs Road,"

Noah said, reading the sign. "Yup, this is it." He hit the blinker, then carefully turned onto a narrow dirt road that cut through the trees.

Katelyn felt the asphalt give way to the forest floor, and the Ford began bumping along the dirt path. Her brows came together as she stared out the window, creating worry lines she knew one day would be a permanent feature on her face.

"How long on this?" Noah asked. "Does it say?"

Katelyn looked down at the Gmail printout. "Go down this for one-point-three miles. The house is on the left. Seventeen forty-nine Scarlett Springs Road."

The Ford jostled its way down the dirt road, Noah having to slow more than once to steer around a pothole or fallen branch. Inside the trees, it was almost gloomy—like a forced twilight when all you wanted was another hour of sunshine. Katelyn felt the worry lines on her forehead deepen, and hastily tried to rub them away with her fingers.

"Do you think they meant scarlet like the color?" she asked.

"What do you mean?" Noah took the Ford over a particularly deep divot in the road, and the car tilted at an awkward angle before leveling out again.

"The name of the road. Do you think they meant scarlet as in the color red? If so, it's spelled wrong."

"Hmm. I think I'd rather it *not* be the color."

"Why's that?"

"Because I can't think of any not-creepy explanations for why there would be a red river in the middle of the woods."

"Good point." Katelyn's eyes caught on a wooden sign in the distance, sticking out of the undergrowth that was attempting to claim it. The wood was cracked and splintered with age, the left side of the sign coming together to indicate a driveway off to the left. Burnt carefully into the wood were the numbers *1749*.

"Looks like we're here," Noah said, and turned the Ford onto yet another dirt path. The driveway was by far bumpier than the dirt road, and he was unable to bring the Ford over five miles an hour as they lumbered along through the woods.

"Yeah, I guess we are." Katelyn watched the wooden sign shrink and then disappear in her rearview mirror. Now there was nothing around them but wilderness.

# Chapter 2

*Thursday, 2:14 p.m.*

The narrow driveway came to a dead end where the trees opened up into a small clearing. The underbrush had been more or less cut away to allow for a small parking area in front of a single-story house that stood at the clearing's edge. The exterior of the house was made of weathered wood the color of brewing storm clouds, and a brick chimney jutted out from a shingled roof that was littered with forest debris. Four windows faced the clearing, the curtains tightly drawn in each one. No other cars were around.

"Are we the first ones here?" Katelyn asked. "I thought your brother said he was coming this morning."

"He did," Noah said, sounding puzzled. He parked the Ford and killed the engine. "Maybe he's already inside?"

They stepped out of the car, and Katelyn immediately withdrew from the cold. She clutched her arms to her chest, trying to keep her body heat from leaking out, like blood from a wound. *Scarlet blood.* Noah said it would be in the fifties, but it certainly felt more like the forties to her. Or colder. "Hey, pop the trunk, would ya? I'd like to grab my jacket."

Noah fished the keys from his pocket and pressed a button on the key fob. The trunk let out a low clunk as it unhitched. Katelyn scurried over and yanked the hatch up. She fished through the contents of the compartment, grabbed her travel bag, and unzipped the front pouch. Inside she found her pastel-pink hoodie. She quickly threw it on and zipped up the front, rubbing her hands up and down her arms to warm herself up. She felt the chill begin to ease off. Her legs were still bare, but with her upper body covered she was already starting to feel a little better. *Take that, desert mouse. I'm gonna be a New England girl in no time.*

"I don't get it," Noah said, more to himself than to Katelyn. "He said we were really going to be impressed with this place. But from the looks of it, it's kinda… boring. Right?"

They stood side by side in the center of the driveway, staring at the front of what appeared to be a fairly simple, ranch-style house. "Maybe the inside is decorated really well?" Katelyn suggested.

Noah shrugged. "Maybe. But it's also kinda small, isn't it?"

Katelyn's eyes scanned the front-facing windows. It might be enough space for two or three bedrooms and a small living room, but that was about it. "Hey, as long as there's a bathroom, I'm not gonna complain."

"From the looks of it, we might all be sharing a bathroom." Noah sighed and put his arm around Katelyn, pulling her close. "Should we try the front door?"

Katelyn leaned into him, grateful for the warmth coming off his body. "If he was here already, wouldn't his car be parked out front? Maybe we should just wait for a little while."

"Let's at least take a look around," Noah said. "He said there was a private park or something. Maybe we can wait there." He pivoted, his arm still around Katelyn, and led her toward the side of the house.

Thick underbrush surrounded the trees that lined the clearing's edge, boxing in the space and making it hard to see out into the surrounding forest. As they neared the tree line, Katelyn was finally able to glimpse what was beyond the trees: nothing. The forest floor suddenly fell away, descending into a deep ravine.

Katelyn stepped forward, away from Noah, being careful not to get too close to the edge. She stood on her tiptoes to see over the underbrush and peered down. Pine trees grew from steeply slanted earth, and the forest floor that was not concealed by undergrowth was covered in decades of pine needles in various states of decomposition. The land sloped lower and lower and disappeared from sight.

"How far down do you think it goes?" she asked. She looked over at Noah, and was surprised to see he was no longer beside her. "Noah?"

"Holy shit," he mumbled, his back to her. He was standing by the side of the house, looking down. "Goddamn, Travis, you did it again," he said to himself. He looked over at Katelyn, his eyes wide with barely contained excitement. "C'mon Kate, you're gonna love this." He gestured with his chin to where he was looking along the side of the house.

Katelyn went over to him, keeping her eyes on the edge of the clearing. The last thing she wanted to do was slip in some aging pine needles and tumble down into the seemingly endless ravine. She could hear soil and leaves crunching underfoot as she carefully walked along the tree line.

Once she neared Noah, he held out his hand. Katelyn reached out and placed her palm against his, his fingers encircling hers in a firm grip. She huddled close to him and followed his eyeline down into the trees.

The ground sloped downward at an even sharper angle here, creating a steep grade that she suspected was all but impossible to climb. The bottom of the ravine lay hidden far below. Katelyn looked up at Noah, confused. "Why would they build a house right at the edge of a cliff like this?"

"This is why," he said, and stepped aside to reveal a staircase attached to the side of the house. The stairs went down, not up, and were made of the same ash-gray cedar that the house was constructed from. The staircase descended along the side of the house, which was three stories tall instead of just one, and built into the side of the ravine. The stairs hovered in the air over the sloped forest floor, which was visible between the wooden planks and easily eight to ten feet down below. A handrail was on the left-hand side of the stairs, the house on the right.

"Jesus," Katelyn whispered. "Where do you think it goes?"

"Only one way to find out," Noah said with unrestrained glee, and started down the stairs.

"Noah, wait." Katelyn pulled on his hand, her eyes not leaving the stairs. The wood was worn, the handrail splintered. "What if it's not safe?"

Noah smiled and pulled Katelyn into his arms. "Allow me to assure your safety, my lady." His lips pressed softly against her cheek and then he was gone, running down the stairs.

"Noah!" Katelyn protested, but he was already midway down the first flight. Her eyes darted from the stairs to the forest floor, then back to the stairs again. She held her breath, waiting to hear a sharp, splintering crack, followed by Noah's screams, but neither occurred. Instead, the woods were silent, save for the whispers of wind trickling through the trees.

Noah bounced up and down a few times, the stairs easily holding his weight. He shrugged. "Seems like they're okay." He threw a hand in the air and waved for Katelyn to follow him. "C'mon, let's go!" He turned and started making his way down the staircase, his head on a swivel as he tried to look everywhere at once.

Katelyn followed, taking her time as she made her descent. Every now and then the stairs issued a soft creak, but other than that, the planks were plenty sturdy and the wood stronger than it first appeared to be.

Noah was down below, standing on the first of two landings. He was looking to the right, toward the house, with a goofy grin spread across his face. *Like a kid on Christmas morning,* she thought as she continued her descent. When she made it the rest of the way down the first flight, she followed his gaze. "Holy shit," she mumbled, her mouth falling open.

"I know, right?" Noah tittered.

The landing was attached to a large deck, which spread across the entire backside of the house. The deck itself extended at least twenty feet out, with a handrail wrapped around its edge. Beyond the deck, the forest opened up into an immense clearing that butted up against the bottom of the ravine, which was still some two stories down below.

The deck housed two sitting areas, one on either side, with cushioned lounge chairs and cast-iron fire pits. In the center there was a large dining table, equipped with eight chairs and an elaborate centerpiece of pinecones. Sliding glass doors opened up onto the deck, one by each sitting area and the largest behind the dining table. Katelyn squinted through the glass door closest to them, and could see bedroom furniture on the other side.

A small balcony hung over the central portion of the deck, shading the dining table but leaving the lounge areas open to the sunshine. Katelyn suspected the balcony was attached to the top level of the house, where they had parked. There were no stairs going from the deck to the upper balcony, so the only way to access it must be from the inside.

"There's more," Noah said, pointing down the main staircase. They made their way down to the next landing, where, sure enough, there was another deck attached. This one was smaller than the first, and only had room for one lounge area and one set of sliding glass doors. The bottom of the ravine was still another level below.

They continued their descent to the bottom of the long staircase, Noah in the lead and Katelyn trailing behind him. Past the bottom-most landing, stone steps led the rest of the way down into the clearing.

Katelyn stepped away from the stairs, grateful to once again be on level ground. The clearing itself was easily eighty yards across, and covered in long, lush grass that was basking in the afternoon sunshine. The woods hung heavily around the clearing's edge, as if waiting for its chance to reclaim the land and cover it in shadows once more.

In the center of the clearing, two large oak trees towered overhead, their crowns level with the roof of the house. Thick ropes hung from their high branches, descending down to the clearing floor and attached to various types of swings and playthings. On one side, nearest the forest, a swing was made from a single plank of wood, a knotted rope attached to each end. On the next branch over was a climbing rope with thick knots at various stages of height. A canvas swing hung from the adjacent oak, looking like a warm cocoon in the chilly breeze. And on the far side, a tire swing made lazy circles in response to the soft wind. There was also a hammock and a picnic table, mostly shaded, but with bits of sunlight dancing across their surfaces as the oaks' crisp, red leaves rustled up above.

Katelyn wandered further into the clearing, speechless. Her eyes scanned the tree line before sweeping up to the multilevel house that stood to her right. It jutted out from the ravine wall, looking incredibly tall and completely out of place in conjunction with the surrounding forest. The central deck monopolized the center of the home, with the lower deck cast in shadows and the top balcony alight with sunshine. How the whole house managed to stay erect on the side of the slope seemed a miracle in itself. Katelyn imagined one good storm would send the whole thing sliding down the ravine and crumbling into the clearing where she now stood. However, the house obviously wasn't built recently, so it must have weathered quite a few storms in its time. "Incredible," she whispered.

"Yahoo!" Noah exclaimed from behind her. Katelyn whirled around to see him on the wooden swing, kicking his legs wildly in the air as he tried to gain height and momentum. Her eyes followed the swing's ropes to where they were attached to an oak branch some two stories up above. The branch bobbed ever so slightly under his weight, and the bough's crimson leaves rustled against a pine tree that stood at the edge of the clearing.

"Not too high, Noah! You don't know how old that thing is!"

"It feels pretty sturdy to me!" Noah called, leaning himself back and forth as the swing shot through the air.

"Twenty-seven going on ten," Katelyn muttered to herself, watching the thick ropes of the swing as they drifted forward and backward through the branches. "You know, if you break your arm we have no way to call for an ambulance, right?"

Noah was too preoccupied with the swing to respond. The oak's branch continued to bob up and down, its leaves caressing the boughs of the neighboring pine tree. Katelyn groaned, imagining the immense crack the branch would make if it broke and sent Noah plummeting to the clearing floor. And then the additional crack his bone would make upon impact. "Noah, I really think you should get off that—"

"Looking good, bro!" a voice yelled across the clearing.

Katelyn spun around and looked up at the house. On the central deck, a tall, dark-haired man was standing near the handrail, his tan forearms resting on top of the wood. He was lean and muscular, and handsome in the same rugged way that Noah was. *Travis,* Katelyn thought, noticing the resemblance right away. Only if Noah was the all-American golden boy, then this man was his dark and enigmatic counterpoint. A woman joined him on the deck and looked down into the clearing. She was trim and petite, with waves of long, brunette hair spilling over her narrow shoulders. She was stunning.

Katelyn felt a pang of imposter syndrome alight in her chest. She didn't belong at this beautiful house with these beautiful people. What was she doing here? A desert mouse in some crazy forest chalet with people she's never met before and a guy she only recently started dating. And no phone. She belonged in the desert, wearing year-round flip-flops and sitting next to a cactus or something. The queasiness returned to her gut. What had she gotten herself into?

A loud *thump!* came from behind her, and she jumped and let out a small cry. Noah had just launched himself off the swing, and he clumsily stumbled up beside her, teetering on the edge of balance.

"Careful, Noah! You're going to get yourself killed!" Katelyn exclaimed, cringing when she heard the anxious whine in her voice.

"I agree," the gorgeous brunette called from up above.

Katelyn and Noah craned their necks to look up at the main deck. "Hello, Brooke!" Noah hollered. "You two women ganging up on me already, huh?"

"It's called common sense, Noah," Brooke called down. "Something the Hayden brothers seem to have been born without."

"Wife! It pains me to hear you say such a thing!" Travis dramatically clutched at his broad chest. "Did you hear that, bro?"

"I sure did!" Noah yelled. "I'm deeply wounded by this insinuation, Brooke."

"Oh, shut it!" Brooke tossed a hand in Noah's direction. "Get up here. I want to meet your lady friend."

"Yes, ma'am!"

Brooke put her hands on her hips. "Don't you *ma'am* me, Noah Hayden. I'm the same age as you. Now come on."

Noah turned to Katelyn. "You ready?"

"Yeah, I think so." Katelyn smiled weakly. "I'm just nervous."

"Kate, it's going to be just fine. I promise. They are really nice people. And I think you're going to love Brooke. She's great."

"And beautiful. And tan." Katelyn sighed. "Noah, I don't know if I fit in here."

"Kate, *you* are beautiful. And they are going to love you. You'll see." He leaned down and kissed her lightly on the lips, and then once on the nose. "You ready?" He waggled his eyebrows at her and grinned.

Katelyn smiled, closed her eyes, and nodded. "Yes, sir. Let's do this."

# Chapter 3

**Thursday, 2:37 p.m.**

Katelyn and Noah ascended the stairs, stopping at the second landing that led to the central deck. Travis bounded over and pulled Noah into a hearty embrace, leaning back and lifting his little brother off his feet. Only Noah wasn't that little.

"Dude!" Noah cried. "Put me down, you freaking hulk!"

Travis set him down with a grunt, laughing. "Sorry. Couldn't help myself." The two brothers hugged again, pounding each other's backs with their fists much rougher than seemed necessary.

Katelyn watched the masculine display with perplexed interest. She was an only child, and never quite understood the bond between siblings. She wished someday she would, even if it was a bond by marriage and not by blood.

Brooke walked past the men, pushing them playfully aside even though they were twice her size. "Geez, you two are ridiculous." She hurried over to Katelyn and hugged her without hesitation. Startled, Katelyn brought her arms up to hug her back. "I'm Brooke," she said, pulling away. "It's so nice to meet you. And I'm so happy you could come!"

Katelyn smiled with relief. "It's nice to meet you, too. I'm happy to be here."

"It's going to be so nice to have another female around," Brooke said, clasping her hands together. "Otherwise, the testosterone is palpable. I mean, look at them." Brooke glanced over her shoulder, where Travis and Noah were doing some sort of bizarre secret handshake. "Thank God you're here, Katelyn. Or do you prefer Kate?"

"I'll answer to either," Katelyn said. "Just no Katy Kat."

"Oh, dear God. Has someone actually tried to call you that?"

"It was a playground nickname," Katelyn said, brushing it off. She didn't want to tell Brooke the nickname was actually part of a teasing chant the kids would sometimes yell at her when she was too scared to jump off the swing or stand on top of the monkey bars. *Katy Kat is a scaredy-cat.* Oh, the joys of elementary school.

"Well, I will refrain from calling you Katy Kat as long as you can refrain from calling me Babbling Brooke. Which I do do, from time to time." She laughed. "Can you tell?"

Katelyn joined in the laughter, marveling at how natural it felt. "You're fine," she assured. Noah was right, she did like Brooke. Katelyn always thought someone as pretty as Brooke would be stuck-up or would have no personality, but neither of those traits described the woman before her. Brooke was kind and friendly, and Katelyn felt instantly at ease in her presence.

"Well, how about I give you the lay of the land?" Brooke asked. "Those two are going to be at it for at least another ten minutes. Best to avoid it if at all possible."

"I heard that, lovely wife," Travis called over Noah's shoulder. "And I detect an insult was mixed in there somewhere."

Brooke spared him a glance. "Your deductive skills are awe-inspiring, my dear. Would you like to meet the lovely Katelyn before we go on our tour?"

"Absolutely." Travis shoved Noah aside. He offered a hand to Katelyn and bowed before her. "Madam, it is a pleasure to make your acquaintance."

"God, you're such a goober," Brooke said, rolling her eyes.

Noah joined them. "Gotta agree with the little missus on that one, bro."

"Nice to meet you," Katelyn said, blushing as she took Travis's hand.

"I'm sorry for acting ridiculous, Kate. I just get excited whenever I get to see this guy." Travis clapped Noah on the back. "It happens not nearly enough. Please, enjoy the tour with my lovely wife. I will return to my usual composed self by the time you have returned."

"Doubtful," Brooke chimed in.

Katelyn giggled. "Okay, sounds good."

"Great to have you with us, Kate." Travis gave Katelyn a nod of his head, then turned to Noah and swiftly put him into a headlock. Noah grunted, and began throwing punches over his shoulder.

Brooke leaned over to Katelyn and whispered in her ear, "Like I said, it would be best if we just skip this manly display of brotherly affection."

"I'm apt to agree with you on that one." Katelyn allowed Brooke to take her hand and lead her across the deck to the sliding glass doors behind the dining table. They stepped over the threshold and entered the warm, although slightly stuffy, interior of the house.

They were standing in the living room, which was filled with dated decor and mismatched furniture. Nonetheless, it was cozy and inviting. A worn area rug covered the hardwood floor in the sitting area, which had a sectional couch and two reclining chairs. A large TV sat on a not-so-large entertainment unit, the TV obviously purchased much more recently than the wooden entertainment unit it sat upon. The left wall was lined with bookshelves, stuffed with an assortment of books in various shapes and sizes. Two closed doors made up the corner of the room, adjacent to the bookshelves.

The kitchen was located behind the living room, connected to the space by a single mustard-colored countertop. Beyond the counter, Katelyn could see wooden cabinets that were aged and chipped, but the appliances looked fairly new. There were no windows in the kitchen, since the back of the house was built into the ravine. A single fluorescent light hung overhead.

To the right of the kitchen was the dining area. A large rectangular table took up the majority of the space, surrounded by an assortment of chairs. Like the other side of the living room, the far corner was made up of two doors, both of which were closed. Various paintings hung on the walls. One was of a sailboat on calm seas with a storm cresting the horizon. Another had children playing in a park next to a pond where ducks floated in the murky, greenish-gray water.

The entire house looked like it was on the verge of greatness, if only someone could afford the upgrades—which the owner of the house obviously could not.

"So," Brooke said, turning to face Katelyn, "this is it." She held her arms up and gestured to either side. "As you can see, a little worn and torn, but it definitely has that warm and cozy mountain cabin feel, doesn't it?"

"Yeah, it sure does," Katelyn agreed, looking from the dining area back to the living room. Her eyes caught on the wall of books on the far side of the room.

"You like to read?" Brooke asked, following her gaze. She skipped past Katelyn and over to the bookshelves, her feet clomping on the wood floor despite her small size. "Who's your favorite author?" She ran her finger over the spines of the books, which weren't organized in the slightest, then plucked one off the shelf and started flipping through the pages.

Katelyn walked across the living room and joined her. "Well, I do like the *Harry Potter* books, I guess."

"Oh, yeah? I'm more of a Stephen King girl myself." Brooke shut the book she was holding and turned it over to show Katelyn. The muzzle of a growling dog was on the cover, with the title *Cujo* scrawled across the top. "I saw this one when we came in. Whoever owns this place has good taste. In books that is, not decorating." She giggled and slipped the book back into its place on the shelf. "You ever read any Stephen King?"

"No, uh, not really. A little too scary for me, unfortunately."

Brooke smiled. "No worries. We'll try to keep the ghost stories to a minimum tonight." She winked.

"Oh, it's okay if you guys like to tell ghost stories, I just—"

"Katelyn, it's *fine*. We want you to feel comfortable here. Noah was so excited to introduce you, and Travis and I were equally excited to meet you. So we absolutely want you to feel at home here. Tacky decor and all."

Katelyn grinned. "It is a little tacky, huh? Or just old, I guess."

The two women looked around the house, taking it in. "Travis loves finding places like this. He says hotels are cookie-cutter crap. His words, not mine. So he spends all this time finding unique looking rentals on Airbnb, such as this lovely abode you see before you."

"The house is pretty amazing, built right into the side of the mountain like this. And the yard is incredible." Katelyn looked out past the sliding glass doors. She could see the two oaks dominating the center of the clearing, their leaves proudly displaying the fiery colors of fall: vibrant gold, burnt orange, and, most of all, scarlet red. *Maybe that's where the name comes from,* she thought. To Brooke, she said, "I bet it will be amazing to sit out there in the morning and drink a cup of coffee."

"I'm looking forward to that, too. And perhaps a glass of wine tonight?" Brooke winked and gave Katelyn a playful nudge with her elbow.

"So how many places have you guys stayed at that are like this?" Katelyn asked, pulling her gaze from the window and the blazing trees beyond. "I already heard about the beach bungalow. And the boat."

"Ha! Thank God I wasn't around for the boat. That sounded awful." Brooke shook her head, chuckling to herself. "So, Travis and Noah have been doing this once or twice a year since before I met Travis. So there have been *a lot* of places. Some great, some..." Brooke waggled her head from side to side, "not so great."

"How long have you been with Travis?" Katelyn asked.

"Together for six years, married for two. We met in college. Travis was in grad school and I was getting my undergrad. He's five years older than me."

"And you're the same age as Noah?"

"Yup." Brooke nodded. "Twenty-seven. And Travis is thirty-two. What about you, my dear?"

"I'll be twenty-four in December."

"Oh, to be so young." Brooke clutched at her chest in mock woe, then giggled. "Okay, so let me show you the rest of the house so we can all get unpacked. We have a few bedroom options to choose from." Brooke walked past the bookcases and opened one of the adjacent doors. "This is one of the bedrooms here. Smaller room and bed, but nice view of the backyard."

Katelyn glanced inside and nodded. The room was a typical spare bedroom, with wood paneling and a faded yellow bedspread. "What's inside this room here?" she asked, pointing to the other door.

"Nothing," Brooke said, and shrugged. "That one is locked. I suspect it's a staircase that leads to the top level of the house, since I haven't seen any other way to access that floor. Just the front door that faces the woods, and what I believe to be a staircase behind this door." She wrapped her knuckles on the wood.

"Yeah, I saw there weren't any stairs outside that connected to the top balcony."

"I think the owner lives up there. Rents out the lower levels, but keeps the top floor to himself. Probably stays there when he doesn't have any renters."

Katelyn inspected the closed door. "No locks on this side. So it only locks from the other side, I guess?"

"Looks like it. I'm sure he has to come down here and fix the place up between guests. Then locks it so said guests can't go poking around upstairs."

"I guess so," Katelyn said, her eyes lingering on the door handle.

"Anyhoo!" Brooke turned away from the door and pointed toward the dining area. "There's another bedroom across the way." They headed over to the other pair of closed doors, the sounds of their feet on the hardwood marking their progress.

Brooke opened one of the doors, revealing another, more spacious, bedroom. She then opened the remaining door and stepped aside. Inside was a modest bathroom, the tub, toilet, and sink cramped together in the small space. The same aged, chipped cabinets were below the vanity, and a mirror hung above the sink with a single crack going down the center.

"Looks like someone is gonna have some bad luck, huh?" Katelyn joked.

"As long as it isn't us!" Brooke closed both doors and turned to face Katelyn. "So, there is this level with its two bedroom options, and then there is downstairs."

"No inside staircase to that level?"

"Doesn't look like it. I think the lowest level might have been a basement or storage space at one point, so the only access is from the outside. But we checked it out already and it's actually pretty cute down there. Let's go take a look." Brooke grabbed Katelyn's hand and led her across the living room and back out onto the deck.

Noah and Travis were gone, but Katelyn could hear them down below, horsing around in the clearing. The oak branch attached to the wooden swing bobbed gently up and down, its scarlet leaves caressing the nearby pines. "Looks like one of them is on that swing again."

"One of those guys is gonna break his neck if they're not careful." Brooke shook her head and crossed her arms over her chest. "Hopefully that branch is strong enough."

They walked across the deck and over to the staircase, heading down to the lowest level of the house. The lower deck was considerably smaller and completely covered in shadows from the deck above. Brooke opened the sliding glass door and stepped inside. Katelyn followed.

There was a small living room in the center with a couch and two chairs. A modest TV was mounted on the wall, with a painting of spring flowers hanging nearby. There was a single door on either side of the room. "Bathroom," Brooke said, pointing to the right. "Bedroom." She pointed to the left.

Katelyn walked past her and opened the bedroom door. A lilac-colored bedspread covered a queen-sized bed, with matching end tables and reading lamps. More paintings hung from the wood-paneled walls, all of which were of blooming flowers. "Looks good," Katelyn said, and stepped out of the room. She walked over to the bathroom and peeked inside. It was roughly the same size as the upstairs bathroom, although the mirror wasn't cracked. She stepped out and looked at Brooke. "So who gets what?"

"That is up for debate," Brooke said. "We're open to whatever you'd be more comfortable with. Upstairs has more amenities, with the kitchen and the dining area. But this level would be more private, since I'm guessing we will be spending the bulk of the time upstairs. So what do you think?"

Katelyn shifted uncomfortably from side to side. Her hands crept up to her waist and she wrapped her arms around her thin frame, her fingers digging into her sides. "I'm, uh, not very good at making decisions. Maybe Noah—"

"Those guys don't care where they sleep." Brooke threw a dismissive hand toward the clearing. "But us girls do. And I want you to be where you feel most comfortable." Brooke raised her eyebrows expectantly, watching Katelyn with blue eyes as she waited for a response. She wiggled her shoulders back and forth, a goofy smile pulling on her lips, as she tried to ease Katelyn's obvious discomfort.

"Then... I guess I would prefer... down here," Katelyn finally stammered. Her cheeks felt warm and she hoped she wasn't being too pushy for choosing the private unit. She couldn't tell which area Brooke preferred, and she didn't want to pick the bedroom that Brooke was secretly wanting for herself. They were the ones paying for this trip, after all.

"Perfect!" Brooke exclaimed, clasping her hands together. "I had a feeling you might like this one."

Katelyn felt a wave of relief wash over her. "Okay, great," she said, a smile spreading across her face. "Now what?"

"Now we go get the guys, enlist their manly muscles to carry our luggage to the agreed upon locations, and then pop open some sort of adult beverage. Sound good?"

"Absolutely." Katelyn followed Brooke back outside, grateful she would be spending the weekend with someone so kind and accepting. Noah was right, after all—this weekend was going to be a lot of fun.

# Chapter 4

"Hey! Are you guys ever gonna stop messing around long enough to come help us with the bags? We're dainty over here!" Brooke hollered once she reached the bottom on the stairs. Katelyn descended the remaining steps and joined her at the edge of the clearing.

Travis looked up from where he was spinning Noah wildly on the tire swing. "C'mon, babe! This is fun. Get your sweet ass over here!"

"Dude, I think I'm gonna throw up!" Noah whirled around, clutching desperately at the tire and flailing his legs in the air in an attempt to slow down. "Stop this thing!"

Travis dipped in and grabbed the swing with one hand, his shirt sleeve stretched taut over his defined biceps. "Sorry, Noah. Got carried away I guess."

Katelyn and Brooke made their way across the clearing, the sun feeling blissfully warm against Katelyn's back. Her eyes ran up the trunk of one of the oak trees, marveling at the sheer size of the thing. She didn't see many trees like this back in Arizona—not in southern Arizona anyway. She walked past the picnic table, wrapping her arms around herself as the oak's shadow stole the light from her back. *Shoulda packed more warm clothes,* she thought as she came up to Noah, who was trying to stand on wobbly legs next to the tire swing.

"Wanna try, babe?" Travis asked Brooke as he gave the tire a smack. A broad grin spread across his handsome face as he waited for her to reply, the sharp angle of his jawline emphasized by the dark stubble of his five o'clock shadow. Noah had always been one to go clean-shaven, but Katelyn wondered if he let his beard grow out a bit if it would look as good on him as it does on Travis.

"Not a chance," Brooke said, and stuck out her tongue. "What about you, Kate?"

"I'm gonna second what Brooke said. Not a chance."

Noah stumbled over and put his arm heavily around Katelyn's shoulders. "You sure? It makes you feel wicked sick."

"Well, when you paint such a pretty picture it certainly is hard for me to resist." Katelyn leaned into him, letting the warmth of his body envelop her.

"Ya know, I think I'm gonna like this girl. I can already tell." Travis winked at Noah, then gave Katelyn another winning smile.

"Hey, what's that over there?" Brooke asked as she looked out toward the forest. She raised her hand and pointed a finger at the tree line.

Everyone turned and squinted through the trees and undergrowth. Katelyn could see horizontal planks of wood in the distance—the distinctive lines of a man-made structure. Her eyes followed what she thought might be a path leading through the trees, and sure enough, she saw a break in the foliage at the far end of the clearing. "There," she said, pointing past Travis to the cut branches and trampled bushes that pressed up against the clearing's edge. "There's a path."

"Awesome!" Noah exclaimed. "Let's go!" He took a step forward, then stumbled back when Katelyn didn't budge from her spot. He turned and looked at her. In a lower voice, he said, "What's wrong? You okay?"

"Yeah," Katelyn mumbled. "But I don't know if I want to go exploring in the woods just yet. I'm pretty chilly already. I really shoulda worn pants." She looked at the break in the shrubbery, and then back to the small structure in the trees, some fifty feet away. "Plus," she added, "it looks creepy in there. What if there's bears or something?"

Travis and Brooke were already heading toward the path, holding hands and talking among themselves. "You guys coming?" Travis asked, glancing over his shoulder.

"One sec," Noah said. He looked back at Katelyn. "Just for a minute? Then we'll go get the bags? Or we can go back right now and check it out another time." When Katelyn didn't respond, he said, "Let's go get the bags now. It's no big deal, I promise." He kissed Katelyn's cheek, grabbed her hand, and turned toward the house.

Katelyn pulled back on his hand, keeping her feet planted in the tall grass. She didn't want to be *that girl*. The high-maintenance girl. The girl that doesn't want to have fun. Or the girl who is too scared to go on an adventure in the woods. She wanted to make a good first impression. "No, let's go with them," she said finally. "I'd like to see what's out there, too."

"You sure?" Noah asked, his eyebrows drawn together with concern.

"Yeah, I'm sure." She rose onto her toes so she could reach his face, then brought her mouth to his. She could feel his smile against her lips when she pulled away from the kiss. *Definitely the right decision,* she thought, and let Noah lead her into the woods.

"Well, what is it?" Noah asked as they came up behind Brooke and Travis on the path.

"Some sort of shed," Travis said, distracted.

The shed was constructed of planks of pine, unpainted and splintering. The roof was slanted and old, with weathered shingles hanging haphazardly across the top. A double door, one side slightly askew, was latched and locked with a padlock. There were no windows.

Katelyn scanned the surrounding woods. Just beyond the shed was a chopping block with an ax propped up against its side and a few pieces of split wood lying nearby. The canopy above was too heavy for any light to penetrate the trees. Tall, fragrant pines stretched up from the forest floor, and shrubs with various colored leaves gathered around many of their thick trunks. Katelyn could hear birds chirping, and a soft, babbling sound coming from somewhere beyond the shed.

"Locked?" Noah asked, looking at the padlock. He stood next to Katelyn, his hand loosely clasped around hers.

"Looks like it," Travis said. "Bummer. I wanted to peek inside."

"Why?" Brooke asked. "To see some old, rusty gardening tools and a bunch of cobwebs? Maybe make friends with a spider or two?"

*"Noooo,"* Travis said, drawing out the word in a silly tone. "I thought maybe the shed was haunted, too."

"Travis," Brooke said in a low voice, tugging down on his hand. She glanced over at Katelyn with nervous eyes.

"What?" he asked, confused.

"Haunted?" Katelyn and Noah said in unison.

*"Travis,"* Brooke said in the same low voice, although with more urgency. "I don't think we should talk about this," she whispered. "We don't want to make anyone feel uncomfortable." Her eyes flicked back up to Katelyn, and then down again.

"What do you mean *haunted*?" Noah asked, taking a step forward.

Katelyn felt her stomach churn. She looked around the forest, as if seeing it for the first time. Her hand tightened around Noah's. Was it always so dark in here? Did the birds stop chirping, or was that just her imagination? She scanned the trees, looking for signs of movement, but saw none. The incessant babbling noise continued, somewhere up ahead.

Her eyes returned to the shed. The old, dilapidated shed in the woods. The *haunted* woods. And the *haunted* shed. It was locked, but why? Why bother to lock a shed in the woods?

Travis tilted his head down and met Brooke's eyes. "What's wrong?"

Brooke looked back at Katelyn, her lower lip clamped between her teeth and her brows turned up into an unspoken apology. "I just don't think we should be talking about haunted anything. I don't want to make anyone feel uncomfortable, or scared. That's all." She kept her eyes on Katelyn while she said it.

"It's fine," Katelyn said, probably a little too quickly. "I'm fine. We can talk about whatever." She shrugged, again, a little too quickly. It felt more like a spasm than a shrug.

"But you said you didn't like scary things," Brooke said in a small voice. "When we were looking at the books."

"Yeah, I know…" Katelyn said, stalling. "But that's just when I'm trying to relax. I like scary stories just as much as the next person." She forced a smile. Noah's grip on her hand tightened into a reassuring squeeze. *He must know I'm lying.* "So," Katelyn said as casually as she could muster, "tell me about this haunted woods."

"You sure?" Travis asked, his eyes ping-ponging between Noah and Katelyn. "We don't have to talk about it. We can just head back and enjoy the house."

"No, I wanna hear it," Katelyn insisted. "But maybe... maybe we can wait until we get back to the house and unpack. I'm kinda cold and wanna change into something more forest appropriate."

"Absolutely," Travis agreed. He glanced over at Brooke and they both smiled, looking relieved.

Noah gave Katelyn's hand another squeeze. "Should we head back then?" he asked.

"Yeah, let's go." Travis took a couple steps back down the path.

"What's that noise, though?" Brooke asked. They all stopped, listening. The babbling sound continued, soft and persistent.

"Sounds like water," Noah guessed.

"Let's go take a look," Katelyn suggested. They all turned and stared at her with raised eyebrows. She took the opportunity to move past them, letting go of Noah's hand. She hoped this would make up for them thinking she didn't like scary stories. Something they can laugh about later—how they all thought Kate was a scaredy-cat and then she ventured into the haunted woods first. Maybe earn her some brownie points with the family. *Take that, high-maintenance.*

Katelyn trudged through the undergrowth, feeling the branches scratching at her bare legs as she went. Her skin prickled with goose bumps when she felt a twig linger on her thigh, then slowly trace along the hem of her shorts before brushing past her. A couple of minutes later she came to a stop, standing at the edge of a stream that cut through the forest. Water trickled and gurgled as it flowed around several rocks that were jutting out of the stream at even intervals. *Stepping stones,* she thought immediately.

Noah came up beside her and snatched her hand back. He sounded slightly out of breath. "Hey there, Lara Croft. Why don'tcha slow down and wait for the rest of us?"

"I just wanted to take a look," Katelyn said, giving Noah what she thought was a sly smile. Or at least not a frightened one. Lara Croft, the infamous Tomb Raider, doesn't get frightened, and she kinda liked the idea of that nickname. It certainly kicks Katy Kat's ass.

He leaned in and whispered in her ear, "You don't have to try to impress them. I think you're pretty impressive already." He kissed her cheek, his lips warm against her skin.

Katelyn glanced back at Travis and Brooke, who were nearing the stream. "I just don't want them to think I'm a party pooper or something. And it's not that big of a deal. It's not like we're gonna be out here at night or anything," she said. Then added, "Which I will *not* be doing, by the way."

"Absolutely not," Noah chuckled. "I don't even have the balls to do that, Ms. Croft."

"Pretty!" Brooke exclaimed as she ran past them and hopped out onto the first of the stepping stones.

"Careful, babe," Travis said, reaching for her hand to steady her. He surveyed the stream for a moment. "Well, I must say, it is very picturesque. Alas, I have left my camera at home. So shall we head back? I'm thirsty."

"Good idea," Noah agreed. "I am quite parched myself."

They left the stream, slowly making their way back through the undergrowth that lined the barely there path.

Katelyn allowed Noah to lead the way this time, his arm stretched out behind him to hold her hand as they went. She threw one last look over her shoulder before the stream faded from view, her eyes catching on the stones as water lazily babbled between them. *Stepping stones,* she thought again, perplexed. *Why are there stepping stones in a haunted woods? Who uses them? And where do they go?*

# Chapter 5

"So where did you guys park?" Noah asked. They were walking through the clearing, the massive oaks rustling their crimson leaves high up above.

"We didn't," Travis said.

"Wait, what?"

"Our damn truck broke down the day before last. Couldn't get it into the shop until yesterday, and then they said it was gonna take two days to get 'er fixed up. So we ended up just Ubering it over here." He laughed dryly. "Had to tip pretty heavy to get him to go down that dirt road, too."

"Why didn't you tell me?" Noah asked, casting a perturbed glare in his brother's direction. "We had plenty of room in Kate's car."

"Yeah, but we were coming from different directions," Travis said. "We didn't want you guys having to drive all the way to our place, just to turn around and go back the other way."

"It's no big deal, really," Brooke said, leaning forward so she could see around Travis.

"What about getting home?" Katelyn asked. "With no reception out here, how are you going to call for an Uber back?"

Travis gave her a sheepish grin. "We were actually hoping you guys could help us out with that part. Not drive us all the way home, but just give us a lift to the nearest town. From there we can call an Uber for the rest of the way."

"Absolutely," Katelyn agreed, eager to help in any way she could to thank them for this weekend.

"You got it." Noah clapped Travis on the back. "Say, what would have happened if we both showed up in an Uber? We'd... what? Just live here then?"

Brooke laughed. "There's supposed to be a landline inside somewhere if we need to make a call."

"I didn't see one," Katelyn said as they mounted the stairs. They had just passed the first landing when she heard a creaking sound somewhere up above. When a man's voice followed, she jumped and nearly lost her footing. Noah clamped his arm around her waist and pulled her against him to prevent her from falling.

"Why, hello there!" the voice called down from the top balcony. It was a deep voice, and raspy from what was probably a lifelong smoking habit.

Katelyn craned her neck and looked up. She could see the figure of a man leaning over the balcony, his forearms resting on the handrail. However, from such a sharp angle, she couldn't make out much of the man's features. Just his hands, which were large, rough, and calloused.

"I'm the owner," he called down. "Sorry to startle 'ya."

"Hello," Travis said, sounding startled nonetheless. "We didn't think anyone else would be here." They continued up the stairs, single file, until they reached the second landing and walked out onto the main deck.

Katelyn could see him better now. The man appeared to be in his sixties, if not older. He was burly in size, had a deep set of wrinkles carved into his pockmarked face, and wisps of gray hair atop his head. He was wearing a red flannel shirt and worn blue jeans.

"Name's Maurice," he called down. "I live on the top level here, but I make sure to keep myself scarce when people are rentin' the place. I just wanted to say hello so you wouldn't go thinkin' the place was haunted when you heard footsteps goin' around upstairs. The floorboards tend to creak when the weather starts gettin' cold."

"He lives here?" Katelyn whispered, tugging on Noah's arm. *"While we're here?"*

"I don't know," Noah said from the corner of his mouth. His eyes remained locked on the man above them. "That does seem kinda weird."

Brooke looked puzzled but didn't speak. She glanced over at Travis, waiting to see how he would react. Katelyn followed suit and focused her attention on Travis as well.

Travis cleared his throat. "It's quite a place you've got here," he said. "Pretty impressive having the house built into the side of the ravine like this."

Maurice nodded, apparently having heard this many times before. "Sure is. But it's a lot of upkeep, I'll tell ya that much. I didn't use to rent 'er out, but with an older house, keepin' the place in shape was gettin' to be too much for my bank account. But with the Airbnb rentals, I'm able to keep the place up and runnin'.'"

"That's great to hear," Travis said, stepping into his role as the de facto leader of the group. "We're happy we get to spend the weekend here. Seems like a lovely place." Maurice nodded but didn't speak, prompting Travis to continue on with introductions. "I'm Travis, and this is my wife, Brooke. And that's my brother and his girlfriend, Noah and Katelyn."

"Nice to meet'cha," Maurice said, and bowed his head. He rubbed his hands together, and Katelyn thought she could hear the roughness of them even from where she was standing, like coarse sandpaper. "Now, I don't have many rules here—other than to have a good time, of course." Maurice chuckled. "But I do want ya to take mind when goin' out in the woods like ya just did."

Brooke's eyes widened, their color almost aqua in the fading afternoon light. She looked over at Katelyn and mouthed, *He was watching us?*

"The woods are mighty pretty," Maurice went on, "but they got some mean poison oak in there." He gestured toward Katelyn with one of his calloused hands. "Bare legs like that, you don't wanna be brushin' up against anything pois'nus."

Katelyn took a step closer to Noah, wishing more than ever that she had changed into her jeans in the car. *Stupid desert rat.* At least the dangerous plants in Arizona *looked* dangerous. She didn't even know what poison oak looked like, let alone how it felt. She shivered.

"Also, there's a stream out there a little ways in. You guys mighta saw it already. Anyway, you can feel free to explore a bit on this side of the stream, but I highly recommend not goin' past it. That's where the poison oak really gets thick."

"Duly noted," Travis said, glancing down at Katelyn's bare legs and then at his own. He was wearing cargo shorts, which were much longer than Katelyn's cutoffs, but his calves were just as exposed as hers. He looked back up at Maurice. "We also saw some sort of building out there."

"Yup, that's m' shed," Maurice said with a nod. "I keep all my equipment in there—lawn mower and tools and such. I'd stay out of there, too, if ya don't mind. I didn't used to lock it up, but then one of the family's stayin' here had a little girl. Curious little thing, and *brave*. Went right into that shed and ended up cuttin' her leg on a hacksaw. Nothin' serious, but still. I put a lock on the damn thing the very next day."

"Good idea," Travis said, glancing around the group. He lifted his shoulders into an exaggerated shrug and let out an audible sigh, clearly eager to wrap up the conversation. "Well, it was very nice to meet—"

"One more thing," Maurice interrupted, holding up one worn, arthritic finger. "And then I'll get out of yer hair and let ya nice folks enjoy yourselves."

Everyone looked up at Maurice expectantly. When he was sure he had their undivided attention, he went on. "I don't wanna scare ya, but I do haveta warn ya that there's a pretty big bear population 'round here. I never had a problem with 'em myself, but they're out there, to be sure. So if you bring any food out into the clearin', please make sure to bring it all inside when you're through. And I would strongly advise ya to not go into the woods at night. Best to stay in the clearin', or better yet, up here on the deck."

Travis nodded somberly. "Understood." A grin twitched at the corner of his mouth. "Is that the *only* reason to stay out of the woods at night? Because we heard… *rumors*… that the woods was—"

"Haunted? Yessir, there's been a lot of talk about that 'round these parts. But, as someone who has lived here for my entire life, I gotta say that it's all just a bunch of poohocky."

*Poohocky?* Brooke mouthed to Katelyn. Katelyn bit down on her lower lip to keep a giggle from escaping.

Travis looked disappointed. "So none of it's true then?"

"'Fraid not," Maurice said. "Nothing worth mentionin' anyway. The woods is just your typical woods, with all its normal, typical dangers. But still, best to stay out of it at night. And remember,"—he lifted up his finger for emphasis— "don't cross the stream."

"But there's stepping stones across the stream," Katelyn blurted out before she could stop herself. Her cheeks heated and she pressed in closer to Noah.

Maurice regarded her briefly, then gave her a curt nod. "There are indeed, little miss. But those were there long before the poison oak got hold of the area. So again, I'd steer clear. Of the stream, and the bears."

Katelyn nodded hastily in agreement and looked away. She didn't like his eyes on her. Or the fact that he had been watching them in the clearing. She thought of the staircase inside—the one that only locked from the other side. The staircase that led up to his living quarters, apparently. She shivered again. Noah put his arm around her, probably because he thought she was cold. She wasn't.

"We'll make sure to avoid the stream," Travis promised. "And we won't leave any food out. Mainly we just want to enjoy the house and each other's company."

"Well, sir, that is a mighty fine idea. I hope ya folks have a wonderful time."

Maurice turned to head back inside, but Travis called after him. "You said you lived in this place your whole life, right?" he asked.

"Yessir, from cradle to grave, I'm afraid. My family's owned this place for generations. We always passed it down from one to the next. Unfortunately, it looks like the ownership is goin' to stop with me, since I got no family to pass it down to. Never married." Maurice looked out toward the woods, a wistful expression on his face.

"Ya know, there have been five generations of Scarlett's here," he went on, turning back to his guests. "My mother bein' the last. I'm not sure if they were named after the road, or the other way around. That's before my time. Anyway, I had always hoped to pass along the name to a daughter, if I ever happened to have one. Turns out, it wasn't in the cards for me. Funny how things go from someday to too late without ya even realizin' it. Sneaks up on ya if you're not careful. Hell, maybe even if ya are."

Katelyn suddenly felt pity for the old man instead of fear. Out here all alone, having to bring in strangers to his family home just so he can pay for the upkeep. And after he's gone, all those generations of his family will be gone with it.

"Anyhow, I've taken up too much of yer time already," Maurice said. "Please go, enjoy the house. Furnishin's are a bit dated, but the appliances are fairly new. There's a lighter and some lighter fluid in the kitchen under the sink, if you wanna light one of them fire pits. And I got some fresh firewood chopped for ya. Can get purdy cold out here at night."

"Yeah, I bet," Travis said. "Well, it was nice to meet you, Maurice. Thank you for allowing us to enjoy your lovely home." Brooke snickered beside him, and he swatted at her from behind his back.

"You bet," Maurice said. "Have yourselves a good night." He nodded to them, his eyes going from one person to the next, and then turned and went into the house.

Once the door closed, Brooke leaned over to Travis and said in a goofy voice, "Thank you for *allowing* us to enjoy your *lovely* home." She giggled. "Since when did you get so polite? Usually all I get are grunts."

Travis made a quick swipe with his arm and smacked her hard on the ass. She jumped, giggling louder. "You, lovely wife, need to learn some manners." He pulled her close, bent her backward until she squealed, and then brought his mouth to hers.

Brooke kissed him back, one hand wrapped around his neck and the other clinging to his arm. When he brought her back to standing, he added a grunt for good measure, and Brooke swatted him away, her cheeks flushed. "And you, lovely husband, need to go get Katelyn's bag out of the car. Poor girl is freezing."

Katelyn blushed. "Yes, that would be very much appreciated. Noah—"

"I got the keys," he said, pulling them from his pocket and jingling them in the cool air. "I'll go with Travis and we'll bring everything down. Travis, where are your bags?"

"We left 'em up top."

"Got it," Noah said. He looked at Katelyn. "Where are we staying, my lady?"

"Bottom level."

"Ooo," Noah cooed, moving in close enough for Katelyn to feel his breath fanning across her face. "How private and romantic." He gave her a quick kiss and headed up the stairs with Travis. She could hear them laughing as they reached the top.

"That guy's kinda creepy, huh?" Brooke asked, jerking her chin toward the balcony.

"Yeah. Creepy, or sad. Remember that locked door? Locked from the other side, I mean. Can't he just come down here whenever he wants then?"

"I suppose he could. But I'm sure he just uses it to get down here and clean everything between tenants. Otherwise he'd have to go around the outside of the house using those steep-ass stairs every time."

"I guess you're right," Katelyn said, trying to shake off the disquiet that had sauntered into her chest without permission. *Don't be a scaredy-cat. You're Lara Croft, remember?*

"Nothing for you to worry about, though." Brooke arched one of her perfectly shaped eyebrows. "Since you and Noah will be downstairs in your private bungalow anyway." She made kissing noises and wiggled her slim shoulders.

Katelyn's mouth fell open and she felt her cheeks growing warm. "Hey now! Enough of that."

Brooke giggled. "Okay, okay. I'm sorry. Let's head inside. You're cold, and I'm thirsty. Ready for some wine?"

"Absolutely," Katelyn said, and followed Brooke inside the house.

# Chapter 6

**Thursday, 8:23 p.m.**

"Now wait just a minute!" Brooke exclaimed, reaching for the half-full bottle of wine in Travis's hand. "Just because I'm a lady doesn't mean I can't drink."

"I am very sorry," Travis said, bowing before her. "Would my lady like another glass?"

"Damn straight," Brooke said, and giggled. "This is my vacation, after all." Travis topped off her glass, then walked over to the dining table in the center of the deck. He set the bottle down and grabbed another beer from a dwindling twelve-pack.

Brooke leaned back on the wicker loveseat and curled her legs beneath her. She took a sip of wine and let out a long, contented sigh. "Now this is the life."

They were all sitting around one of the fire pits on the main deck, a fire crackling and popping inside. The pit was a black bowl made of cast iron, with pine trees etched into the sides and extending up into the mesh grate that covered the top. The trees looked like silhouettes against the flames—a forgotten forest on the brink of extinction. Overhead, stars twinkled in the night sky, and the darkness of the woods loomed around them. The only source of light came from the fire, and it danced across their faces as they sat around it, laughing and drinking.

Katelyn leaned against Noah, his body strong, warm, and inviting. He had his arm wrapped around her slight shoulders, the other hand holding a beer. He took a long swallow and pressed his cheek against the top of her head. Katelyn closed her eyes and breathed in the earthy smells of the woods and the intoxicating aroma of burning pine from the fire pit. She thought she could stay in this moment forever, given the opportunity. Slightly buzzed, snuggled up with a man she very well may love, listening to the sounds of laughter and the crackling of the fire.

Upstairs, floorboards creaked, pulling Katelyn out of her serene trance. Everyone fell silent and tilted their heads to listen as Maurice came out onto the balcony briefly, then went back inside.

Once they heard the door shut, Brooke leaned in and whispered, "It's freaking weird, isn't it? Him being here like this. Shouldn't he go somewhere else when he rents the place out? Or at least stay out of sight?"

"And where is he supposed to go, babe?" Travis asked. "He already said he can't really afford to take care of this place. If he rented it out and then had to stay somewhere else, he might come out making little to no profit on the whole thing. Might as well not do Airbnb at all."

"Stop being logical, husband. It's annoying. All I'm saying is that it's a little weird that he's here, is all. Listening to us."

"Not that we have anything of interest to say," Noah laughed. "Movie critiques and a seemingly endless supply of dirty jokes doesn't exactly make us worthy of eavesdropping."

"Hey now, baby brother, I thought that joke about the blind hooker was top-notch stuff." Travis leaned back on the loveseat and pulled Brooke against him. "Warm me up, my sweets. It's a tit bit nipply out tonight."

"I think you meant to say a *tad* bit," Brooke said with a grin.

Travis looked at Noah. "No, I didn't," he said, and they both laughed.

Noah took another pull from his beer. "So are we going to get to this haunted woods thing ever? Or do I need to call Maurice down here to join us? I'm sure he'll start talking after a couple of drinks."

"Dear God, no," Brooke said. "Having him upstairs is enough."

"I second that," Katelyn chimed in.

Travis looked from Brooke to Katelyn, trying to read her expression across the flames. Flickers of orange glinted off the emerald green of his irises, again making Katelyn think of a scorching, forgotten forest. "You okay with hearing a ghost story, Kate?"

"Sure," Katelyn said, nodding. "Why not?"

"It's completely fine if you want to skip it. I have plenty of dirty stories to keep us entertained."

"He ain't lying, neither," Noah snickered.

"Oh God, Travis," Brooke groaned. "Nobody wants to hear about your college escapades." She took a sip of wine and turned to Katelyn. "You sure you're okay with hearing this?"

Katelyn closed her eyes, feeling the heat of the fire against her cheeks and the warmth of Noah beside her. It was like nothing else existed outside of this burning circle. No clearing, no woods, no shed. She was safe here, somewhere where nothing bad could penetrate. "Yeah, I'm sure," she said, opening her eyes. "Isn't that what nights like this are for anyway? Outside, in the woods, sitting around a fire? It's the ideal ghost story setting."

"Hell yeah!" Travis exclaimed, and slapped his hand down on his knee. "I shoulda brought stuff for s'mores."

"Damn, I knew we forgot something." Noah made an aw-shucks motion with his free arm. A bit of beer sloshed out of his bottle and splashed onto the deck.

"Okay, well I guess we're gonna have to proceed sans s'mores then," Travis said regretfully.

"Oh, here we go." Brooke pushed herself upright and crossed her legs, holding her wine glass in front of her chest with both hands.

Travis rested his forearms on his knees and leaned closer to the fire, the shadows caressing the sharp angles of his face. "So, when I was looking for a place for us to go this weekend, I was thinking mountain cabin all the way. But I didn't want just *any* mountain cabin.

"I kept hearing about this part of the Appalachian Mountains that is supposed to be haunted. Hikers disappearing, campers hearing strange sounds at night. Ya know, things like that. Turns out, when I investigated where a lot of these strange occurrences were taking place, it wasn't too much of a trek from where I was already planning for us to go. So I thought, why the hell not find a place to stay *in* this so-called haunted woods, instead of just nearby. I'm sure Noah told you, Kate, that I'm always looking for new and exciting locales for these little trips."

Katelyn nodded and took a drink from her glass. "He sure did."

"Of course, this was before I found out a haunted woods might not be your idea of a good time. Sorry about that." Travis offered her an apologetic smile.

Katelyn smiled back. Noah's family really did care about her. "It's no big deal, really. Like I said, this place is amazing. I don't think a ghost story is going to ruin anything."

"Well, it's not exactly a *ghost* story," Travis went on. "But before I get to that, let me tell you a little background information first."

"Oh, goody," Noah said in a sarcastic tone.

"This is a history lesson, jackass. So listen up." Travis took a moment to look each person in the eyes. "So, the First Nations are Indigenous peoples from Canada. Their cultures go back *thousands* of years. There are over 620 First Nation communities in Canada—or maybe it's 630. I might have the numbers a little mixed up."

"This from an engineer," Brooke snickered.

"Hush now, lovely wife." Travis ran his fingers over her face, stopping on her mouth. She playfully slapped them away. "Anyway, the Algonquian people are part of the First Nations. They live in Eastern Canada. One of the Algonquian-speaking tribes is the Abenaki, whose territory once spanned Quebec and northern New England—including Maine, New Hampshire, and," Travis paused for emphasis, *"Vermont."*

"So far I'm not exactly shaking in my boots, bro," Noah said, and kissed Katelyn on the top of the head. She giggled.

"I'm getting to it," Travis snapped. He rolled his eyes and downed half his beer. "You people have no respect for history. *Anyway,* one of the Algonquian legends is that of a malevolent creature that stalked the forests. One that was brutal, violent, and"—another pause for emphasis—*"cannibalistic."*

Travis's eyes scanned the circle, the flickering orange light kissing his parted lips and cascading down his neck. He swallowed, and his Adam's apple bobbed through the shadowed landscape of his throat. "This creature had a voracious appetite for human flesh," he went on, "and would eat any man, woman, or child who ventured into its territory. It stalks the woods at night, preying on those who wander too far from the tribe."

Katelyn looked over at Brooke, who was shaking her head and quietly sipping her wine. *Good idea.* Katelyn took a large gulp from her own glass, hoping it would calm the sinuous stirrings of disquiet in her stomach.

"This creature was called the wendigo. It roughly translates to 'the evil spirit who devours mankind'. It—"

"I've heard of that!" Brooke declared, breaking the unnerving quiet that had taken over the circle. She sat bolt upright on the loveseat, her wine sloshing in her glass. A few drops flew out and splashed onto the deck next to Noah's spilled beer, looking eerily like blood splatter. She shot her hand up in the air, like a child in school who wanted to be called on by the teacher.

Travis glanced over at her. A brief moment of irritation swept across his face and then was gone. "You've heard of it?"

"Yeah!" Brooke nodded with excitement. "It's in a Stephen King book. *Pet Sematary*, I think. It's what cursed the cemetery." A broad smile spread across her face. "Okay, I'm excited now. Tell the rest." She settled back into the loveseat, her blue eyes sparkling.

"You know, lovely wife," Travis said, "sometimes I think you might love that Stephen King more than you love me." Brooke stuck her tongue out at him, then leaned over and kissed him on the cheek.

Travis looked over at Katelyn. "You know where she made me take her for our honeymoon?" Brooke reached over to swat Travis's arm, and he swiftly grabbed her hand and pulled it to his side. *"The Stanley Hotel."*

Katelyn looked over at Brooke, who had a sheepish grin on her face. Puzzled, she craned her neck to look up at Noah. He was smirking. "I don't get it," she said.

"The Stanley Hotel is from *The Shining*," Travis explained. "King stayed there one time and got the idea for the book.

There's this specific room that's supposed to be extra haunted and terrifying. You know which room we stayed in?"

Brooke was giggling behind her wine glass. Katelyn couldn't help but join her. "I'm guessing that's the room you stayed in."

"Bingo!" Travis patted Brooke's hand. "Literally the day after I proposed she said I had to call The Stanley and book room two-seventeen for our honeymoon. No 'what style dress should I get?' or 'what should our first dance be?'. Hell, our *wedding date* was chosen based on when room two-seventeen would be available."

Brooke pulled her hand away from Travis with mock outrage. "Hey now, husband. You are making me sound unromantic. You know that I love you very much." Brooke made kissy faces at him. "And as I recall, you ended up loving The Stanley."

"I loved it because you loved it." Travis snatched Brooke's hand back and kissed it. "Anyway, we are getting off topic. Back to the wendigo."

"Yay!" Brooke jostled her wine glass as she settled in, causing a few more drops of blood to appear on the wooden deck. "Let's hear it!"

Katelyn's eyes lingered on the not-real blood splatter, glints of orange flame dancing across the almost-black splashes. "You didn't know what the story was about tonight?" she asked, pulling her eyes away from the fake bloodshed. "I thought you already knew the woods was haunted."

"Travis told me it was a haunted woods, he just didn't tell me what haunted it. I thought it was going to be the ghost of a hitchhiker or something. Or a guy with a hook for a hand that preys on teenagers trying to get some in the back of Daddy's Buick. This is so much more exciting. The wendigo..." Brooke shook her head wistfully. "It's a classic."

"It's *supposed* to be terrifying," Travis corrected, and downed the rest of his beer. He set the bottle on the deck next to the definitely-not blood splatter and continued. "The wendigo is a giant humanoid creature. It is said that when it eats a person, it grows in size instead of filling its stomach. So it is *always* hungry. And as it grows and grows, its ashy gray skin gets stretched taut over its bones and face, pulling its tattered, bloody lips back to reveal yellow, jagged fangs. It can be fearsomely tall—some say taller than a tree—but it is gaunt and emaciated, always starving and never able to satisfy its appetite. Eating one person never satisfies its hunger, so it is always looking for its next victim..."

"Sounds like me and tacos," Noah said. Everyone laughed, and the comforting sound traveled over the clearing until it was devoured by the surrounding woods.

"Does it... look like a person?" Katelyn asked, her voice soft against the crackling fire.

"Sort of," Travis said with a shrug. "It has human characteristics, but it cannot be mistaken for a normal person. *Although*, it can mimic a human's voice in an attempt to lure someone away from safety and into the woods. A lot of recent depictions show it with horns or antlers—like the devil—but in the traditional Algonquian legend it didn't have horns."

"Is there only one?" Brooked asked. "Stalking all of the forests?"

Travis chuckled. "Not even close. It is believed that *anyone* can be turned into a wendigo. It is a creature of greed and gluttony, and anyone who is overpowered by those traits can be possessed by the evil spirit."

"How many beers counts as gluttony?" Noah tilted his bottle in the firelight to reveal that only one sip remained.

"I think you hit gluttony about two beers ago," Travis said.

"Uh oh, sounds like I'm in trouble. Or more likely, *you guys* are in trouble." Noah made a strange sucking noise with his lips and teeth. "Anybody have any Chianti? Or perhaps some fava beans?"

Katelyn forced a smile to go along with their laughter, but inside she wasn't feeling much humor in all of this. Ghost stories around the campfire were supposed to be fun, and even though Travis's story wasn't exactly terrifying, she still couldn't help but notice how the forest suddenly seemed so much darker, and the light from the fire so much dimmer. The branches of the oak trees in the clearing seemed to be reaching out for her with gnarled, knotted hands of wood, hoping to grab her and pull her into the woods, where in their depths a creature was hiding. One with an insatiable appetite. Waiting for her to wander too far from the tribe.

Brooke's voice cut into her thoughts. "If that's how you become a wendigo, then half the country would be wendigos by now."

"That's more of just the concept of a wendigo," Travis said. "Someone who is overcome with greed and excessive consumption. But in the legends, most transform into wendigos in a way that is much more disturbing than a little greed and gluttony."

"And I have a feeling you're about to tell us about that other way right about now." Noah grinned and pulled Katelyn closer to him.

"After I get another beer, I am." Travis jumped up from the loveseat. He went to the table, saw that the twelve-pack was depleted, and then headed inside the house.

Once he was gone, Noah turned his body so he could look at Katelyn. "You okay? We can call it quits now if you want. Say we're tired and we're gonna go to bed."

Katelyn gave her head a small shake. "No, it's okay. It's interesting. Like a history lesson."

"A history lesson of gore." Brooke leaned forward in her seat, her eyes locked on Katelyn's. "Look Kate, if my husband is making you uncomfortable with this shit, we can talk about something else."

"*I'm fine.* Really."

Brooke nodded, although she didn't seem convinced. She turned her head and watched Travis as he came back from inside the house. He held two bottles of beer in one hand and an uncorked bottle of wine in the other. "Refills?" he asked.

Noah took the extra beer, and Travis filled both women's wine glasses. He sat back down with an oomph. "Cannibalism!" he announced. "That's the other way you become a wendigo. *Cannibalism.*"

Brooke and Noah groaned. Katelyn said nothing. Travis's eyes locked on hers—the one person he might actually be able to scare with his campfire story. "You see, Kate," he said, leaning in, "the wendigo is an evil *winter* spirit. Tribes that got into hard times during the harsh winters would sometimes have to resort to cannibalism to survive. And after consuming human flesh, that person transformed into a wendigo—cursed to crave human flesh for all eternity and never have its hunger satisfied."

Travis fell silent, his eyes gleaming as he stared at Katelyn from across the fire. Finally, he continued. "After becoming a wendigo, that poor soul was forced to hunt down the ones it loved. It lured them to their deaths with haunting calls, then tore them limb from limb, drinking their blood as their hearts pumped it out into the snow. It pulled the flesh from their shattered bones and devoured them while they screamed."

"Enough!" Brooke exclaimed. "You're terrifying the poor girl. She's pale as a sheet." She threw a hand in Katelyn's direction. "We're done with the human flesh talk, okay? No more."

Travis looked at Katelyn, as if seeing her for the first time. "I'm sorry, Kate. Too far?"

"Maybe a little," she squeaked.

"Okay, no more human flesh talk." Travis held his hand up as if taking an oath. "I promise."

"Thank you," Katelyn and Noah said in unison.

"Yes, thank you," Brooke agreed. "You gotta read the room, babe."

"Sorry. I get a little carried away with my stories sometimes."

"Yeah, you should hear the one about him getting diarrhea on Space Mountain." Noah snickered. "On second thought, maybe not."

"I told you that story in confidence, bro." Travis pointed an accusing finger at Noah.

"No, you didn't," Brooke said. "I was sitting right next to you when you told him. No one needs to describe excrement in that much detail."

"You must not have minded, seeing as you married me." Travis quirked an eyebrow at Brooke, the corner of his lip curling up into a small smile.

"I must have lost my mind there for a minute."

"Speaking of losing your mind…" Travis turned back to Katelyn. "That's another part of the wendigo curse. It's called wendigo psychosis. It's when someone gets possessed by the evil spirit and becomes a cannibal. Or at least has intense fears of becoming a cannibal. Eventually they can't stop themselves from eating human fl—" Travis clamped his jaw shut. "Err, sorry Kate. Eating people, I mean."

"Okay, let's wrap this up," Noah said. "Wendigo—bad. Greed and gluttony—bad. Anything else?"

"How about how to kill it?" Travis leaned back in his seat, draping one of his arms over Brooke's shoulders.

"Finally some useful information." Brooke rolled her eyes, but leaned into him nonetheless.

"It is said that the wendigo has an ice-covered heart. So the only real way to kill one is by burning the heart."

"Well, that sounds easy enough," Noah said, nodding. "Find the wendigo. Don't get eaten. Don't get wendigo psychosis. Pin it down. Cut out its heart. Light said heart on fire. Easy peasy lemon squeezy."

A shrill scream shot across the clearing, coming from the direction of the woods. Everyone fell silent, except for Katelyn, who let out a startled gasp. The cry carried on for a full five seconds, then was gone.

They sat in silence, hearing nothing but the crackling of the fire. Katelyn felt herself growing dizzy, and realized she had stopped breathing. She forced herself to take in a slow breath through her mouth, careful not to make a sound.

*"What in holy fuck was that?"* Brooke asked in a harsh whisper.

They all looked across the clearing to the tree line, which was shrouded in inky darkness. The leaves of the oak trees rustled gently in the soft breeze.

The cry came again, sharp and piercing in the quiet of the forest. Katelyn's entire body went rigid, and she felt gooseflesh prickle into existence on her arms and legs. Noah felt tense beside her, his body stiff and unmoving.

A third call drifted out from the foliage, sounding less like a shriek and more like a melody. Katelyn reached for Noah's hand. Once she found it, she clutched down hard, feeling the bones shift inside. She was sure it was painful for him, but he didn't so much as wince—just stared out at the blackness of the tree line.

"It's a loon," Travis whispered. Another melodic call filled the night air, followed by more silence. "Just a loon," he said again, louder this time. He leaned back in his seat, his shoulders relaxing. "Jesus Christ, for a second there *I* even had myself freaked out."

Brooke let out a nervous laugh. "A loon? You're sure? Like the bird, right? Not a crazed killer with a machete?"

"The *bird*, Brooke. We grew up not too far from here, back in Lyndonville. I recognize the call. Right, Noah?"

"Yeah," Noah said, although he sounded unsure. "Yeah, I think that's what they sound like." He nodded, as if in agreement with himself. The tension in his body eased off, and after a long, shaky exhale, disappeared completely. He took a long pull from his beer. "God, that scared the shit out of me!"

Katelyn didn't speak. She stared out at the tree line, struggling to make out any shapes in the darkness. Anything tall and gaunt lurking in the shadows. Tall as a tree and horrifically thin. But there was nothing. She strained to hear anything over the relieved laughter of her companions, but again, there was nothing.

"Kate?" Brooke's voice. "*Katelyn?* You okay?"

"Huh? Uh—yeah. Sorry. I just never heard a loon before, I guess."

"Yeah, I got myself a cute, little desert mouse," Noah said, and kissed the crown of her head. "There's no loons out in Arizona, are there?"

Katelyn shook her head. "No, not that I know of. We're more of a birds of prey kind of place. Owls, hawks, condors."

"Tucson," Travis said, shaking his head. "You're a long way from home, huh? What brought you out to these parts anyway?"

"Well, I just recently moved to Boston to live with my cousin after I finished vet tech school. I wanted a change of scenery."

"You certainly got it," Brooke agreed. "And by the looks of it, you haven't gotten used to the cold yet. Let me get you another sweater."

"No, it's okay. I think I'm fine."

"Nonsense," Brooke said with a wave of her hand. "We're practically the same size, and I brought a ton. I bet forty degrees is probably pretty dang chilly for you."

"Yeah, I am a little cold." Katelyn leaned into Noah, greedily trying to steal his warmth for herself.

"Then I'm getting you a sweater. Just a sec." Brooke hopped up and headed toward the sliding glass doors directly behind them. Once inside, she flipped on a light, and Katelyn could see her rummaging through a drawer in the bedroom. She pulled out a mint-green sweater, looked it over, then closed the drawer.

Katelyn's eyes drifted back to the clearing, and to the dark line of the surrounding trees. So many trees, and so little light. But still nothing there—not that she could make out anyway. She thought about the sounds coming from the forest. The last few calls did sound melodic, and she could already feel her mind accepting them as the possible call of a bird—a loon or whatever. But that first call… that didn't sound like a bird at all. That was a scream. A shriek. That was the cry of something else. Something that was waking up.

# Chapter 7

**Thursday, 11:19 p.m.**

Noah burrowed under the covers, snuggling up to Katelyn, who was already curled into bed with the comforter pulled up tight to her chin. She was shivering. They had forgotten to turn the heater on in the lower bedroom when they brought in their bags, and the room was only now starting to thaw. The covers felt like sheets of ice as she slipped between them, and it took a thorough thrashing of her legs to get the blankets to warm up to an acceptable temperature.

Noah pressed his body against hers, wrapping his arms around her waist and pulling her close. His breath felt hot against her neck. "God, you feel like an icicle, girl." He rubbed his hand up and down her arm, trying to warm her up. "You really aren't from around here, are you?" he joked.

"Yeah, well, someday I'm gonna take you to Tucson in June and then laugh when you fall down from heat stroke,"

Katelyn snapped back. Despite her irritation, she leaned into him, wanting all the warmth from his body that she could get.

"Oh, yeah? You gonna introduce me to your parents when we go?"

Katelyn's cheeks began to burn, a sensation of heat she was *not* yearning for. She hadn't meant to suggest they go to her hometown together—not this early on in the relationship. She didn't want to scare him away just yet. Her tongue felt glued to the roof of her mouth as she struggled with how to respond to his question, which hung in the air like the smoldering smoke of a recently extinguished campfire.

"I wouldn't mind," he whispered against her neck. "Meeting your parents, I mean. Seeing where you grew up."

"Really?" she asked, turning her body to face him. "You'd want to meet them?"

"Absolutely." He kissed her gently, the warmth of their cumulative breath hanging in the air between them. "Just not in June," he whispered.

Katelyn giggled. "I accept those terms." Her lips brushed against his as she spoke.

"You know, if you're cold, there is a proven method that can help warm you up." Noah's hand slid down Katelyn's side until it reached the elastic band of her pajama bottoms. "You're from a pretty hot environment, so I'm not sure if anyone has disclosed this life-saving information to you yet."

Katelyn's hand traveled through the covers until it found Noah's, lingering on her hip. "A proven method, huh? What about Brooke and Travis?"

"I'm pretty sure they are already familiar with this method."

Katelyn giggled. "No, I mean they might hear us."

Noah kissed her neck once, just below the jawline, and then again, lower. "I promise not to scream like a loon if you don't," he whispered.

She laughed in spite of herself, then stopped when the sounds in the forest flickered through her mind. That first sound, that screech…

"I'm sorry if that story upset you," Noah said, feeling her body tense. His finger traced the line of her flannel shorts. *Shorts—not pants. Dumb dumb dumb.* She shivered under his touch.

"It's okay," she whispered. "I'll be fine. Maybe you could help me think about something else." She gently pushed Noah's hand downward, south of her waist.

"Oh, yeah?" Noah shifted his weight on top of her. "I can definitely help with that."

The sounds of their breathing, ruffling sheets, and the gentle rattle of the heater filled the room. And Noah was right—Katelyn did forget about the sounds of the loon calling out in the darkness. Or whatever it might have been.

# Chapter 8

"Good morning!" Brooke called down to Katelyn as she climbed the steps from the lower level up to the main deck. Brooke was standing at the railing, looking out at the clearing. Her small body was dwarfed by a large maroon hoodie, and she was wearing fuzzy white slippers with pink pom-poms on the top.

"Good morning," Katelyn said as she walked across the deck.

"Coffee's in the kitchen," Brooke said, gesturing with her chin.

"Thanks." Katelyn turned and went inside to the kitchen. The door to the main bedroom was closed, and she saw no sign of Travis. She poured herself a cup of coffee from the steaming pot, reveling in the rich aroma, and then headed back outside to join Brooke. "Where's Travis?" she asked.

Brooke gave her a sly smile. "Sleeping off the beer from last night. I'm guessing Noah is doing the same?"

"Yeah. Snoring like an elephant, actually."

"Did you guys sleep okay?" Brooke asked.

"Yeah, once we got the heater working."

"Oh God, we never turned that on for you guys did we? Shit, I'm sorry."

"It's okay. We managed to stay warm." Katelyn grinned and looked away.

Brooke bumped her shoulder against Katelyn's. "I bet you did." She gave Katelyn an exaggerated wink, then looked back out at the clearing.

Katelyn followed her gaze. A hazy mist was creeping along the top of the tree line, the pines beneath looking so green they were almost blue. The oaks in the clearing reached up into the mist, their scarlet leaves dulled by the shrouds of fog. The grass far down below twinkled with dew, looking like crushed emeralds. A hushed silence hung over the landscape. "Beautiful," Katelyn said.

"I bet you didn't have mornings like this very often at home."

"Never," Katelyn whispered, taking in the beauty of the surrounding forest.

"Look, I wanted to say—before the boys get up—that I'm sorry if Travis upset you last night. He gets so excited to see Noah, and then sometimes gets carried away with his stories. He means well, though."

Katelyn nodded. "It's just fine, really. I'm having a great time so far. And thanks for the sweater last night, I meant to bring it up this morning, but—"

"Girl, keep it for now. You can give it back to me when we're leaving. Like I said, I have a ton." Brooke looked back out at the clearing, her delicate eyebrows pulled together and her lips scrunched to one side. She looked puzzled.

"What is it?" Katelyn looked out at the trees. "A loon?"

Brooke laughed. "No, no loons. I'm just trying to remember which one of us moved the chair."

"What chair?" Katelyn scanned the clearing, and finally saw what Brooke was looking at. One of the chairs from the picnic table had been moved. Someone had taken it out to the tree line and left it there, facing outward toward the woods. It sat at the forest's edge, looking pathetically small compared to the surrounding trees. "Why would someone put it there?"

"That's what I can't figure out," Brooke said. "I don't remember any of us moving it. Weird, huh?"

"Yeah," Katelyn agreed. "Weird." The stirrings of disquiet awoke in her stomach again, where she suspected they had been lurking in the shadows all along. Tall. And gaunt. And hungry.

"I can't decide if it's creepier that the chair is pointed out toward the forest, or if it would be creepier if it was pointed toward the house." Brooke took a sip from her coffee. Steam rose steadily from the cup, joining the hovering mist.

A board creaked upstairs, soft but audible. They both turned and looked up at the balcony, but Maurice wasn't visible. He was there, though. Katelyn was certain of it. Was he just enjoying the misty morning as well, or was he listening to them? And was he listening to them last night, when Travis told the legend of the wendigo?

Brooke brought her stormy blue eyes from the balcony down to Katelyn. In a lower voice, she said, "It's freaking weird. Him being up there like that. I know what Travis said about him not having any other place to go made sense, but still. It feels weird. Like we're being watched."

Katelyn glanced back up at the balcony. She couldn't see him, but still sensed his presence. "Yeah," she whispered, "because we are."

They looked back at the lone chair at the edge of the clearing. "You think he moved it?" Brooke asked softly, throwing a thumb toward the balcony.

"I don't know, maybe. But why?" Katelyn took a sip of her coffee. The bitter taste across her tongue was soothing.

"I have no idea," Brooke said, her eyes not leaving the chair. "Why would anyone just sit at the edge of the forest and stare into it? What's he looking at?"

"Or, more importantly, what's he looking out for?" Katelyn asked.

The two women stared out at the tree line, watching as the mist wound its way sinuously through the treetops.

# Chapter 9

"No, I'm telling you dude, it was 2004. The Red Sox won the Series for the first time in eighty-six years in *2004*."

"I coulda sworn it was 2005," Noah said, grabbing another Dorito from the bag.

They sat at the picnic table in the clearing, bickering over a collection of snack foods and beer. Brooke was lounging in the hammock, reading the *Cujo* book she had found on the bookshelf in the living room. Katelyn was on the wooden swing, feeling the breeze tug at her hair as she swayed backward, forward, and backward again.

They had spent the day at a nearby lake, the guys tossing a football back and forth while the water lapped at their feet, and the girls lying on the beach, sucking up the remnants of the summer's sun. Brooke was lean and tan in her shorts and tank top, and Katelyn as pale as the sand beneath her. She wanted to throw her sweater back on against the chill from the lake, but thought a little vitamin D might do her body some good.

"I thought everybody from Arizona would be tan," Brooke commented, oblivious to the chill.

"That's what everyone thinks," Katelyn said. "But really, it's too hot to go outside in the summer. We just run from air-conditioned building to air-conditioned car and back again."

After having a picnic lunch at the lake, they headed back to the house to take a nap. Travis snoozed on the couch, but Brooke spent the quiet time curled up in a recliner reading *Cujo.* That's where Katelyn found her when she came back upstairs after showering and taking a quick nap herself. The sun had made her drowsy, much like it did in Tucson. Some things never change, regardless of where you might be.

Now they were down in the clearing, the sun already below the tree line and the swing Katelyn was sitting on blissfully in the shade. She could feel the beginnings of a sunburn spreading across her chest and shoulders. *Shoulda worn sunscreen,* she thought. She wasn't used to the New England sun just yet, but it turns out it could burn you just as easily as the desert sun, even if the temperature was only fifty-eight degrees.

They had moved the lone chair back to the picnic table when they came down, and other than the chair itself, nothing seemed to be out of the ordinary. Travis joked that the wendigo had moved it in the night, but everyone eventually agreed that it was probably Maurice, and that nobody wanted to ask him why.

Katelyn snapped some pictures with her iPhone while they were down there, hoping to capture just how lush and green the forest was so she could show her mom back home. No matter how hard she tried, though, she couldn't convey the beauty of the Vermont landscape inside her lens. It was like seeing the most beautiful, grandiose harvest moon, but then when you photograph it, it only looks like a tiny speck of light on the screen. Eventually she gave up and tossed the iPhone at the base of the tree so she could use the swing. The branch barely moved with her weight, and the oak leaves only made the slightest bit of rustling against the neighboring pine's boughs.

The guys were arguing over something. First it had been about every sport imaginable, but now it was something else. Brooke looked up from her book, which she was already more than halfway through. She watched them briefly, then returned to the secret world that was hidden inside the pages of her novel.

Katelyn stopped pumping her legs and let the arc of the swing dwindle before eventually ceasing completely. She wasn't about to jump off the damn thing like Noah had done. She would almost certainly break her neck in the process. She carefully hopped off the wooden seat, feeling the crease from the plank burning across the backs of her thighs as blood flow returned to the area. She strolled over to the picnic table, purposefully keeping her eyes off the woods and the strange path that led to the locked shed.

"Whatcha guys talking about?" she asked, coming up behind Noah and resting her hands on his broad shoulders.

"The pepper eating contest," Travis said simply.

"The what?"

"I think you guys are dumb," Brooke called from where she was lounging on the hammock.

"Every time we meet up we have a pepper eating contest," Noah said, ignoring Brooke. "We each bring some peppers, and see who buckles first under the heat."

"Last time we did red habaneros," Travis said, "and poor Noah almost puked it all up on Brooke's shoes."

"I did not appreciate that, by the way," Brooke said, not looking up from her book.

"So what's this time?" Katelyn asked.

"Ghost peppers," Noah said.

Travis grinned. "Get it? Ghost peppers… haunted woods. It's perfect!"

"Dumb dumb dumb," Brooke said in a singsong voice.

Katelyn sat down in one of the chairs and zipped up her hoodie. "How hot is a ghost pepper?"

"Well, peppers are measured on the Scoville scale—by degrees of heat, that is. A bell pepper is zero. A jalapeño can be up to eight thousand. A habanero, up to 350 thousand. A ghost pepper is over a million."

"Holy crap," Katelyn mumbled.

"And the big daddy of all peppers—the Carolina Reaper—is two-point-two million," Noah added.

"That's the goal," Travis said. "Maybe next time I think we could do it."

Noah took Katelyn's hand, smiling at her bewildered expression. "We've been working our way up the Scoville scale, a hotter pepper each time we meet up."

"Why don't you guys just drink pepper spray?" Brooke asked, still not looking up.

"It is something to consider. Thanks, lovely wife!"

"You got it, husband. That's what I'm here for—helpful suggestions."

"Pretty clever, Travis," Noah said. "Picking a haunted forest for our ghost pepper."

"I aim to please. So, are we doing this now?"

"As good a time as any," Noah said. They stood up from the picnic table in unison.

Katelyn looked at Noah, then over at Travis. "Is this safe? Eating those things? We won't be able to call 911 if one of you guys swells up or chokes or something."

"It's perfectly safe," Noah assured her, bending down so his eyes were level with hers. "Hurts like a bitch, but it's safe." He kissed her on the nose.

"Then why do it?"

"Manly male bonding," Brooke said, and finally shut her book. She flailed her legs, struggling to get out of the hammock, and Travis jogged over to help her.

"C'mon babe. You think it's hot, right?" He tickled her ribs. She let out a cry and swatted him away. "Pun intended."

"Dumb dumb dumb," Brooke said again, and stuck out her tongue.

They left the clearing, each couple walking side by side. Upstairs, a door quietly closed on the top balcony. Nobody noticed.

"Okay, here we go." Travis held a small, misshapen red pepper between his thumb and index finger. The pepper's skin was warped and glossy, and it did not look appetizing in the slightest. Like nature was screaming at you not to eat it. Nonetheless, Travis and Noah intended to do just that. They held their deformed peppers, jumping up and down with anticipation. "Count it down, babe," Travis said.

Brooke sighed and rolled her eyes. "Yes, dear. Three... two... one... be stupid!"

Katelyn watched as Travis and Noah both bit their peppers off at the stems, chewing noisily with anxious expressions on their faces. They swallowed, then stood across the table from one another, eyeing each other closely. Noah's eyes began to tear, and Travis began to hiccup. Noah bent over the table, perspiration beading on his brow and then dripping from his forehead. His breath hissed in and out from his clenched jaw. Travis started pacing the length of the deck, smacking his hands together and hiccupping rapidly.

Dumbstruck, Katelyn turned to Brooke and asked, "They do this for *fun*?"

Brooke shrugged. "Some sort of testosterone thing, I guess. They asked me to participate once, but I can barely handle a jalapeño, let alone what they're eating now." She took a sip from her beer. "Sure you don't want one?" she asked, holding up the bottle.

"Not yet," Katelyn said. "I wanna eat something first. I'm feeling a little icky from the sunburn."

"Well, how about you and me go start dinner? We'll get you a snack while we're at it, and we can leave these two crazies out here to sweat, cry, and dry heave in peace."

"You know, Brooke," Katelyn said, "I'm really starting to like you."

"Right back atcha, sister. Let's go."

# Chapter 10

*Saturday, 12:07 a.m.*

Katelyn sat at the edge of the bed, listening to Noah's not-so-soft snores beside her. Her lower lip was trapped between her teeth, and she chewed at it absentmindedly in the dark. She had woken up a few minutes ago to pee, and that's when she realized it was missing. Her cell phone. She had left it down in the clearing, next to the trunk of the oak tree.

Katelyn sat in the dark, her knees pulled up to her chest and her mind furiously debating her options. She could go down to get the phone now, or wait until morning. Everything inside of her screamed to wait until morning—no one was around, it's not like the phone was going to get stolen. It would be right there by the tree when she went down to get it in the morning. *After* the sun was up.

But then she remembered all the dew that had collected on the grass overnight. When Brooke and her went down to the clearing that morning, they were soaked almost to their knees in freezing dew. If she left her iPhone out there in the grass, would it be damaged by the water and ruined before the sun came up? It was a fairly new phone, and she couldn't afford getting another one right now. She could barely afford her half of the rent. So she sat in the dark, chewing on her lip and trying to decide.

Inside her head, the song "Should I Stay or Should I Go" was running on repeat—promising her trouble if she went, but even more so if she stayed. Double, even. Katelyn shook her head, silencing The Clash and wishing she had remembered her damn phone in the first place. *Stupid pepper contest. Stupid ghost peppers. Stupid ghost stories.*

She looked over her shoulder at Noah, who was sleeping soundly in the bed beside her. She could wake him up, ask him to go with her. But then she would be *that* girl. The dreaded high-maintenance girl. The girl that wakes you up in the middle of the night to go retrieve a cell phone she could very well go get herself.

Katelyn looked at the sliding glass door, and to the inky blackness that lay beyond. How long would it take her to go down the stairs, cross the clearing, grab the phone, and then come back to the room? Two minutes? Maybe less, if she hurried. That's not so bad. Two minutes of fear, and then back under the covers with Noah. She could tell everyone in the morning how she went down in the middle of the night to get her phone—wendigo or no wendigo, bears or no bears—and they would all be impressed. Even Travis. "Damn bro, your girl is a badass." That's what he would say. And Noah would throw an arm around her and say, "Hell yeah, she is." Brooke would mention how even she wasn't brave enough to do that, not alone in the dark anyway.

Katelyn looked longingly at Noah. Or she could just wake him up and have him go with her. He wouldn't mind. She was sure of it. He might even go do it himself, so she wouldn't have to go out into the cold darkness at all.

*Or* she could just wait until morning. If the phone is ruined, then it's ruined. It's just a phone, after all. Only it *wasn't* just a phone. She had saved up for months to afford that damned overpriced iPhone. A phone she stupidly didn't even get insurance on because she didn't want to pay the extra monthly charge. Now that phone had droplets of dew collecting on its surface; droplets that would eventually accumulate to the point that they started dripping into the charging connector... the speaker... the microphone...

Katelyn set her feet on the ground, her mind made up. Half a year of saving up for that phone, or two minutes of being scared to get it back. Was it really even a choice? She got up from the bed and squinted in the dark to find her hoodie and some shoes. She found her shoes near the door and sat down to pull them on, doing a mediocre job of tying the laces. It's not like she was going to be wearing them for that long anyway. She then felt around for her hoodie, but couldn't find it in the dark. Instead, her hand landed on something soft and fuzzy: Brooke's sweater.

Katelyn tied her hair up into a messy bun and threw the sweater over her head. She wiggled it into position, then gave one final look over at Noah. She wasn't sure why she was creeping around so much—that guy could sleep through a nuclear explosion. She envied him that. She was such a light sleeper, if someone three apartments down sneezed, she'd wake up. Well, that might be a bit of an exaggeration, but not *that* big.

Katelyn's hand hovered just shy of the door handle. Inside her head, The Clash started its chorus again, asking her if she should stay or go. She took a deep breath and placed her hand on the lock. *I'm going,* she thought. They hadn't seen any sign of bears out there, and there is no such thing as wendigos. Or a haunted woods. So there really is nothing to be scared of. Just a fairly new iPhone sitting in the wet darkness on the brink of getting ruined.

The latch clicked up as the lock disengaged. Katelyn almost opened the door, thought better of it, and instead reached along the wall for the porch light. *Duh,* she thought. *Was I just gonna go out there with no lights on at all? What did I think I was gonna use? The flashlight on my phone?* She would have laughed at her small joke, if the fear wasn't so thick in her throat. It made it hard to swallow. She clicked on the porch light and looked outside. The deck was now cast in an eerie orange glow. The scant light made it to the edge of the clearing, and was then sucked away by the night. Katelyn scanned the trees, but saw nothing.

She slowly slid the door open and stepped outside. The air was cold and humid, the mist already settling onto the land. It felt damp and sticky, and she could see particles of moisture floating in the air, illuminated by the porch light. Katelyn let out a shaky breath, and closed the door behind her.

She stood on the deck, listening for signs of life in the forest. She heard none. No loons. No bears. No wendigos. She crept across the deck and over to the staircase. Just one flight of stairs and she would be in the clearing. Then just a hundred feet or so, maybe two hundred, and she'd be at the tree. Then back across the clearing, up the stairs, and back inside and under the covers. *Easy peasy lemon squeezy.*

Her footfalls were silent on the steps, the darkness seeming to steal sound as well as light. She reached the bottom of the staircase and scanned the tree line. Her eyes had adjusted to the darkness by now, and she could make out the first row of trees at the clearing's edge—like sentinel guards watching over the midnight forest. And amongst their trunks: nothing. *Just a whole lot of nothing,* she thought, and started making her way across the clearing. She felt wetness around her ankles; the dew was already collecting in the grass. Hopefully her phone wasn't ruined already. She might have already waited too long while singing songs from the eighties.

She beelined for the tree, casting glances in either direction for signs of movement. Nothing. She looked back up at the house. The lower deck's porch light was on, as was a light in one of the top floor windows. *Huh,* she thought. *Doesn't that guy ever sleep?*

She looked away, dismayed that her vision was momentarily altered by the lights of the house. She stopped where she was, blinking rapidly and willing her night vision to return. Slowly, the shapes of the night started to take form again. She crept forward, the damp grass lapping at her ankles. She was only twenty feet from the oak tree now. She could make out the swing just beyond the trunk, unmoving in the stillness of the night. There was not even a breath of wind to rustle the autumn leaves above.

Katelyn reached the oak tree and said a silent prayer of gratitude. She went around the side of the trunk and reached down to scoop up her phone, right where she had left it near the swing. Only it wasn't there. *It wasn't freaking there.* She jerked upright, and looked frantically around the grass. It was so damn tall, it would be hard to find it in all that grass. *But I left it right here,* she thought. *Right fucking here.* She looked back at the trunk of the oak tree, convinced she had just missed it the first time. *Nope. Not there. Definitely not there.*

A shriek filled the air. Katelyn crouched down, throwing her hands up to defend her face. And then there was complete darkness. Someone had turned off the porch light. She was all alone in complete darkness with the shrieking thing. Panic set in, reaching up from the grass and clawing its way up her body, onto her face, down her throat. She was choking on it. Choking on panic. *Why was it so dark? Where did the light go?*

Katelyn opened her eyes. She had squeezed them shut when the shriek came out of the forest. She released a heavy sigh and let her hands fall to her sides. The porch light was on, and she was in near—but not total—darkness. *God, fear can really screw with your brain,* she thought, embarrassed if not for the panic.

Another shriek came out of the trees. It was high-pitched, piercing even, and trailed off into a wail. *Is that really what a loon sounds like?* It didn't sound like a bird to her. *Fuck it,* she thought. *I'll get a new phone. This isn't worth it. It might not even be out here anyway.*

Katelyn started to turn toward the house, but stopped when the glimmer of something at the edge of the clearing caught her eye. Right where the chair had been that morning. She tilted her head to the left, to the right, trying to make out what it was. It glinted with each turn of her head. *Her phone?* She hadn't even gone over there, had she? The guys had moved the chair back to the picnic table, but she hadn't gone over there with them. She didn't want to, specifically because she didn't want to see what the chair was pointed at. But something was in the grass over there now. Something that reflected the little light that was available.

She went toward it, ignoring the third shriek. *It does sound a little like a melody. And birds sing, so yeah, a loon. Definitely a loon.* She approached the edge of the forest, not realizing she was hunched over into a crouch, as if ready to fend off a blow. As she drew near, her mind began singing that pesky song again. Trouble if she goes. Double if she stays. Should she stay or go…

Katelyn reached the object and looked down at it.

It wasn't her phone. *It wasn't her phone, it wasn't her phone, it wasn't her phone.* She took a step back, tripping over her own feet and falling hard onto her hip. The wetness of the grass soaked through her pajamas, and she felt her skin prickle at the unforgiving coldness of the heavy dew.

A branch broke. One single crack, just past the tree line. She looked up from where she was sprawled across the grass, and stared into the darkness. She might as well have been staring at a black wall, for the good it did her. She couldn't see anything—nothing past the first row of trees.

Her breath hitched in her throat. *It preys on those that wander too far from the tribe.* She wanted to look over her shoulder, toward the house, but couldn't pull her eyes away from the blackness before her. *I wandered too far from my tribe.*

Katelyn shoved herself up just as another branch cracked. She pivoted on her heels, slipping in the wet grass but catching her balance just before she lost her footing again. She lurched forward, made it one step, then felt something heavy connect with her back, just between the shoulder blades. She stumbled and fell onto her hands and knees. Her back felt wet. Wetter than the dew beneath her. Only this wetness was warm and smelled of copper.

She attempted to shove herself back up, but the heavy thing struck her again, lower this time. Her arms gave out and she collapsed onto the ground, the grass soaking her front. She thrust her hands out, attempting to break into a crawl, but her legs weren't working properly. She couldn't seem to bend her knees, or her hips. She grabbed at the grass with her hands, pulling out chunks of green blades and sodden earth.

She tried to scream, but the wind had been knocked out of her with the first blow. Instead, she dragged herself along using her elbows. The porch light burned her eyes, impossibly bright and impossibly far away. She dug her elbows into the ground to pull herself forward again, but something pulled her back. She went backward one foot—three feet—five—eight.

Katelyn clawed at the ground, digging her fingers into the soft earth, searching for purchase. A root, a branch... *anything*. Anything at all. And then something was on her back, pushing her into the earth, and she heard more than felt a sickening crack across her spine. Warm wetness flowed down her sides, mixing with the cold wetness beneath her.

She reached forward again, clawing at the ground, the air. Reaching for Noah's hand, even though he was sound asleep back in their room. A room she would never get to return to, and a bed she would never get to crawl back into, safe and warm under the covers.

She was dragged backward again—toward the trees, toward the darkness. Katelyn sucked in a gulp of air and managed to get out one long, anguished scream before she was dragged the rest of the way into the forest. She tried to scream again, but something stopped her before the sound could escape her throat.

Brooke

# Chapter 11

Brooke Hayden jerked awake, consciousness slamming into her with sudden, violent clarity. Her breath caught in her throat, and for a second she thought she was choking. It wasn't until she took in three shaky gasps of air that she realized where she was: in a mountain cabin in northern Vermont. Not in her safe, reassuringly normal house back in Syracuse. The house where she knew every creak and every squeak. The house where she had set up the nightlights just right so even if she woke in the dark she could still make out everything in the room. Here, it was far too dark—a darkness that consumed the furniture and anything else that might be lurking amongst the shadows. She had meant to pack a few nightlights for the trip, but after the truck blew a gasket—or whatever the hell it was that made it make that awful grinding noise—she had been too frustrated and preoccupied to remember all of her packing essentials. Going on vacation in an Uber to a place without cell reception had thrown her for a loop, and when they arrived at the Airbnb she was just happy she had remembered the toothpaste and the deodorant.

Travis didn't care about nightlights. The darkness never seemed to bother him in the way it had always bothered her. He claimed her fear of the dark was because she had such an overactive imagination—all those horror movies and King novels had put frightening ideas into her head that only came out at night. And perhaps he was right on that account, because no matter how much she tried to convince herself she would feel silly in the morning, those fears always felt impossibly real in the depths of the night. As real as the shadows she sometimes saw lurking in the bedroom corner—and did those shadows just move?

Despite the more-than-occasional fear of the dark a certain book or movie might instill in her, Brooke still couldn't get enough of the haunted tales and bloodthirsty beasts inside her stories. Horror was like an amusement park ride, one where the second the ride ends, you're already running around to the back of the line so you can do it all over again. Even if it makes you queasy. And even if it makes you need a nightlight. Another thrill, another scream, another peek over your shoulder to make sure nothing is sneaking up behind you.

There was no nightlight now, though. Just that all-consuming darkness, blending everything in the world into one giant black blur of foreboding mystery. She lay in bed, her eyes struggling and failing to make out the ceiling above her. If she can't see the ceiling, what else can't she see?

*And what the hell was that noise?* she thought. Her eyes scanned the room, staring at everything and nothing at the same time. Something had woken her up, and her mind was having trouble deciphering what it was. Had something fallen over in the room? No—the room was as silent as it was dark. *Something outside then?*

She lay in the darkness, her body as rigid as a corpse in one of her stories, feeling on alert even though she wasn't sure why. Something had to have woken her up. *A scream—that's what it was. I heard a scream. Outside somewhere.* Brooke strained to hear anything coming from outside now—a cry for help, another scream, something. But there was only silence. She brought her hand out from under the covers to reach for Travis, then stopped herself.

*He'll just think I'm silly,* she thought. *Just another moving shadow in the dark. Just another Cujo, or Ghostface, or Poltergeist. It was probably just a loon again anyway. Stupid freaking loons, they sound like the goddamn boogeyman.* With the thought of the boogeyman entering her mind, her eyes darted across the room to where the closet was located. She couldn't see it. If the door was ajar she wouldn't even know…

Brooke rolled over onto her side, away from Travis and the closet, facing the sliding glass door that opens out onto the deck. The curtains were closed tight, and she was unaware that the porch light was on down below. If only she opened the curtains, she would have had the nightlight she was yearning for.

Instead, Brooke lay on her side, listening for another call from the loon, wondering if wendigos could mimic the songs of a bird. *If they can mimic a human's voice, then they must be able to mimic a bird's call as well. Maybe there are no loons in this forest at all, only wendigos. Forever starving and forever searching for their next victims.* No other calls came from the forest, wendigo or otherwise, and eventually, Brooke fell back asleep.

# Chapter 12

*Saturday, 3:26 a.m.*

Awareness filtered into Brooke's mind, slowly and laboriously, like someone dredging up a lake. She felt like she was stuck in molasses, trying desperately to open her eyes, but feeling too tired to do so. Her sleep was sticky and thick, holding her down and refusing to let her surface.

Something had awoken her again, but instead of jolting awake in a sudden panic, she felt like the intruding consciousness was fumbling around as it tried to find the light switch to her brain. *Should have brought a nightlight...*

Another thump, from up above. Brooke's eyes finally opened and she peered into the blackness. *What time is it?* The morning light had not begun to filter in through the edges of the curtains yet, and the room was still shrouded in a heavy layer of darkness. *Not morning yet.*

*Thud thud thud... thump... bang... thud thud thud.*

*What in the name of God is he doing up there?* Brooke thought, rolling onto her back and staring at the invisible ceiling. Maurice was up there, walking around and moving things. But why? It was still the middle of the night. She listened as his footsteps went across the ceiling above her, there was another thump as he opened or closed something. Then more footsteps.

Brooke grunted. *"What the fu—"*

"Babe? Are you okay?" Travis's voice, hovering somewhere off to her right. He was awake, and from the sounds of it, propped up on his elbows.

"I'm sorry, I didn't mean to wake you," she mumbled. She reached through the dark until she found his arm, then slid her fingers down his warm skin until she reached his hand. He wrapped his around hers, the comforting pressure of his grip causing her heartbeat to steady.

"You didn't wake me. Damn ghost peppers. I've been up and down all night. It's like the ring of fire down there."

"Ew. God, babe. Overshare."

"Marriage is about sharing things with one another, lovely wife. Even bowel movements." The mattress shifted as he rolled onto his side, facing her. "Is something wrong?"

"I—" she paused. Maurice was making another trek across the room directly above them. *Thud thud thud.* "Well, you tell me. What the hell could he possibly be doing up at this hour? It sounds like he's in the middle of a particularly enthusiastic round of spring cleaning or something."

"Maybe he couldn't sleep," Travis suggested. "I'm sure it's nothing to worry about."

"Has he been doing this all night? You said you've been awake a lot."

"No, not really. Why? Does it matter?"

"I guess not," she said, and sighed. She was doing it again—making shadow monsters out of clothes piles. In the morning she will laugh it off and think about how silly she was to lie awake, fretting about Maurice's insomnia. "It's just… creepy, I guess."

"You were reading that horror novel all day…" Travis trailed off. "What's it called?"

"*Cujo*. And that's about a rabid dog. Not a psychotic innkeeper."

"Babe, why do you read that stuff if it freaks you out so much?"

"Because I love it." She could hear Travis laugh softly beside her.

"I know you do, babe," he said. "Well, since there probably isn't a homicidal dog upstairs, do you think we can try to get some sleep now?"

"Yeah okay, sounds good." Brooke leaned over and kissed what she thought was her husband's cheek. She missed, and felt his eyelashes brush against her lips. She giggled. "Sorry."

"I'll take any kisses from you that I can get," he whispered. He felt through the darkness, found her cheek, and then gently guided his lips to hers. "Get some sleep, lovely wife."

"Yes, sir." Brooke rolled onto her stomach and pressed her forehead into the pillow, willing herself to fall into a deep and dreamless slumber in the safe cocoon of the bed. She was just starting to feel the pull of sleep tugging at her mind when a thought flashed through her head and brought her back to reality. "Travis?" she whispered.

"Yeah, babe?"

"You said you were awake a lot. Did you hear anything earlier? Outside? Like a scream, or a—"

"Loon?"

"Um, yeah. I thought that's what it was. Never mind. I'm being silly."

"It's because you forgot your nightlights, isn't it?" He wiggled closer to her and wrapped his arm around her. "Don't worry, I'll protect you from the big bad birdie."

"My hero," she whispered, and let the safety of Travis's embrace carry her off to what turned out to be a blissfully dreamless sleep.

# Chapter 13

*Saturday, 8:17 a.m.*

To Brooke's relief, the next time she opened her eyes, sunlight had seeped beneath the curtain and she could now see all the shapes in the bedroom. Dresser, suitcase, lamp, chair—all present and accounted for. Travis snored peacefully beside her. She slipped out of bed and threw on her hoodie and slippers, wanting nothing more than to go out onto the porch and bask in the morning sunshine.

She stepped out onto the deck and felt the damp morning air brush against her cheeks. She closed her eyes and drew in a deep breath, relishing the feeling of daylight on her skin. Already she felt foolish for getting worked up in the night, first from the loon and then from Maurice. Poor old guy probably has trouble sleeping for whatever reason—back pain, prostate issues. It was nothing to get worked up about. Neither was the damn loon. *That's why they probably call it that. A loon. Because it turns you into a loon.* She snickered to herself. Not her best joke, but Travis might still think it was cute.

She turned at the sound of footsteps on the stairs below her. Probably Katelyn, coming up for her morning coffee. Brooke was beyond excited she was here—it was so nice having another female around when Travis and Noah got into their brotherly shenanigans. She enjoyed their company, but sometimes she felt like the odd one out when she was with them. They had all their inside jokes from growing up together, and she had her books. As they rehashed childhood traumas and teenage triumphs, she read her stories, one after another, sometimes making it through more than one in a single weekend get-together. But now with Katelyn around, Brooke felt she finally had someone to connect with. She hoped her and Noah would work out; she'd love to go on more trips like this one with Katelyn to keep her company.

To her surprise, Noah's head appeared on the stairs instead of Katelyn's. He made his way up the remaining steps and walked across the deck to join her by the railing.

"Morning," he said, sounding groggy.

"Good morning to you, too." Brooke glanced toward the stairs, expecting to see Katelyn's head next, but she didn't. "Kinda early for you, isn't it? Where's Kate?"

"She's not up here?" Noah asked, alarm flashing across his bedsheet-imprinted face. "She came up here and had coffee with you yesterday. I just figured she did the same thing today." Noah's eyes darted around the deck, as if Katelyn might be hiding behind one of the lounge chairs.

"I haven't seen her," Brooke said, following Noah's gaze. "I did just wake up, though."

"Maybe she went up to the car to grab something. I'll go check." Noah spun on his heels and went back to the staircase, this time heading up to the top level. Brooke listened to his ascent, then turned back to face the clearing and the stillness of the morning. Rays of sunlight cut through the mist, coming from somewhere behind her. Before long, the mist would burn away completely, and the sun would conquer the sky once again.

She was just thinking about getting the coffee going when she heard Noah's footsteps coming back down the stairs, faster than before. He reached the landing and hurried over to her. A deep crease had emerged on his forehead, and his eyes were wide with worry.

"Our car's gone," he said. "Why the hell is our car gone? Where would she go? We're in the middle of nowhere. Why would—"

"Noah, slow down." Brooke put her hands on his shoulders, trying to calm him at the same time her insides abandoned the concept of calm. He was looking around the deck again, searching, and she had to stand on her tiptoes to try and catch his gaze. When he finally focused on her, she said, "It's going to be okay. We'll figure this out. I'm sure she's just fine."

"Then why is our car gone?"

"I don't know. Maybe there's something she needed at the store bad enough to drive to town."

"Like what?"

"Us ladies are mysterious beings, Noah. Sometimes we require certain products and we don't have the time to dillydally with explanations."

"You're talking about period stuff, aren't you?"

"Maybe. Who knows? Or she might have a prescription that ran out. All I'm saying is there is no reason to panic just yet."

Noah's body relaxed, although not completely. "So now what? We just wait for her to come back?"

"Let's take a look around. Maybe we'll be able to figure it out. Did anything look out of place in your room?"

"No." Noah shook his head. "But I didn't really look around all that much. I just figured she was up here and headed out the door."

"Then that's where we'll check first. Let's go." Brooke turned him around and gave his back a gentle push. He started walking toward the stairs, with Brooke trailing behind him.

They made their way down to the lower level and headed inside. The rooms looked the same as Brooke remembered them, except for the bed being unmade and two suitcases lying on the ground, both with clothes piled in or around them. Noah's suitcase had a lot of blue and black clothing, while Katelyn's was mostly pastels.

"Do you see her purse anywhere? Or her phone?" Brooke asked.

"Why would those be in here if she went to the store? She would have taken them with her."

"I know, I know. I'm just checking. Trying to solve the mystery."

"Well, I don't see them," he said, exasperated. He walked across the room, rummaged through her suitcase briefly, then returned to where Brooke was standing. "Everything else seems to be the same, though."

"What about the bathroom?"

"What about it?"

"Whenever I want to leave a note for Travis, I leave it in the bathroom. That way I know he'll see it. A lot of people do that. Post-it notes on the mirror or whatever."

Noah hurried across the living room and into the bathroom. He came out a moment later with a single sheet of paper. He held it with both hands, his hazel eyes eagerly scanning the page. His brow furrowed.

Brooke watched as his eyes went back to the top of the page to read the note again. She walked over to him, and by the time she reached him, Noah's expression had gone blank. His arm fell to his side, and the note teetered there, on the brink of slipping from his fingers and falling to the floor.

"What is it? Is it from her?" Brooke carefully removed the sheet of paper from his hand. He made no move to stop her.

She looked down at the note. It was a lined page torn out from what must have been a journal. The page was light pink, and the ruling a darker shade of pink. A hand-written message was hastily jotted down in purple ink.

Noah,

I'm sorry, but I can't be here. I have to go home. Tell Brooke and Travis I'm sorry. Goodbye.

Love, Katelyn

Brooke read it again, equally taken aback. They stood in silence until a board creaked above them. Travis was up. Footsteps went across the ceiling, in the direction of the bathroom. The pipes began to hum. The shower.

"Noah, I—" Brooke began. She didn't know what to say. Was it the house? The woods? Travis's stupid-ass wendigo story? She seemed just fine last night, not nearly as freaked out as the night before. Why would she just leave all of a sudden? And not even wake Noah up to tell him goodbye? "Noah—"

"Did she just break up with me?" he asked softly.

Brooke looked at the note again. *Love, Katelyn.* "No. No, I don't think so. Love, Katelyn? Have you guys said that to each other yet?"

"No, we haven't. But I mean, people often sign notes that way, don't they?"

"I guess," Brooke said. She looked at the note once more, then handed it back to him. He took it from her and set it down on the table without looking at it again.

"I don't think it necessarily means she broke up with you," Brooke said. "Maybe she was just too spooked out by the woods to stay and she was embarrassed. She might be waiting for you when you get home." She reached out and rubbed Noah's arm, trying to comfort him.

"Then why didn't she *tell* me?" he whined. "I would have gone with her, if she was scared. Hell, I could have at least helped her pack up her stuff, if she didn't want me to come."

"I'm really sorry, Noah. I thought she was having a good time." Silence followed, and Brooke didn't know what to fill it with. Finally, she said, "Should we go back upstairs and tell Travis?"

Noah looked around the room, his eyes welling up as he took in the vacancy of the space. He nodded. "Yeah, I guess so." He looked down at the note, then walked away, leaving it on the table. Brooke followed him out the door and slid it shut softly behind her. Her gaze caught on the wall near the door, where an orangish glow hovered above her.

"The porch light is on." She pointed to the lantern mounted on the wall, where an incandescent bulb burned inside the dusty glass. "Were you guys sitting out here at all? Maybe that's what got her spooked. That damn loon was at it again last night."

"No, we never..." Noah trailed off. He stared up at the porch light. A cobweb hung haphazardly from the metal frame, bits of dew clinging to the finely spun silk. "We went to bed as soon as we came downstairs. Katelyn was feeling a little tired from her sunburn. And I was regretting those ghost peppers. So we decided to crash early."

"So you didn't turn it on?"

"*I* didn't. Do you think Katelyn was sitting out here by herself?"

Brooke looked at the collection of patio furniture on the small deck, then up to the clearing and surrounding forest. "I highly doubt it. She was a little spooked out by the forest and Travis's story. I don't think she'd go out here to sit by herself. But if she left early enough this morning, before dawn, then she might have needed the light to make her way to the stairs."

*"But why the hell wouldn't she tell me?"* Noah asked, nearly shouting. He walked over to one of the wicker chairs, dropped down into it, and put his face in his hands. "Why would she just... *leave?*" He threw a hand toward the empty room. "And why the hell didn't she take any of her stuff?"

Brooke sat down in the chair beside him, the dampness on the cushion sinking into her leggings. She reached out and took Noah's hand. He resisted her at first, then gave up and let his arm go slack. Eventually, he loosely wrapped his fingers around hers.

"If she was really freaked out, she might have just wanted to leave in a hurry," Brooke offered. "It doesn't mean she broke up with you. Now that it's light out, she might already be feeling silly for leaving in such a rush. What seems scary in the dark almost always seems silly in the morning. That's how it is with me anyway."

Noah nodded, not convinced.

"She might already be wishing she could call you and apologize for taking off like that. Maybe she'll even turn around and come back."

"Maybe," Noah muttered. He looked out at the forest, as if seeing it for the first time. "It was the fucking wendigo shit, wasn't it? I shouldn't have let Travis tell that stupid story. He never knows when to quit."

"*I* should have stopped him. He's my crazy husband."

"And my crazy brother."

They sat in silence for a while. "I guess we should go up and tell him what happened," Noah said. He gave her hand a squeeze, and let go.

"Yeah, I guess so," Brooke agreed. They stood up and crossed the deck to the stairs. In the clearing, birds were chattering as they hopped from branch to branch among the oak trees.

*Everything sounds better in the daylight,* she thought. *During the day, the birds' calls sound like cheerful little songs. At night, their calls sound like death.*

# Chapter 14

**Saturday, 9:14 a.m.**

"Noah, I am so freaking sorry," Travis said for the umpteenth time. "God, I feel like such an asshole. I never should have told that damn story in the first place." They sat in the house's main living room, the TV off and the room quiet.

Noah had informed his brother of Katelyn's sudden departure once he got out of the shower. At first, Travis thought it was a joke, but when he saw how distraught Noah was, he became concerned. Now they sat side by side on the couch, Noah staring at the blank TV with an equally blank expression, and Travis looking ashamed. "It's all my fucking fault."

"No, Travis. It's mine, too," Noah said. "I didn't tell her about the no-reception thing, even though I knew it would bother her. And then I let you tell that story on top of it. It's all my fault, really."

"I didn't stop you from telling that story either," Brooke said softly from the chair beside the couch. "Even after she told me she didn't like scary books." She stared at the various books on their shelves, then over at the locked door next to the spare bedroom. Her eyes lingered on the door. Locked from the other side. Not from their side.

Travis and Noah had moved on to what Katelyn's sudden departure meant for her and Noah's relationship. "Did either of you hear anything weird last night?" Brooke asked, cutting Travis off mid-sentence.

"Oh, c'mon babe. I know you were letting your mind run wild last night, but this—"

"What do you mean?" Noah asked, shifting forward on the couch so he could get a better look at Brooke. Travis sighed and leaned back, shaking his head.

"I didn't hear anything crazy," Brooke said defensively, more to Travis than to Noah. "But I did keep getting woken up by something. Noises."

Noah watched her, his eyes wide and not blinking. He didn't speak.

Brooke continued, "When I woke up the first time, I could have sworn I heard a scream. Coming from outside, down in the clearing. But I was all groggy and confused, and when I heard it again, it was that damn loon. I fell back asleep, and then when I woke up a second time, an hour or two later, I heard the guy upstairs clomping around."

"Maurice?" Noah asked, his eyes going up to the ceiling. He looked back at Brooke. "What do you mean, *clomping around*?"

"Well, he kept going from one side of the room to the other. Opening and closing stuff. I'm not sure. Travis heard it, too."

Noah shifted in his seat and looked at Travis.

Travis sighed. "Yeah, I did hear him walking around up there. I thought it was kinda weird that he was up in the middle of the night, but who knows? Maybe he's *always* up in the middle of the night. I don't know the guy's damn schedule."

"When I woke up in the morning, I just figured he has trouble sleeping and that's why he was up," Brooke said. "I was creeped out while I was lying there in the dark listening to him, but in the daylight it didn't seem all that weird. But…" She looked at the locked door again.

Noah followed her gaze. "Do you think he could have—"

"Dude, no," Travis said, grabbing Noah's arm. "How could he do that?"

"He has keys to all the rooms, I'm sure," Noah said. "He could have—"

"What? Come into your room in the middle of the night?" Travis glared at Brooke, clearly irritated with her insinuation.

Brooke shrugged helplessly. "It's weird that he's here," she said. "He was listening to Katelyn and I the other morning, while we were out drinking coffee. We could see his shadow up there, like he was hiding or something. And he was also watching us the day before, too, while we were down in the clearing."

"That doesn't mean he's an ax murderer," Travis grumbled. "Babe, you know how your imagination can get. I don't want you guys convicting this guy just because he has insomnia."

"We're not *convicting* him of anything," Brooke snapped.

"Not yet." Travis turned back to his brother. "Noah, I'm so sorry she left. But she obviously left of her own free will. Not because the guy upstairs attacked her."

"But he could have—"

"No, he couldn't. How could he sneak into your room, grab Kate, and then drag her outside without you waking up?"

Noah looked like he was about to say something, thought better of it, and slumped back down on the couch. "I am a heavy sleeper," he muttered.

"That heavy?" Travis asked, his eyebrows raised.

"No, I guess not."

Brooke drummed her fingers on the arm of the chair. "So what should we do now? Stay? Leave?"

Travis looked at Noah. "It's up to you, bro. We can pack up and head home right now if you want."

"How are we going to leave?" Brooke asked. "We can't call for an Uber. And now we don't have a car."

"Maurice must have a landline. He runs an Airbnb, for Christ's sake. I'm sure guests have had to call out before. It even said it on the site—landline telephone available upon request."

Noah ignored them, his eyes lingered on the locked door. "No, I want to stay," he said slowly. "She might end up coming back, and if we're not here, she'll be all alone with that guy." He jerked his chin toward the locked door. "And if she doesn't come back and it turns out she really did dump me, at least I'll still get to spend some time with you guys."

"You sure?" Travis asked.

"Yeah, I am. I'm just gonna go down and take a shower and get dressed." Noah stood up. He looked shorter somehow, defeated.

"Do you want to move up here?" Brooke asked. "We have the spare bedroom, if you don't want to be down there by yourself."

Noah shrugged. "Yeah, maybe. We'll see how I feel tonight, and if she comes back."

"Okay, sounds good," Brooke said. Then added, "Noah, I'm so sorry."

"Yeah. Me too," he said, and went out the door.

# Chapter 15

*"Kate? Kate..."*

Brooke stirred. She had fallen asleep in a lounge chair on the deck. *Cujo* lay against her chest, her finger curled inside, marking her page. She sniffled, looking around for the bookmark as she wiped sleep seeds out of her eyes. *Not enough sleep last night,* she thought, finding the bookmark in her lap and sticking into the book where her finger had been.

*"Kaaate..."* The call came again, from down below, in the clearing. Noah's voice.

Brooke stood from the chair, her legs feeling stiff and her low back grumbling at her for falling asleep in such an awkward position. She set the book down and walked over to the railing, rubbing at her lower back as she went. Noah was down at the edge of the trees, looking around and calling for Katelyn with his hands cupped over his mouth.

She was about to call out to him, thought better of it, and headed toward the stairs instead. Travis was inside taking a nap, and she didn't want to wake him. They had all decided to crash for a bit after having lunch, tossing a Frisbee around for a while, and then watching a movie. *Lethal Weapon*—their choice, not hers.

Brooke reached the bottom of the stairs and entered the clearing. She walked past the hammock, the picnic table, the swing, then slowed as she neared Noah at the edge of the forest. "Whatcha doin'?" she asked. They hadn't spoken about Katelyn's departure since the morning discussion in the living room, although her absence hung heavily in the air.

"I couldn't sleep, so I came down here to take a walk and clear my head."

*"Okaaay,"* Brooke said, drawing out the word. "But why are you calling for Katelyn?"

Noah shrugged and kicked at a clump of grass. "I don't know. Her taking off like that just doesn't seem like something she would do. She'd at least," he shook his head, frustrated, "wake me up or something."

Brooke looked out into the woods, the dense foliage making it difficult to see more than a few yards inside. "What makes you think she'd be out here? She took the car, left a note."

"When I got down here I noticed some broken branches." Noah pointed to the undergrowth near one of the oak trees.

"And the grass... I thought maybe it looked like something happened here."

Brooke looked over to where he was pointing. "Was it like that before?" She walked past him, heading in that direction.

Noah followed her. "I don't think so. But—I don't really remember. It's not like I was paying attention to that sorta thing."

Brooke looked at the grass near the edge of the clearing. There was a small section, three or four feet in diameter maybe, that looked like it had been pressed down recently. She knelt beside it and ran her hand along the surface of the grass, following the bent blades as they headed toward the trees. Closer to the oak, some tufts of grass looked like they had been pulled out. Chunks of dark soil, more black than brown, hung loosely to their roots.

"Well?" Noah asked hopefully.

"It definitely looks like something's been through here," Brooke said, "but I can't really tell what. The damn grass is so thick. Maybe it was an animal? Maurice did say there were bears around here."

"A bear came into the clearing, rolled around, tore up some grass, then ran off?"

"Maybe?" Brooke said, although her voice didn't sound very convincing. Her knowledge of typical bear behavior was limited at best. "We should wake up Travis. Maybe he will have a better idea—"

Noah brushed past her and entered the forest, parting the underbrush with his hands before stepping through. He marched forward without turning back, and before she knew what she was doing, Brooke followed him into the trees.

Branches clawed at her calves and tore at her skin, which was bare up to her knees thanks to her capri leggings. Brooke paid them no mind, her focus on the ground as she tried to find the path of least resistance through the undergrowth. When she stumbled out of the bushes she collided with Noah, his body feeling as rigid as a tree trunk.

Brooke felt herself go off balance, and grasped at Noah to steady herself. He stuck his arm out and wrapped it around her before she could fall, without so much as looking in her direction.

"Noah, what the—" Brooke began. She followed his gaze, still clutching at his arm, and then all the breath was sucked from her lungs. Her insides suddenly felt hollow and empty, like they were devoid of oxygen and blood. They stood side by side, staring at the mess before them, not speaking.

The earth had been trampled, branches from the surrounding bushes cracked and torn away. Pine needles covered the forest floor, and splattered on top of them, more blood than Brooke had ever seen in her life. As an elementary school teacher, she saw her fair share of bloody noses and scraped knees, but this amount of blood was immense. Overpowering. Life-ending. This was a life-ending amount of blood.

It had already congealed, and stuck together in a sticky syrup of dirt, pine needles, and clots of red. Everywhere red. Brooke's stomach lurched, and she let out a retching sound.

Stomach acid burned at her throat. She tried to swallow it back down, but couldn't.

"Holy shit," she mumbled. Her head felt swimmy and off-kilter, like she might stumble and fall at any moment if she didn't have Noah's arm firmly wrapped around her. "Noah," she whispered.

"I don't know," he whispered back.

Blackness danced at the edges of her vision, then slowly faded out of her periphery as her breathing returned. The swimmy feeling in her head subsided as something else replaced it. Fear. Her adrenaline peaked, and she began tugging on Noah's arm, trying to pull him back toward the clearing. "We need to get out of here. We need Travis. Noah, we need to—"

"Do you think it was a bear?" Noah asked, not hearing her. His arm didn't move from around her waist, pinning her in place. Brooke continued to tug on him, but he was nearly as strong as Travis was. She was like a mouse tugging on a damn lion—he wasn't going to budge. She stopped trying.

"They're gonna hibernate soon," Noah went on. "Maybe they killed a deer and—"

"Then where's its body?" A deer hadn't even crossed Brooke's mind. For some reason, the second she saw all that blood, she was convinced it was human. That it was Katelyn's blood. But it could have been from an animal—was most likely from an animal. It was the freaking woods, after all.

*Definitely from an animal,* she thought. *Freaking horror movies. Now they have me imagining the worst even in the daylight.* Although the daylight was fading all around them as they stood in the midst of all that red. The forest sucked the light away, just like it did to her breath. Before long, it would be twilight, and not normal twilight—*woods twilight.* It came on faster and sooner than one would expect, turning the woods into nothing but shadows. Shadows that moved. Shadows that a nightlight couldn't chase away.

"Let's look for it." Noah released her unceremoniously and started carefully stepping around the bloody smears of pine needles.

Brooke immediately wanted his arm back. She didn't want to stand next to that life-ending amount of blood feeling alone and exposed. "What? *No!* Noah, no. If it's a bear, it might still be around here. *Noah!*"

Despite her protests, Brooke was already stepping from one unbloody patch to another, deeper into the woods, following him. Her flip-flops made it difficult to navigate the forest floor, and she stumbled more than once. She followed him blindly through the trees for an unknown amount of time, all her attention on her feet so she wouldn't trip and fall.

When Noah's legs finally came into view, unmoving and pointed to the right, Brooke slowed to a stop and looked up. The shed was there, around thirty paces away, vines growing against its posterior. The door was on the opposite side, where they had come through the other day.

"Why the shed?" she asked. "If it was a deer that died, it could be anywhere. Anywhere but inside a locked shed." Brooke felt her stomach fluttering, not with butterflies, but with bats. Bats with leathery wings and claws, tearing at her insides and making her feel weak and queasy. She didn't want to go near that shed. She didn't want to be following blood trails into the woods either. She wanted to be curled up in her lounge chair, reading a book about *somebody else* following blood trails into the woods. Not her. She wasn't in a horror novel. Her life was not a fictional tale. And if it was, a rom-com would sure be nice right about now.

Noah turned and looked at her. "Brookey, stay here," he said, calling her the pet name Travis always used to use when they were dating. She thought it was a dumb nickname—at least Babbling Brooke was clever—but Noah saying it now did seem to soothe her for whatever reason. Even so, she wasn't going to just stand here in the woods by herself. Not a chance in all of hell. When Noah started walking toward the shed, she followed at his heels, her fingers grabbing at the back of his sweatshirt.

They wrapped around the side of the shed closer to the clearing, and then came up to the double doors. The padlock was still there, and the doors still locked. The shed looked the same as it did when they discovered it on their first day. The weathered pine planks were old and cracked, the shingles aged and sagging. The only part of the shed that looked even remotely new was the padlock itself, glinting in the rays of late afternoon sunlight that managed to filter down from above.

"A deer wouldn't be in there, Noah," Brooke whispered, although she wasn't sure why she felt compelled to whisper. "What are you looking for?"

"I don't know. I was looking for the deer—or *something*—and then I saw the shed." He looked from Brooke to the shed, then back at Brooke. "Do you really think it's lawn equipment in there?"

"Why wouldn't it be?"

"Why's it so far from the clearing?" he asked. "You're telling me that guy lugs his lawnmower through the forest every time he wants to use it? Or the hedge trimmer or whatever? Why not have it closer to the house?"

"Maybe because it's an eyesore? Nobody who stays here wants to be looking at that ugly thing."

"This shed has been here for what looks like forever. Way before he started renting the place out."

Brooke felt like she was in a horror novel again, and she didn't like it. "Noah, I don't think we should mess around with it. *He'll know.*"

"Who?"

"The guy. Maurice. You go poking around that thing, he's gonna know."

"How will he know?" Noah walked up to the doors of the shed and jiggled the lock. "Heavy," he muttered, and dropped it back into place. He placed his palms against the double doors, one on each side, and pushed. The doors arched inward a few inches, then came back to the center. He pushed again, harder. The doors swung inward again, but no more than before. Noah was about to rejoin Brooke, but her words stopped him.

"Do it again," she said, curiosity taking over her brain, squashing down her common sense and striding right over the top of it. Noah looked at her questioningly. "The door," Brooke said. "Push it again."

"It's not gonna budge," he said. "That's a pretty heavy-duty lock."

"I just mean push it. Push the doors in like that again, and try to hold them there." Brooke joined him by the shed. She looked at the ground directly below the doors. It was a single slab of concrete, dusty with forest grime. "Push it. Now."

Noah pressed his hands against the doors again, pushing inward with a grunt. He spread his legs, leaning his body weight into the doors to keep them slightly arched. "What are you looking for?"

Brooke stared down at the concrete slab with mounting horror. With the doors arched inward, she could see a little bit of the floor inside the shed. And it was red. Dark, blackish red. Smeared red, just like the pine needles. "Oh God," she murmured, and stumbled backward.

Noah let go of the doors and they came forward again, concealing the blood-splattered concrete inside. "What the hell, Brooke? What did you see?"

"Red," Brooke said. "I saw red." Her voice didn't sound like her own. It was high-pitched, almost childlike.

Noah pushed the doors in again. They creaked on their hinges, a rusty grating sound. He looked down as he pushed. "What the fuck?" he uttered in surprise, and jumped away from the shed as if it was on fire. "What is that?"

"Red," Brooke said again.

*"Kate!"* Noah ran up to the doors and pounded on them with his fists. "Kate! Are you in there? *Katelyn!* Are you hurt?" He rammed one of the doors with his shoulder, putting

his full weight behind it. The hinges grinded together, but the doors wouldn't budge.

"Noah, she's not in there," Brooke said in the strange little-girl voice, but she didn't believe the words as they left her mouth. She stood there, like an idiot, her arms wrapped tightly across her body, feeling like the little girl she sounded like. Helpless and afraid.

Noah dropped to his stomach and pressed the side of his head against the concrete, trying to look beneath the doors. "Katelyn?" he called. "Ka—" he stopped, her name cut off. Brooke imagined the letters of her name, cut through the center and dripping red. Dripping blood.

"There's something under here," Noah said from his position on the ground. "Brooke, get over here."

"I—" Brooke squeaked. She took a step backward instead, and bumped into a tree she didn't realize was behind her. Her entire body spasmed, and she felt like the lump in her throat was actually her heart, pressing against her tonsils and threatening to leap from her mouth if she didn't swallow it back down. The jolt did get her moving, though, and she walked over to the shed in a trance.

"Push the doors in," Noah said from the ground.

Obediently, Brooke pushed the doors in as hard as she could. Her shoulders ached with the effort, and she felt her toes sliding out of her flip-flops as she tried to brace herself on the forest floor.

"Stop," Noah said. He came onto his elbows, looked around the ground for a moment, then picked up a twig. He inspected it, then tossed it aside. "Hey, do you see any—"

Brooke knelt down, grabbed a stick that was near her foot, and handed it to Noah.

"Perfect," he said. He got back onto his stomach and peered under the doors, stick in hand. "Okay, go."

Brooke pushed the doors again. She struggled to keep them arched inward, but her feet were slipping. One foot came out of her shoe completely, and she felt rocks scraping against the arch of her foot and pine needles jabbing in between her toes.

Noah fished around with the stick, and Brooke heard something scrape across the concrete floor inside the shed. She pressed harder into the door, her second shoe sliding off. The scraping sounds continued, and then something shiny appeared, brought out by Noah's stick. A phone. An iPhone. Noah snatched it from the ground and stood up. Brooke let the doors go, and they quickly swept back together, the padlock jiggling in the latch.

"It's Katelyn's," Noah said without a hint of uncertainty. He flipped it over. The case had a cartoon puppy and kitten snuggled up against each other. "Definitely Katelyn's."

"Why would it be in there?" Brooke asked. A stupid question, but she didn't know what else to say.

"There's no blood on this thing at all," Noah said, turning the phone over in his hand. "Maybe that means she's alright. That she got away…" His voice trailed off when he saw Brooke's expression. "You don't think she got away?"

"I don't know what I think. I—we need to go get Travis. He'll know what to do. He always knows what to do."

Noah nodded. "Yeah, you're right." Without another word, he turned and started following the path that led back to the clearing.

Brooke watched him go. She wanted out of the woods, but she also didn't want him to ask her if she thought they would be able to save Katelyn. Because she didn't believe Katelyn needed saving—not anymore.

A breeze trickled through the trees, somehow colder than the surrounding air. *Cold like in a ghost movie when the ghost is standing right behind you.* And with that thought, Brooke shoved her feet back into her flip-flops and hurried up the path. *No more haunted, bloody woods for me. No fucking thank you.*

Noah was waiting for her when she emerged from the forest a moment later. He was looking up at the house, his knuckles white from the death grip he had on Katelyn's phone. "It was him, wasn't it?"

"Who?" Brooke asked. She followed his gaze up to the house, momentarily confused when she didn't see anything amiss. And then she saw it—on the top level, in one of the windows. The curtains were pulled to the side, and beyond the dirty panes of glass, a shadowed figure stood just out of view. Maurice was watching.

# Chapter 16

**Saturday, 6:25 p.m.**

"We have to confront him," Noah seethed. *"Right fucking now!"* He paced the living room, his hands shaking by his sides. Brooke watched him go back and forth, back and forth, his rage an almost palpable presence in the room.

Travis was sitting on the couch beside her, his chest expanded and his spine so rigid she thought his vertebrae must be constructed of steel and bolts instead of bones and ligaments. He kept one of his arms wrapped firmly around her waist, as if she might float away if he didn't keep her tethered in place.

Brooke knew what this puffed up posturing meant for her husband; she had seen it from time to time during their courtship and marriage. Travis was scared. And he was doing the only thing he knew to do at the moment: protect her. Every other time he puffed up with alpha male bravado, it turned out to be for something silly—a noise outside that ended up being a raccoon, a man stepping out from the shadows in a parking garage that ended up being the security guard—but this time it didn't feel so silly. This time she leaned into his broad frame, grateful for the safety his arms provided.

The brothers had returned from the shed not ten minutes ago, Travis seeming to have lost his tan in only a few moments' time. He now looked pale, worn out. Creases marred his brow and his lips were compressed into an almost invisible line across his face.

After their cryptic discovery in the woods, Brooke and Noah had woken Travis and informed him of what they had found. In true Travis fashion, he had insisted on seeing it for himself, and Noah had agreed to go down with him. Brooke, however, refused to go back out there. She didn't want to see it again. Not the blood, not the shed. Not the *bloodshed*. And she especially didn't want to go traipsing around out there at dusk. No freaking way. In the woods, it was probably already night.

Instead, she sat on the couch, absentmindedly picking at her fingernails as she thought about Maurice—lurking on the balcony and listening to their conversations, peeking out from behind the curtains and watching their every move. It was creepy enough, at least to her, that he was here at all, but when you added his constant surveillance into the mix, it wasn't just creepy—it was sinister. And what about him running all over the house in the middle of the night? *Insomnia, my ass,* Brooke thought as she tore viciously at a hangnail, her eyes glued to the door handle that led to the locked indoor stairwell. Locked from the *other* side. She kept expecting the handle to jiggle, the knob to slowly twist back and forth like it does in the movies, but it never did.

Even now, with her men returned, she still found her eyes straying to that doorknob. That unmoving doorknob. Was Maurice on the other side? With his ear pressed to the door and a butcher knife in his hand? Brooke thought of *The Shining*, and how easily Jack had broken down that bathroom door with only a few swings of his ax. Only this was different, because Maurice didn't need an ax. He had a key. He had *all* the keys.

"Dude, we can't just march up there and start accusing him of stuff," Travis insisted, his arm tightening around Brooke's waist. Before long, it would start to hurt.

Brooke forced her eyes away from the doorknob. It's not like it was going to move when she was looking at it anyway. Instead, she watched the brothers as if they were in the midst of a heated tennis match, the argument volleying from one side of the living room to the other. At least no one was throwing backhands. Yet.

"Why the hell not?" Noah snapped. "He obviously killed Katelyn! God knows what else the sick fuck did to her in that shed."

Brooke shuddered. She didn't want to think about that shed anymore, or what possibly could have happened inside of it. Her eyes drifted back to the locked door, again waiting for the doorknob to turn. *It won't move right now,* she thought. *Not when you're waiting for it. In the movies, it always happens when you least expect it. After you thought you were safe.*

"We don't know that Katelyn is dead," Travis volleyed back. "This can all be some sort of… misunderstanding."

"How can you *misunderstand* Kate's phone being in that fucking murder shed?"

"We don't know that it's a murder shed. That might not be blood on the ground. It might be—"

"What? Might be what?" Noah stopped pacing and fixed Travis with a contemptuous glare, his arms folded defensively across his chest.

Brooke sighed. Now Noah was the one that was puffed up. And if this situation didn't deescalate real quick, Travis was gonna puff up right alongside him. And then what would she do? Watch them fight it out in the murderous innkeeper's living room? *And that's when the doorknob will turn. While they're fighting and I'm standing helplessly on the sidelines. I'll get pulled inside and they won't even notice. Not until it is too late.*

"Paint?" Travis ventured, wincing as he said the word. As if he knew how pathetic the explanation was even before the syllable had left his lips.

*"Paint?"* Noah repeated, his voice on edge. "You think someone went out there and decided to smear a bucket of red paint around? Just for the hell of it?"

Travis sighed. "Yeah, that's bullshit," he muttered. He slumped down on the couch, his bravado deflated and steel spine cracked with rust. Now he just looked tired.

Brooke jumped as a hand brushed against her leg. "You okay, babe?" Travis asked. "You've been really quiet."

"I'm—I don't want to be here anymore," she murmured, her eyes darting back to the doorknob. "I think we need to call the police. And then we need to leave."

"How?" Travis asked. "The car's gone."

"And how in the hell is the car gone?" Noah quipped. He was standing near the sliding glass door and looking out at the woods. If this was a cartoon and not a horror movie, Brooke thought she would be seeing waves of heated rage radiating off his body right about now. "If she was taken out there," he said, jutting his chin toward the woods, "then why the fuck is her car gone?"

"That's why I'm saying maybe it's a misunderstanding," Travis said cautiously. "The note she left for you, the car being gone. It's still possible she left because she was scared. Probable even. What you found in the woods… it could easily have been from a bear. A completely unrelated incident."

"And the shed? With her phone inside?"

*"Fuuuuck,"* Travis said, drawing the word out into a long exhale. "That I don't know." He squeezed his eyes shut and leaned his head back against the couch, thinking. "Maybe she left it somewhere, or dropped it when she was leaving," he suggested. "Maurice stumbled upon it, didn't know it was one of ours, and put it in the shed for whatever reason. Or he accidentally left it in there when he went to go get something."

Noah grunted, unconvinced. "He fucking did it, bro."

"We don't know that," Travis countered. "Not for certain."

Their heads swiveled in unison as they both turned to look at Brooke, the elected tiebreaker. "I have no idea what happened," she mumbled, unnerved by the ensuing silence as they waited for her to choose a side. Instead of giving in to their heated stares, she said, "I *do* know that we can't stay here, though. It's time to leave. Past time."

Noah's eyes narrowed. "If we leave, and Katelyn's still here and in trouble, we're effectively killing her. You know that, right?"

Travis cleared his throat. "And if you're right about him being a killer, and we do stay here, he could go after Brooke next. Is that what you want?"

Noah's mouth fell open. "Of course I don't want that! I would die if something happened to her."

"So would I," Travis said in a clipped tone, his shoulders tense.

Brooke's eyes went back to the doorknob, the men's voices fading from her mind. If Travis was right, Katelyn was fine and this was all just some sort of big misunderstanding. On the other hand, if Noah was right, they were sharing the house with a murderer. A *serial killer*, most likely.

Brooke could feel her imagination working on overdrive, much like it did in the depths of the night. Logic was gone, and so was reasoning and common sense. And in their wake, they left ample room for the clothes pile monster to form and grow. Room for a murderous innkeeper to take shape, and for a rogue bear to acquire a taste for human flesh.

"Do you think he could have done this before?" she asked softly, knowing Travis wasn't going to be happy with her, but still unable to keep the words from tumbling from her mouth. "It's such a perfect setup, isn't it?" she went on. "'Come to my mountain retreat, where there is no way to call for help. And I will be staying right above you, waiting until the time is right to take you to my murder shed.'"

"Enough with the murder shed!" Travis exclaimed, exasperated. "Jesus, Brooke. Not you, too." He lifted his hand and rubbed at the stubble along his jaw, shaking his head irritably. "We have no concrete evidence that Maurice is a deranged killer, or that anything sinister happened to Katelyn. All we have is a bunch of what-ifs. And I'm not going to go up there and confront this guy based on what-ifs."

Travis's gaze swept from Brooke to Noah. "And if by some off chance he *is* what you think he is, then we sure as hell shouldn't be going up there and accusing him of it. God knows what the hell he'd do."

Noah's jaw ticked, but he didn't argue. "Then what do you suggest we do?"

"Well, we can't call for a ride out of here, because we'd have to go up there with him to use his phone. Same thing with calling the police. And we also can't stick around here waiting for what happens next."

"Well, that's a whole lot of we-can'ts, bro. What the hell *can* we do?"

"We can hike the fuck out of here, that's what we can do. But not in the dark."

"So you expect us to stay the night? In here. With him." Brooke's eyes darted to the unmoving doorknob. "The goddamn door only locks from the other side, Travis. He can come right in here whenever he wants to. No fucking way!"

Hot tears stung at Brooke's eyes, feeling more like acid than saline. She had unwittingly jumped onto the 'Maurice is a killer' train, and now that she was on board, she couldn't stand the thought of sticking around to see who he picked off next. "I don't want to stay here," she whined. "It's better to leave right now. We're able-bodied. We can hike through the night if we have to."

"With the bears?" Travis asked. "It's miles and miles to the nearest town, babe." He patted her thigh, which felt more condescending than he probably intended it to. She fought the urge to smack it away. "Think what you want about Maurice," Travis went on, "but he wasn't lying when he said there are bears out there."

"I'd rather take my chances with the bears," Brooke snapped, although she could already feel the determination draining from her voice. She did *not* want to take her chances with the bears. She had been terrified of bears since she was a little girl. Ever since she realized they were a lot more teeth than they were snuggle. *Screw you, Charmin.*

Brooke slouched in her seat, refusing to make eye contact with either of them. Travis was right, and judging by Noah's silence, he had come to the same conclusion. "So we stay?" she asked, her shoulders slumping. Her voice sounded small again, the little-girl voice.

"Start walking at first light," Travis said, nodding. He looked over at Noah. "Maybe you should stay up here with us? Not alone downstairs."

"Why not the other way around?" Noah asked. "This is the level that has that creepy locked staircase."

"I'm sure he has keys to all of the levels," Travis pointed out. "Here we at least have a kitchen, and two beds."

"What about that door?" Brooke asked. "If we're all asleep he can—"

"We'll sleep in shifts," Travis said, cutting her off. He probably didn't want to hear how she was going to finish that sentence. Truth be told, neither did she. "Someone can always keep an eye on the door then. Sound good?"

"Not really," Brooke muttered. "But I guess it will have to do."

"I'll go get my shit from downstairs then." Noah stood from the chair. He walked over to the sliding door, paused, then looked back. "Do you really think this might all be some sort of big misunderstanding?" he asked Travis. "And some day the four of us will be sitting on the beach or in some desert lodge out in Arizona, laughing about that time Travis picked a haunted forest with an evil innkeeper for our weekend reunion?"

"God, I hope so," Travis said with a weary laugh. It sounded hollow, empty.

Brooke didn't respond. Instead, she looked back at the doorknob, watching for signs of movement. She had a sneaking suspicion this would be their last weekend reunion together, but she didn't want to say the words out loud.

# Chapter 17

**Sunday, 3:56 a.m.**

Brooke sat in the armchair next to the bookshelves, tapping her feet on the worn carpeting. The Ramones were playing on an endless loop inside her head, singing about pet semataries and how they didn't want to be buried inside one of them. Neither did she.

She scrunched her nose and squeezed her eyes shut. Not that song. Why couldn't she have something cheerful and optimistic stuck in her head? Not a song about the woods. About being brought back from the dead. About being *buried*. Her eyes darted to the locked door. Was it still locked? Was he on the other side?

Her feet resumed their anxious tapping and the Ramones filtered back in, louder and more foreboding than ever.

Brooke let out a frustrated sigh and shoved herself up from the chair. Despite the hour, she felt alert and on edge, her anxiety playing an unsynchronized symphony on her central nervous system. Sitting still was difficult, and she often had to fight the urge to pace the room. If she did, she'd wear a hole in the floor before this night was up.

Noah and Travis were asleep in either bedroom, leaving her alone in the living room. Each of them had only six hours to sleep, and if they were going to be walking for God knows how many miles in the morning, they all needed what rest they could get. Noah had taken the first shift, staying awake from nine until midnight. Poor Travis got stuck with the middle shift, sleeping for three hours, then staying up from midnight until three a.m., which was when he went back to sleep and Brooke took over.

So far nothing out of the ordinary had taken place, and Brooke had not heard so much as a footstep from upstairs. At six she was supposed to wake up everyone, and then they would set out at first light to walk to town.

For the first half hour of Brooke's shift, her mind wavered between the possibility that something actually did befall Katelyn, or if there was a perfectly logical explanation for everything. Something to laugh about during their next vacation, as Noah had said.

However, as three a.m. gave way to four, without so much as a peep from upstairs, Brooke was really starting to wonder if what they saw in the woods was just from a bear, after all. She had always been one to jump to conclusions, especially when she was scared. Was that what she had done? Jumped to conclusions? And Katelyn was back at home, safe and sound, feeling guilty for leaving but unable to call Noah to explain why?

Brooke walked over to the locked staircase door. She leaned forward, bringing her ear just an inch from the stained oak. *Nothing.* No movement. No footsteps. No heavy breathing from the supposed madman up above. Her hand hovered over the door handle as she thought seriously about attempting to open it, then decided against it and moved away.

She wandered over to the bookshelves instead, her finger meandering from one book's spine to the next. She had gone through some of the shelves when they first arrived, but after finding *Cujo*, she had stopped perusing. Now, with *Cujo* finished, she thought she might as well start reading another one just to pass the time until sunrise. Preferably something a little more upbeat. Something about kittens, and fuzzy blankets, and ice cream sundaes. Brooke wasn't sure what kind of book that would be, since all her shelves at home were overflowing with horror and suspense novels. Maybe a romance book would be better this time, if the psychotic innkeeper happened to have any.

She scanned the plethora of titles as she went. There was quite the variety on the dusty shelves, with no sort of order or categorization. *Jurassic Park* was leaning against *The Chocolatier's Kitchen*, which was up against *Pride and Prejudice*. Brooke traced her finger along the colorful spines, her fingertip making its way over the mountains and valleys of the various novels.

She was just about to give Mr. Darcy and Elizabeth Bennet a try, when her finger flicked a piece of paper that was sticking out from between two books. The paper was wedged between them, its torn edge making a rasping sound as her finger dragged across it. Brooke stopped and looked down. Half an inch of paper protruded from between the books— *Lord of the Flies* and *Auto Repair For Dummies*—and she could see a bit of handwriting scrawled across the page.

She carefully dislodged the piece of paper, holding it by the edges like it was a piece of forensic evidence. It was a book page, cream paper torn from one of the novels on the shelves. The page was blank save for the handwriting, which was scrawled across the page next to a few brown smudges.

Brooke recoiled as she read the words. She dropped the page and jumped back, as if the paper had grown teeth and bitten her. It fluttered down to the back of the armchair, slid across the cushion, then tipped and made its final descent to the floor. It landed faceup, the words pointed toward the bookshelf.

Not safe here. Get out. NOW

A gasp clogged Brooke's throat as she looked down at the page, its scrawled words and brown smudges staring up at her defiantly. Not brown—red. Red smudges. Something that was once red and then faded to an ugly brown when it dried. Blood. Dried blood.

She was fixated on the last word—*NOW*—more than anything else. No punctuation. No period, no exclamation point, nothing. The other sentences had periods, but the last word... *NOW*... nothing. Like the person who wrote it didn't have time to scribble an exclamation point before they hastily shoved the paper into the stacks, leaving it out just enough to be discovered, but not enough to be conspicuous. *NOW*

Brooke whirled around and stared at the door to the staircase. Her eyes landed on the doorknob. Had it just moved? Jiggled slightly from side to side? He was on the other side of the door. He must be. Listening and waiting. Somebody else who stayed here—some poor girl that also wound up in his bloody murder shed in the woods—had scrawled a warning on a piece of paper torn from a book, then jammed said paper back onto the shelf before he came down and grabbed her. The girl knew she wasn't going to escape, so she did the one thing she could do: wrote a note of warning to whoever came next. *Not safe here. Get out. NOW*

Katelyn was dead. Noah and Travis will be dead. And she would be next—dragged out by her hair, down the stairs, across the clearing, and into that shed. Her back would be bleeding, from where the wooden stairs scraped across her spine, vertebra by vertebra. The dew from the grass would then soak her clothes as he dragged her across the clearing. And then dirt and leaves and twigs would stick to her body, abrading her bare shoulders and clinging to her hair in clumps. She would try to scream, but he would stop her somehow. Not that anyone was around to hear her anyway. He would incapacitate her—hit her over the head or kick her hard in the stomach—and then unlock that heavy padlock. She would roll over onto her stomach, clawing at the dirt and undergrowth, trying to get away from him. But he would overpower her, like he did with all his other victims. He would take her into that shed—that dark, dingy shed in the woods that smelled like old pennies and rusted iron. He'd shut the door, lock it from the inside somehow, and then he would... he would...

Brooke stumbled, her legs threatening to give out from beneath her. Her head felt light and unfocused, and she grabbed the armrest of the chair to steady herself. She let out a shaky exhale and breathed in, willing the lightheadedness to fade enough for her to no longer require the chair for support. Her balance regained, she let go and stared at the door handle. Had it moved? Or had she just imagined it?

*I imagined it. I panicked and imagined it. Just like I always do. Making monsters out of clothes piles. Making murderers out of innkeepers.* The note she didn't imagine, though. The note was real. She looked down at the floor to confirm this, saw the note lying in the same spot where it had fallen, and nodded. *Not completely batshit crazy. Not just yet.*

A loon's haunting call drifted out from the woods. Brooke jumped at the sound, her heart crashing against her rib cage with each beat, threatening to snap her ribs like twigs. *Fuck waiting 'til six,* she thought, and hurried across the living room toward her and Travis's bedroom.

Cold, blue moonlight drifted across her body as she passed the sliding glass door. The ripples of light and shadow across her sweater looked like silver fingers—like claws—that were trying to wrap around her and pull her outside into the darkness.

Another shrill call came from the forest. Brooke stumbled to a stop and looked out at the clearing, which was cast in an eerie silver glow. The last two nights the moon had been concealed by a thick layer of gauzy fog, but tonight the air was clear. Stars, brighter than any she had ever seen, covered the sky like broken shards of glittering glass. The moon, full and impossibly bright, splashed frozen beams of light across the vacant clearing. Brooke could see the picnic table, the hammock, the tire swing—all casting elongated shadows in the icy light. *A nightlight,* she thought, stepping closer to the window. The moon was her nightlight.

The two oak trees in the center of the clearing were fighting the light, struggling to keep the moon from revealing the forest's secrets. Their heavy branches, thick with crimson leaves, enshrouded the far end of the clearing in a blanket of shadows. The wooden swing at the clearing's edge was also swallowed by the shadows. Its ropes reached up from the darkness and grasped desperately at the branch above, as if trying to keep itself from falling into the blackened abyss forever.

Brooke froze, feeling shards of broken glass sliding down her spine, like the stars had fallen free from the sky and become embedded between her vertebrae. *The swing is moving.* She watched the ropes drift forward, then backward, then forward again. In turn, the branch it was tethered to bobbed up and down, bending with the weight of whatever was on the swing. Just like it did when Noah and Travis were horsing around on it the other day. And Katelyn, too, although the branch had barely budged under her slight weight.

Now it was moving freely, the leaves rustling in the moonlight and rubbing against the nearby pines. A few of the leaves managed to break free, and fluttered down into the black pit that was the oak's shadow.

Brooke's eyes followed the drifting ropes as she squinted against the blackness, straining to see what was hidden down below. *Something* was there, that much she was certain of. Something was on that swing, and its weight was causing the oak's branch to sway to and fro. More leaves trembled and fell, descending through the air to join the others in death and darkness.

Brooke's fingers crept onto the glass, which felt like the frigid wall of a freezer. She pressed her hands against the window, her breath momentarily fogging the glass. She sucked the air back in and held it, not wanting to further obstruct her view. Slowly, the fog vanished from the glass and the silver clearing reemerged. The oak's bough was still moving, and the swing still swaying silently through the night.

Another call came from the woods, piercing in its shrillness, and closer this time. Gooseflesh prickled her arms, coldness and fear moving across her flesh in an intricate dance.

Brooke watched the branch, almost entranced by its rhythmic perturbations, when suddenly the swing stopped moving. Not a slow, dwindling stop, but one that was harsh and abrupt. One second the swing was sailing through the night, and the next it was frozen in place, with only a few final leaves fluttering down to affirm that it had ever been moving at all.

Brooke took in a sharp breath and stepped away from the window. Whatever was on the swing wasn't anymore. It must have seen her. Which meant it was coming toward her, or retreating back into the forest. Only the darkness refused to reveal what course it had taken.

Brooke's hands trembled. The blood in the forest. The thing on the swing. The haunting calls in the night. *That note wasn't about Maurice.* Something was out there. Not lurking above them, but out *there*. It was watching her right now, from where it stood concealed in the shadows. It was watching, and it was waiting.

She took another step back. They weren't safe here. They never were. They needed to get out. *NOW*

# Chapter 18

*Sunday, 4:11 a.m.*

Brooke stumbled backward, banging into an end table as she went, and fell to the floor with a thud. The table lamp went over with a crash, and the warm, comforting glow in the living room disappeared, replaced by frozen moonlight. A sharp pain shot up from her knee where she landed, and she instinctively reached for it and began rubbing, gritting her teeth as she waited for the brilliant pain to subside. Before it did, the bedroom door swung open and Travis appeared.

"Babe, what the hell? Did something happen? Is it Maurice?" Travis knelt beside her and wrapped his arms around her, his body tense and muscles twitching. "I knew I shouldn't have left you alo—"

"No," Brooke stammered. "Not Maurice." She pointed a shaky finger at the window. "Something's outside."

"What?" Travis asked, tension giving way to confusion. "What's out there?"

The pain in Brooke's knee was transitioning to an angry throb. She moved her hand away and wasn't surprised to see a red spot on her jeans, just to the side of her kneecap. It looked almost black in the moonlight.

A door swung open on the opposite side of the room. Travis's body went rigid and he shifted his weight to place himself between her and the sound. *Maurice?* she thought. *Coming down here right when we're distracted.* Brooke dug her fingers into the meat of Travis's arm.

"Dude, what the fuck?" Noah muttered, his voice thick with sleep.

Brooke and Travis's bodies relaxed in unison. She peered around his shoulder, to where Noah was standing in the darkened doorway of his bedroom. The door to the stairs remained closed, the handle still.

"What's going on?" Noah asked, rubbing sleep seeds from his eyes as he walked across the room. "I heard—" he stopped, looking down at them. "Brookey, are you okay?" He knelt down beside Travis. "What happened? Why are you guys sitting here in the dark?"

"Careful," Travis said, gesturing with his chin. "There's glass."

"I tripped," Brooke muttered. "It doesn't matter." She waved her arm toward the window. "*Something is out there.* In the clearing."

Travis and Noah exchanged nervous glances, then looked over at the window, where a cool glow was spilling in from the outside. The moonlight's claws tore at their faces as they approached the glass, making their features look grotesquely broken. Brooke turned away, not wanting to see what the frozen light did to the men she cared for. It turned them into ghouls.

They stood at the window, side by side, peering out into the night. Brooke sat on the floor, watching their silhouettes as they surveyed the clearing. She expected murmurs of horror and disbelief, but neither man said a word. Before long, she couldn't take the silence anymore. "Well?" she asked in her little-girl voice.

"Babe, I don't see anything," Travis said softly. He still had his back to her as he continued to scan the clearing.

"Me neither," Noah said, and turned away from the window. He looked down at Brooke, the pity in his eyes clearly visible despite the darkness of their surroundings.

Frustrated, Brooke shoved herself up from the floor. Her left knee buckled, and Noah reached out and steadied her. She gave him a small smile of gratitude, then brushed past him and limped over to the window.

"It was on the swing. It was going back and forth and the branch was moving." She looked out the window. Everything was silent and still, like an eerie moonlit photograph. "It was there. I *swear*. I saw it moving."

"Babe, it's okay," Travis said. He wrapped an arm around her and led her away from the window. "Noah, could you find a light? It's dark as hell in here."

Travis reached the dining table and pulled a chair out for Brooke. She allowed him to guide her over to the seat and sit her down. There was another scrape of wood against wood, and then he was sitting in the chair beside her.

Golden light overwhelmed the room, and she squinted against it. She carefully opened her eyes again, one at a time, just in time to see Noah sit down in the chair opposite them. He had turned on the dusty chandelier above the table, which made her feel like they were items illuminated in a display case. She looked back at the window, but now all she could see were their own reflections. *This whole house is a display case,* she thought, and shuddered. *For whatever is out there.*

"Okay, babe. Tell us what happened." Travis reached out and enfolded her hand in his. The gesture was supposed to be comforting, but Brooke could barely feel his touch. Only the burning in her retinas registered, and the throbbing in her knee. And the prickly feeling of being watched—can't forget about that one.

"I—" she started. "I don't know. I was going to read a book, and then..." Brooke jerked her hand away from Travis and shoved herself up from the table. Her knee screamed in protest, but she stubbornly refused to acknowledge it. "The note!" she exclaimed. "I found the note!" Relief flooded through her system like a broken dam. She wasn't crazy, after all—the proof was lying on the floor on the other side of the room.

"The note?" Travis's voice.

"What note?" Noah's voice.

Brooke ignored them. She hurried across the living room to retrieve the torn page from where it had fallen next to the bookcase. For one horrible moment she thought it wouldn't be there, like she had imagined the entire chain of events that left her on the floor with a busted knee and an even-more-busted lamp. But the note was there, right where she had left it. She brought it back to the table and set it down in front of Travis, a trickle of triumph running through her veins. *Take that, clothes pile monster. I didn't imagine it this time, did I?*

Travis looked at the paper, his expression unreadable. He then used his index finger to twirl the page around so it was facing Noah.

Noah leaned in, his brows drawing together as he read the words. "What the hell is that?"

"I found it shoved between two of the books. I thought it was someone trying to warn us about Maurice. I was about to wake up Travis and tell him about it, but then I saw the swing moving outside. And then I fell."

Noah picked up the note, turned it over, saw the back was blank, and then set it back down. "I don't like this," he said nervously. He pushed the note away, as if it was contaminated somehow and he didn't want it near him. "What are those smudges?"

"It looks like..." Travis picked up the page and held it to the light, "blood, I think." He looked over at Brooke. "Where did you find this again?"

"On the bookshelf, between two of the books. *Lord of the Flies* and—"

"How'd you see it, I mean? Was it sticking out?"

"Yeah, a little bit. But not a lot. I must have missed it when I was looking at the books the other day."

"What's it mean?" Noah asked. "'Cause to me it sounds like Maurice is an even sicker bastard than we originally thought, and we need to get the ef out of here right now."

"Yeah," Travis agreed. "We need to leave right now. Fuck this place."

Travis tried to stand, but Brooke grabbed his arm and pulled him back down. "We can't, Travis," she said. *"It's out there."*

"There's nothing out there, babe." Travis sounded concerned, but his eyes said differently. She had been married to him long enough to know when he was growing impatient with her. This was just another clothes pile monster to him, conjured up from his lovely wife's overactive imagination. "We didn't see anything when we—"

"It was on the swing," Brooke insisted, cutting him off. "I know you guys didn't see it, but I'm telling you Travis, something was out there. Something big enough to move that branch."

"Like a bear?" Noah asked from across the table.

Brooke looked over at him, relieved to see genuine concern in his hazel eyes instead of mock sympathy. "Not a bear," she said. "Bears don't use swings."

"It was *using* the swing?" Noah's eyes widened. "Like… like a person?"

Travis sighed, loud enough to cause both of them to turn and look at him. "Brooke—" he started.

"Travis," Brooke said, cutting him off, "I really saw it. I didn't imagine it."

"Babe, I don't think you imagined it. Maybe there was a strong gust of wind or something that pulled on the swing and rattled the branch. It might have made it look like something was on it, but there isn't anything out there."

"Yes there is!" Brooke exclaimed. She threw a hand toward the window. "There isn't any wind, Travis. If you don't believe me, go take another look."

"Hey, uh, guys," Noah interrupted. "Let's not fight, okay?"

Travis looked at Brooke with a pained expression. In response, she slouched down in her chair and crossed her arms over her chest, directing her gaze to an arbitrary spot on the wall.

Noah turned his attention to Travis. "If Brooke is certain she saw something, maybe we need to consider—"

"Brooke is certain she sees a lot of stuff," Travis interrupted. "Prowling serial killers, shadow monsters in the closet." He turned his eyes to Brooke. "I'm not trying to discredit you, babe. But you have to admit, I've had to investigate a lot of scary shadows and spooky noises back at home, and they never amounted to anything." He tilted his head to the side to try and catch her attention, but she stubbornly refused to meet his gaze.

Instead, Brooke looked at Noah. "I saw the swing moving, Noah. And I heard something scream."

"You heard a loon calling," Travis corrected. "We've all heard them, every night we've been here."

"This sounded different." Brooke finally allowed herself to meet Travis's stare. "It was violent. And angry."

"I'm sure it *sounded* that way after you found that scary-ass note."

Brooke quirked a brow. "So you believe me about the note then?"

"How can I not?" Travis shoved the note away. "That shit's fucking creepy."

"Finally something we can all agree on," she muttered. "So what's your explanation for the note then?"

Travis craned his neck and looked at the ceiling, Noah and Brooke following his gaze. "I think you guys were right about Maurice being a sick fuck. And I think we need to get out of here immediately, like the note said. We can leave right now."

"I'm not going out there," Brooke said with a defiant shake of her head. She hugged her arms to her chest, her eyes fixated on the floor. "You guys can go if you want to."

"Babe, there is no way in hell I'm leaving you here alone with that guy."

"Well, I'm not going out there. Not at night. Not a chance."

Travis sighed, exasperated. "Noah, what do you think?"

Noah fidgeted in his chair, clearly uncomfortable with the decision landing on him. Instead of answering, he stood and walked over to the window. He cupped his hands around his eyes and peered through the glass. Finally, he said, "I don't *see* anything."

Brooke felt her stomach drop. They were going to make her go out there, where the thing on the swing was possibly still standing in the shadows. Waiting.

"But that doesn't mean there isn't something there," Noah continued. "Even if it's just your run-of-the-mill black bear, I still don't like those odds. Us versus bear? Doesn't sound too promising."

"What about us versus crazy psychopath upstairs?" Travis asked, also standing.

"Can't we at least wait until morning?" Brooke begged. "Like we were planning to do in the first place?" She remained seated, the note glaring up at her from the brightly lit table. She closed her eyes, willing the scrawled letters and brownish-red smudges to fade from her mind. They didn't.

Travis came up behind her and rested his hands on her shoulders. "The note says leave now. And I want to get you somewhere safe as soon as possible." He squeezed her gently, her shoulders feeling so small beneath his strong grip.

"Well, outside isn't safe," Brooke said, her mind made up. He could squeeze her shoulders as much as he wanted to—hell, give her a damn back massage while he was at it—and she still wasn't going to go out there. No freaking way.

"It will be light in just a couple hours," Noah said. "Can't we just wait until then? We're all awake anyway. If Maurice tries anything before sunrise, I think the three of us could take him."

"And what if he has a gun? My top priority is making sure my wife is safe. And I'm a lot more concerned about what's upstairs, not what's outside."

"You were okay with waiting until morning before," Brooke quipped.

"That's before you found that note. God knows who wrote that thing. And if they're even alive anymore"

"Could Katelyn have written it?" Noah asked, leaving the window. "She left that other note. And Brooke, she knows you liked looking at the books. Maybe she left it for you."

Brooke raised her eyebrows. She hadn't even considered that possibility. "What's her handwriting look like?"

"Hell if I know," Noah said. He went over to the note and looked it over again, then shrugged.

"How could you not know?" Travis asked.

"Who the hell writes handwritten notes anymore?" Noah snapped, immediately defensive. "All anyone does nowadays is text. Do you even know what Brooke's handwriting looks like? I mean, could you pick it out from a bunch of samples and say, 'Yeah, that's hers, alright'?"

"Okay, okay. How about we compare it to the note she left in your room."

"Can't do that right now," Brooke interjected. She looked out the dark window, and to the world of blackness lingering just beyond the glass. "We'd have to go outside and down the stairs, closer to the clearing. Not gonna happen." She pulled her eyes away from the window and reached for the note, which Noah relinquished without complaint. "I don't think this is from her anyway."

"Why's that?" Travis asked from behind her.

"Because of the ink color. The note to Noah was written with a purple pen. And on pink paper. This one is in pencil. Why would she write one note in purple, and then switch to a pencil for the second note? Why write two notes at all? Especially if she was in a hurry."

"Okay, regardless of who wrote what note and why, I still think we need to get out of here. Agreed?"

Brooke and Noah nodded in unison.

"But not until sunrise," she added.

*"Jesus."* Travis rubbed at his jaw, the disturbed stubble sounding like rough sandpaper. He went to the couch and sat down with a grunt. "You two are freaking ridiculous, you know that? Waiting around here like sitting ducks could end up getting us killed."

"Leaving before daybreak could do the same thing." Brooke went to the couch, sat down beside Travis, and gingerly took his hand in hers. "It's better this way, babe. Really. That note is about what's out there, not what's in here."

"And if you're wrong?" Travis wrapped his arms around her and pulled her close. He was staring at the staircase door, his eyes locked on the doorknob. "I would die if anything happened to you."

"I'm not wrong," she whispered, and kissed his cheek. She may have imagined a lot of stuff in the past, but this time she was certain of what she saw.

A troubling thought surfaced in Brooke's mind, one she was unable to shove back down into the shadows where it belonged. *You were certain all those other times, too. And if Travis is right and you imagined it, that means you have something else to fear other than a psychotic innkeeper and a mysterious playground visitor. You might actually be going crazy. And you can't hide from what's inside your own head.*

# Chapter 19

The incessant chirping and chattering of birds pulled Brooke back into consciousness. Her neck ached something fierce—like she was coming to after a particularly violent fender bender—and she felt sluggish and disoriented. She was curled up on the couch, leaning against Travis's body with her head awkwardly draped into the crook of his arm. Her neck shifted with each rise and fall of his chest, twinging the already-angry muscles inside.

Slowly, the shapes in the living room came into focus. She surveyed the space with sleepy eyes, and saw Noah sprawled across the adjacent armchair, one leg draped over the side and his head cast backward over the cushion. *His neck is gonna hurt, too,* she thought absentmindedly. He was snoring softly. Travis, not so softly.

The darkness of night had faded away, and the light coming through the windows was not the cool and hazy sunlight of early dawn. Instead, it was bright and unyielding—the strong light of a sun that had risen hours ago.

Brooke sat up with a jolt, the previous night's activities rushing back to her. They were supposed to leave at first light, which was, by the looks of things, hours ago.

Travis woke with a grunt, startled into consciousness by her sudden movements. "What time is it?" he slurred, his voice still drunk with sleep.

"I don't know," Brooke stammered. "Late, I think."

"We fell asleep? Jesus Christ... *I* fell asleep?" Travis shot up from the couch, going from groggy to furious. "I can't believe I fell asleep. He could have come in here. He could have attacked you. I'm the worst fucking protector ever." He punched his fist into his hand. *"Damnit."*

Brooke went over to him and grabbed his shoulders, tilting her head from side to side until she caught his gaze. "But he didn't," she said, her voice calm. "We were all exhausted. You didn't do anything wrong, babe."

"Easy for you to say," Travis grumbled. "I'm supposed to be taking care of you." He wrapped his arms around her, pulling her into him and hugging her tight. "I can't lose you," he whispered into her hair.

"You won't lose me, babe. I'm right here."

Noah, miraculously, was still asleep. Brooke went over to him and gently shook his shoulder, then again, not so gently. He cracked an eye open, looking equally disoriented to how she felt when she first woke up. His eyes then widened with realization, and he groaned. "God, if this was a horror movie, we'd all be dead by now," he muttered, standing up. "Anything happen while we were asleep? Any more cryptic notes to decipher?"

"Not that I can see," Travis said. He was already in the bedroom, throwing on a hoodie and shoving his wallet and cell phone into the pockets of his jeans. "Time to go. It's morning, all the playground monsters and black bears are sleeping off a crazy night of rattling the 'ol tree branches, and we are safe to get out of here." He raised his eyebrows and looked at Brooke expectantly. "Right?"

"Not funny," she said, but a touch of a smile twitched the corner of her mouth up anyway. They had made it through the night, and now they were getting out of here. The nightmare was almost over.

She grabbed her tennis shoes and slipped them on, then tried to stretch out her swollen knee as best she could. It ached with her movements, but it didn't scream, so at least that was something.

"I just gotta take a piss," Noah said, and trudged over to the bathroom.

Brooke stood from the couch, her sneakers tied and knee somewhat mobile, and looked out at the clearing. The grass twinkled with heavy drops of dew, as if the shards of ice that were last night's stars had melted and fallen to earth. The wooden swing hung in its usual spot, offering no hints as to what disturbed it in the night. There were no frayed ropes, no scrapes in the wood. As if the thing on the swing was just another clothes pile monster conjured up by her own imagination.

*Which means you might be losing your mind,* she thought as a knot took form in the pit of her stomach. She pulled her lower lip between her teeth and clamped down on it in an effort to keep it from trembling.

"Hey," someone said from directly behind her. Brooke jumped at the intrusion, her hands shooting up as if to ward off a blow. It was Noah, standing so close she could feel his breath on her neck.

Brooke turned to look at him, dread instantly flooding her system. Noah's complexion was ashen, and the worry lines marring his face had deepened. He leaned closer, his body almost vibrating with an emotion she couldn't quite place.

"What's wrong?" she asked.

"Can you come take a look at something?" he whispered into the shell of her ear.

"Um, yeah. Where?"

"In the bathroom."

"Noah… maybe this is a job for Travis."

"Just come on," he said, grabbing her hand and pulling her toward the bathroom door. Reluctantly, Brooke followed, allowing him to usher her into the cramped space before quickly following her inside. "I just didn't want to upset Travis with more fantastical theories until you saw it," he said, still whispering.

Brooke's brow furrowed. "Saw what?"

Noah pointed his finger at the ceiling, his eyes not straying from her face.

Brooke looked up, her neck twinging as she tilted her head back. The white paint was chipped and peeling, and the corners were yellowed with either age or mildew. Over the toilet, the ceiling dipped downward, like it had suffered considerable water damage at some point and never been repaired. In the center of the curvature, the paint looked off-color, like something dark was pooled above it.

The deformity had also created a small separation between the damaged ceiling and the adjacent wall, and from that opening, a few trickles of red had managed to slip through. Red that definitely wasn't there before. Red that was *still dripping*.

Brooke felt like she was going to faint, the periphery of her vision fading into a murky nothingness that was threatening to claim her. She could hear a singsong voice somewhere out in the blackness, calling her name. Luring her away, she thought. Trying to separate her from the others.

The singsong voice continued to call out her name, but now it sounded more urgent—no longer a song but a command. *"Brooke!"* Noah shouted, his voice chasing the lingering darkness away.

The bathroom faded back into focus, and she realized with sudden and almost crippling embarrassment that she was sitting on the toilet. Mortified, she reached down for her pants, overwhelmed with relief when she saw that they were still on. She wasn't *using* the toilet; she was merely sitting on it.

Noah was kneeling in front of her, his eyes searching hers. "Are you okay, Brookey?"

"I'm sorry, I just got dizzy there for a moment," she mumbled, her mind still clouded with haze.

"What are you guys doing in here?" Travis asked from the doorway, his voice alarmed and with a hint of an edge to it.

Noah jerked away and stood up, his hands fumbling with the pocket of his hoodie. "I was just asking Brooke if this was here before. On the ceiling. When she saw it she almost passed out."

Travis looked up and the color drained from his face. Brooke wondered if she was going to have to stand and offer him the toilet to sit on next. But then he grabbed the wall to steady himself, and she decided to remain seated. It was already a big enough clusterfuck in here as it was.

"No," Travis said, "that was *not* there before. What the hell is going on?"

"Is it… blood?" Brooke asked from her porcelain throne. "It looks like it. Like blood." She craned her neck and looked up at the drips of red, and then at the discolored circle of pooling liquid directly above her. The sight instilled a sudden, almost overwhelming urge to flee the bathroom. Before that pooling liquid came down through the ceiling and splattered all over her, just like Carrie at the prom.

*Nope nope nope.* Brooke jumped up from the toilet, almost knocking Noah into the shower in the process, and pushed past Travis. She went over to the couch and sat down, clutching her knees to her chest and shivering. All she wanted to do was go home. Why the hell did they come to this place? With no car and no reception. How freaking stupid was that? They should have canceled the trip when the truck broke down. Or at least got a rental car. *So. Freaking. Stupid.*

The guys were still in the bathroom, looking at the ceiling and whispering amongst themselves. They seemed to agree on something, and then came out of the bathroom together.

Travis walked over to her, stopping near her feet and waiting for her to look up. Brooke stubbornly resisted, knowing whatever he was going to say wasn't going to be a good thing. Otherwise, they wouldn't have been whispering.

"We're going up there," he said when she finally met his stare.

Brooke shot off of the couch like a gymnast, her knee shooting a bolt of pain up her leg. "Like hell you are! Why would you even consider doing that, Travis? I thought we were going to walk to town—"

Travis stooped down, lowering his face so his eyes were level with hers. He tilted his head toward Noah, then quietly said, "It might be Katelyn."

Noah was still standing by the bathroom, shifting his weight back and forth as he fidgeted with the cords of his hoodie. He kept glancing up at the ceiling, then looking away again, like some horrible game of visual tug-of-war.

"And what if it is?" Brooke asked, her voice not matching Travis's subdued tone. "What are you going to do? If she's up there bleeding, that means Maurice is guilty. And armed. Why on earth would you go up there?"

"If she's only injured, maybe there's still a chance we can save her," Noah said softly from his sentinel position by the bathroom door.

Brooke laughed, but it was humorless. Nothing good could come from going up to investigate a congealing blood puddle in a possible murder's living quarters. Which she said, loudly and repeatedly, as the guys went into the kitchen and looked around for weapons. Noah came back with a hammer, and Travis with a kitchen knife.

"You freaking idiots," Brooke whined, her voice bordering on shrill. "You acted like I was insane for not wanting to stroll down the road in the middle of the night, and now you're doing this. It's not going to end well. Giant blood puddles don't end well."

Without a word, Travis pulled open the sliding glass door, stepped through it, and went straight for the stairs. Noah followed, pausing at the door to look back at her. "Brookey, if there's a chance for me to save Kate, then I have to do it. You know that. Travis wants you to stay here. *Please stay here.*"

"Noah, even if it is her, you know it's too late, right? That amount of blood... enough to soak through a ceiling..."

"I know. But if it was you up there, do you think either of us would have even given a second thought about going up and trying to save you?"

Brooke's lower lip quivered, and her mouth suddenly felt impossibly dry. She knew Travis would have gone up there to save her, even if there were two or three killers armed with guns and knives. Hell, even if there were five. She bit down on her lip to stop it from trembling, then nodded grimly at Noah, her mouth too dry to speak.

Noah gave her a wan smile, then pulled the door shut behind him. Brooke listened to his footsteps as he crossed the deck and then started up the stairs. When the sound of his retreat faded completely, she was left with nothing but silence.

# Chapter 20

Seconds ticked by, each revolution of the clock feeling excruciatingly longer than the last. The wind had picked up, and the oaks' branches were quivering in the quickening breeze, their leaves rustling together and spilling onto the clearing floor. Brooke stood at the sliding glass door, hypnotized by the scarlet leaves fluttering through the air, and by the gentle sway of the pines beyond. It sounded like they were murmuring together, whispering secrets of the forest, of which, she was quite sure, they had many.

Brooke fidgeted from side to side, the muscles in her legs twitching and ready—for what, she didn't know. To run upstairs and help? To flee to safety? But where was that? Safety seemed a long way off, if attainable at all.

The incessant whispering was beginning to hurt her head, the sounds filling her senses and making it difficult to listen for signs of movement upstairs. It had been so easy to hear Maurice moving around the other night, but now, it might as well have been cement between them instead of just floorboards.

She was about to leave the room and go out onto the deck, as if she could hear better out there, but a sharp, crackling sound from above stopped her. It was muffled, but she was almost certain it was the sound of breaking glass. Not directly above her, but somewhere in the depths of the house.

Brooke's stomach lurched into her throat, and she felt her heart rattling inside its ivory cage. She moved to the center of the living room, her eyes searching the ceiling for answers. She heard footsteps now, going across the ceiling and coming toward her. More than one set. But was it three sets? She gritted her teeth and strained to decipher how many people were up there, but she just couldn't tell.

The steps moved past her—over her—and went toward the bathroom. She followed them, stopping at the bathroom door, where her eyes involuntarily locked on the red drips descending from the ceiling. There were murmuring voices directly above her, and then a clearly audible groan. Another voice, possibly Travis, yelled something that sounded like, *"Oh fuck!"* And then silence.

There might have been more, but Brooke was already out the door, running for the stairs.

Brooke catapulted up the stairs, almost slipping on the loose gravel that spanned the driveway as she ran for the front door. It was ajar when she arrived, hanging open like a gaping wound, and the adjacent window was broken. She hurtled herself through the doorway, then came to a clumsy stop inside Maurice's foyer. It was empty inside, but she could hear mens' voices coming from somewhere deeper inside the house.

Brooke looked around frantically for a weapon, wishing she had grabbed one before carelessly throwing herself into harm's way. *What a moron,* she thought bitterly. *In the movies, I'd be the first one to go. Without question.*

The interior of Maurice's living quarters came at her like blurred snapshots as she searched desperately for something to defend herself with. The floor beneath her sneakers: aged hardwood, with a frayed carpet runner going down the center. The walls: covered in faded, peeling wallpaper, with an assortment of yellowed photographs hanging in dusty frames. To the right: two rooms, one a bedroom and the other an office space. Both empty. To the left: a living room. The broken window belonged to this room, and the cream-colored curtain that framed the shattered glass was billowing in and out with each gust of wind.

Muffled talking drifted down a hallway that was across from the foyer. Brooke crept forward, her knee throbbing dully from her sprint up the stairs. The hallway was empty except for a long, narrow table that was butted up against the right-hand side. Beyond that, there was another open space, with a glass door that was almost certainly connected to the top balcony that overlooked the woods.

Brooke took one small step after another, silently willing the wood beneath her feet not to creak and give away her position. When she reached the narrow table, she snatched up one of two available candlesticks, the heavy weight feeling good in her trembling hands. She curled her fingers around the brass base, then went forward a few more feet.

She stopped at the edge of the hallway and pressed her back against the wall, being careful to keep herself concealed. She strained to make out the words of who she was now quite certain was Travis and Noah—and *only* Travis and Noah.

"—don't know, man! We have to—" Noah's voice.

*"We can't."* Travis's voice. "She's already upset enough as it is."

Brooke peered around the corner, unable to restrain her curiosity any longer, and saw Noah and Travis standing in an aging dining room. The table in the center of the room could easily fit a family of eight or more, but only one seat was set with a placemat. In the opposite direction, she saw an empty kitchen and not much else.

Brooke returned her attention to the brothers, who were huddled together in front of what could only be a bathroom. Maurice was nowhere in sight.

"I can't keep this shit a secret, Travis! We have to get the fu—"

Brooke stepped out of the hallway, the heavy candlestick feeling slippery in her sweating palms. Noah stopped mid-sentence, his eyes widening when he saw her. He was ghostly pale, the hammer he brought with him hanging limply by his side. Travis whirled around and stared at her, momentarily speechless. They looked almost comical, like a movie that had been paused on an unflattering frame.

When neither of them spoke, Brooke asked, "What the hell is going on? Where's Maurice?" It was then that she noticed Travis's knife resting on the dining table, shiny and silver and free of gore. *If nothing violent happened, then why the hell are they looking at me like that? And what the hell is that smell?*

Travis cleared his throat. Noah swallowed. They exchanged nervous glances and then looked back at her.

"Somebody say something!" Brooke nearly yelled, her nerves vibrating with anxious anticipation. She stomped over to them, anger and fear swirling around in her chest in a nauseating dance. Or was it the smell that was making her feel sick?

As she drew near, the two men shifted their positions so they were standing shoulder to shoulder, their bodies blocking her view of the bathroom. Brooke stopped in front of them, her eyes darting from one face to the other. Travis looked at her head-on, his expression unreadable. Noah was staring intently at an arbitrary spot on the wall in an obvious attempt to avoid her gaze.

Travis reached forward and took her arm, but she pulled it away, not wanting to be touched until she knew what was going on. And even more so not wanting to relinquish her hold on the candlestick. They were planning on keeping something from her—that's what they were talking about when she walked in. They were going to lie to her, and she wasn't letting go of this damn candlestick until she knew what they were hiding. Brooke tightened her grip and repositioned herself so she was standing just out of reach.

A hurt look crossed Travis's face as she withdrew from him, and then his expression faded back to neutral. "Babe, you don't need to see this," he said simply.

"Brookey, he's right," Noah agreed. "You should go." The pasty color of his skin had taken on an almost greenish sheen, like he was about to throw up. Or had just thrown up. Brooke's eyes went down to the floor, where, sure enough, a splattering of vomit was seeping into the wood. More liquid than solid. And fresh.

Well, that explained some of the stink that was hanging in the air—but not all of it. There were other pungent aromas lingering in the stagnant room, and none of them good. One was thick and almost rotting, like decay. Can rotting wood smell that bad? Doubtful. The other was uncomfortably metallic, and made the air taste of pennies.

"Where is he?" Brooke demanded in the toughest voice she could muster. She didn't want to sound like the frightened little girl, but she could still hear her buried down in the depths of her throat. "Tell me, goddamnit. I'm in this mess just as much as you are."

"Babe, please just go back downstairs."

Brooke looked from Travis to Noah, her eyes wide and nostrils flaring. Travis wasn't going to break; she knew it from his tone. But Noah… maybe there was still a chance he would tell her.

The greenish tint of Noah's skin transitioned to red as he struggled to avoid her gaze. Finally, he let out a shaky breath and his eyes dropped to hers. "You're going to regret it," he said softly.

*"Dude!"* Travis grabbed Noah's arm, but he shook it off.

"She has a right to know, Travis." Noah took a step to the side, away from the bathroom door.

Travis looked from Noah to Brooke, then back at Noah again. He let out a frustrated grunt and begrudgingly stepped aside, revealing the bathroom behind them.

Brooke stared into the space, feeling momentarily confused as to why Maurice would leave the rest of the house so dated yet paint the bathroom such a vibrant color. Scarlet—just like the name of the road. And just like Maurice's ancestors.

Realization dawned, and with it, a paralyzing surge of fear. Brooke's whole body wanted to turn away from the violent scene, but she felt frozen in place, her eyes refusing to look away. Like a car accident. Like a plane crash. Like the scariest part in a movie where you want to cover your face, but seeing nothing is by far worse than seeing the monster creeping out of the closet.

The bathroom was so red inside. So red it almost seemed black in places. A giant puddle of deep, sickening crimson was on the floor, congregating in the corner where the floor curved slightly downward. Brooke imagined the blood seeping through the floorboards and traveling sluggishly down to the bathroom ceiling below. Smears of scarlet were on the cabinets, the walls, the toilet, the tub.

And then there was Maurice. He was sprawled in the center of all that red, his skin an ashen shade that could be mistaken for nothing other than that of a corpse. His plaid shirt sleeves were rolled up to the elbows, exposing forearms cut so deep that glimpses of sheer white bone could be seen from within. Each arm was cut from elbow to wrist, some twelve inches on either side. The left side was deeper than the right, with fleshy muscle and tubes of blood vessels and tendons severed into shreds. A long kitchen knife, its blade tacky with blood, lay next to his body.

Brooke had time to wonder where the screaming was coming from before she passed out. It was a sharp, piercing scream—nothing like the sounds she had heard coming from the woods. It sounded like a child's scream maybe; eerily similar to the little-girl voice she sometimes heard slipping from her own lips when everything was falling into chaos. It wasn't until right before everything faded to black that she realized the screams were coming from her.

# Chapter 21

*Sunday, 11:05 a.m.*

Brooke's sweater was hiked up in the back, and the carpet below her was coarse and scratchy against her skin. She tried to wiggle away from the discomfort, but something was holding her in place. Strong, masculine arms, wrapped so tightly around her that they were almost suffocating with their embrace.

Brooke knew those arms anywhere. The dark hairs that swept across the forearms. The hooked scar that blemished the flesh just below the right elbow—a fishing mishap from what she had been told. The heavy, tungsten ring wrapped around the third finger on the left hand. "Travis," she mumbled groggily from where she lay, cradled inside his arms.

Travis pulled her in closer to his chest. "Babe, are you okay?" he asked. "You passed out. Thank God Noah was right next to you. He was able to catch you before you hit your head." Travis rocked her gently back and forth, his hand caressing the curvature of her face. "I'm so sorry you had to see that. I shouldn't have let you. I knew better, I just…"

Brooke pushed herself up, wanting the rough carpeting off her skin. She was on the floor, her legs sprawled out in front of her and Travis's sturdy body cradling her from behind. She surveyed the dining room as if she was seeing it for the first time. Worn rug, old furniture, dated wallpaper. Maurice's home. Except…

Brooke's eyes darted to the bathroom doorway, but with Noah kneeling beside them, his broad frame was blocking her view. Brooke could see part of a foot sticking out, but other than that, Maurice was out of sight.

As if in a drunken stupor, Brooke clumsily shoved herself up from the floor. She stumbled, and Travis jumped up to steady her. "Did he—" she began, but stopped when the rubberiness of her legs demanded her full attention. She curled her fingers around Travis's arm, which was firmly wrapped around her waist.

"Yeah," Travis said, placing his palm over Brooke's hand. "It looks like he killed himself. Cut his wrists with the knife that's in there."

Brooke looked from Travis to Noah, who was standing beside them and still blocking her view of the bathroom. On purpose, she was sure.

"Why would he do that?" Brooke asked nobody in particular.

"Travis thinks—" Noah's breath hitched and his eyes returned to the same arbitrary spot on the far wall. "Travis thinks he did it because he felt guilty about Katelyn. About… what he did to her."

Brooke's head swiveled in Travis's direction. "But why would he do that?"

Travis gaped at her. "Jesus. Why do you think, Brooke? He obviously couldn't live with himself after killing Kate."

"Yeah… but why *now*?"

"What do you mean, Brookey?" Noah's eyes met hers, a trickle of hope brightening his dark expression. It was the kind of hope that does more harm than good—like when a kid is waiting for his parents to tell him that Grandma was just sleeping, or that his missing dog would return home any day now. *False hope.*

"I mean why would he kill himself *right now*?" she asked. "The blood in the shed"—she shook her head, remembering the grotesque amount of red smears—"that was too much to be from just one person, right? And the note in the books. That warning. If it *was* about him," she jerked her chin toward the bathroom, "that means he's done this before. Possibly lots of times. Why would he just up and kill himself with remorse when he's been doing it for God knows how long? That doesn't make any sense."

Annoyance passed over Travis's face, renewed hope over Noah's. "So you think this might not have anything to do with Katelyn then?" Noah asked, taking a step away from the bathroom door. Angry, red splashes appeared behind him before Brooke could look away.

"I just think it's weird that he would kill himself all of a sudden when it seems very likely he's done this before. Many times. In the movies, the killer never gets struck by a sudden wave of guilt because he killed one coed too many."

"This isn't a horror movie, Brooke." Travis met her eyes, and his expression was hard. Unwavering. "He obviously was feeling pretty bad about something. We can't compare this to a Michael Myers movie."

Noah ignored him, his gaze fixated on Brooke. "You think maybe Kate got away then? Just like we thought she did? She got scared for whatever reason and took off, and maybe this"—he threw a hand toward the splattered bathroom—"had nothing to do with her leaving?"

"But she didn't leave, bro," Travis said, his voice raising.

"She could have," Noah shot back. "She could have left!"

"She's in the fucking shed, Noah! And this asshole right here killed himself over it!"

"Hey!" Brooke hollered, letting out a frustrated growl. "Stop it! Both of you!" She stepped between them and placed one hand on each of their chests, pushing them away from each other. Not that it did any good; it was like pushing two pillars of cement.

"I know everyone is on edge right now," she went on, "but yelling isn't going to fix anything. Now can we just find the damn landline and call 911? We're in over our heads here. *Obviously*. And anything we do in this place is just tampering with evidence."

Noah and Travis eyed each other over Brooke's head. She kept her ground between them, wondering if the stress of everything was going to launch them into a full blown fist fight.

Finally, Travis's posture slouched, immediately followed by Noah's. Without another word, they turned away from each other and began looking for the phone.

Brooke let out a breath she wasn't aware she had been holding. She followed Travis into the hallway, where he was looking over the narrow table that was now missing a candlestick. She reached out and tried to rest her hand on his shoulder, but he pulled away from her touch. *Ouch.* "Travis—"

He turned and faced her, lingering anger still etched into his brow and smoldering in his eyes. "Brooke, this is serious. That man is a killer, and giving Noah false hope that Katelyn is still alive isn't going to help anything. I need you to be on my side here."

"There are no sides, Travis." Brooke reached out and rested her hand on his arm. He didn't pull away this time, and the hard crease between his brows finally smoothed over. "Katelyn might very well be gone. And Maurice is definitely gone. I'm just trying to be sensible about why."

"It could have been you," he stammered, his voice breaking. He pulled Brooke in and wrapped his arms around her, so tight she could barely breathe against his chest. "It could just as easily have been you that he attacked. Jesus Christ, I don't know what I would have done if it was you." He drew in a deep breath, his face buried in her hair.

Brooke brought her arms up to him, finally understanding the reason for his outward hostility. It wasn't anger, it was fear—an emotion she rarely saw in her husband. Instead of the realization calming her nerves, it did nothing but amp them back up. Travis was the one that was supposed to tell her the stalker was a raccoon and the monster was a clothes pile. But this time he couldn't. What could he say to comfort her now that the monsters were real?

"Guys?" Noah called from the kitchen.

Travis pulled Brooke into an urgent kiss, crushing his lips against hers. "I'm going to get you out of here," he whispered. "I will protect you. I promise." He kissed her once more, then took her hand and led her out of the hallway.

Noah was standing at the kitchen counter, holding up a thin piece of rope in each hand. Puzzled, Brooke walked over to him, peering curiously at the frayed ends. It wasn't until she got to the counter that she realized it wasn't a rope, but a wire or cord of some kind. Her eyes traveled along one end until it disappeared into the wall. She then followed the other to where it was attached to a telephone. "Oh shit," she groaned.

"He cut the wire?" Travis asked, reaching around her and grabbing the severed telephone cord. "Why would he do that?" Travis lifted the receiver and pressed it to his ear anyway. When he didn't hear anything, he tossed it onto the counter, the clatter causing both Noah and Brooke to jump. "What the hell are we going to do now?"

"Why bother to do that?" Brooke asked, staring at the severed wire. A disconcerting sense that something was wrong was tugging at her. Hell, there was a lot that was wrong about their current situation, but this was something else. Something that said that the pieces didn't add up—that there was something she was missing. And that part scared her the most. It's the monsters that you can't see that are the scariest. Where was a nightlight when you really needed one? Not for the darkness, but for her own mind. One that could light up her thoughts and find the illusive answer that was lurking in the shadows. The missing puzzle piece.

"No more horror movie theories, Brooke. It doesn't matter why." Travis stormed out of the room and back down the hallway.

Noah and Brooke exchanged nervous glances, then scurried after him. Travis was in the hallway, back by the narrow table. "Where the hell would he keep them?" he muttered, more to himself than to his companions. His hands traveled over the various knickknacks, and he let out a frustrated grunt when he couldn't find what he was searching for.

"What are you looking for?" Noah asked.

"Car keys." Travis said, his eyes scanning the hallway as he decided which way to go first. He zoned in on the foyer, then strode in that direction with long strides that Brooke had difficulty keeping up with.

She stopped at the entrance to the living room, watching as the guys searched the chairs, the couch, the coffee table, the end tables. Unsuccessful, they divvied up the remaining portions of the house and then continued on their search, leaving her standing in the living room.

Brooke wanted to help, but she also didn't want to go anywhere near Maurice's body. She turned toward the spare rooms she saw when she first came in, but Noah was already stepping out of one and going into the other. She stopped where she was and instead started tugging on a strand of hair, not sure what else to do.

Travis was back down the hall, presumably checking the kitchen and the dining room. When he returned a few minutes later empty-handed, Brooke noticed the cords in his neck were taut with strain. He let out a curse when Noah emerged from the second spare room shaking his head.

"What about…" Brooke trailed off. She chewed on her lower lip, not wanting to finish the sentence. "What about his pockets?" she asked finally. "Couldn't the keys be inside one of his pants pockets?"

Travis's jaw ticked. Noah cleared his throat and started kicking at the dingy floor runner beneath his feet. "Shit, man—" he began.

"I'll do it," Travis said, his expression grim. He rolled his shoulders and shook his hands out. "One sec." He disappeared back down the hallway, and they could hear muffled thumps and the rustle of clothing coming from the direction of the bathroom. When he reemerged a moment later, he gave them a quick shake of his head.

This time, Noah cursed. "Then where in the hell would he keep them?"

"In the garage maybe," Travis suggested. "Just leaves them in the car since there's no one around to steal it?"

Noah nodded in agreement. "Worth a shot." He turned to Brooke. "We'll be right back, Brookey. You okay here?"

Brooke nodded, and without another word, they hurried out the front door. She watched them go, the disquiet she felt in her gut increasing instead of lessening. *Why commit suicide? And why cut the phone line? What the hell happened here?*

She scanned the house with renewed unease. The hallway felt darker, almost oppressively so. She went to the front door, eager to follow the guys out into the light, then stopped. She didn't want to be alone in the house with what was inside the bathroom, but she also didn't want to be standing out by the garage door with her back to the woods. At least the threat in here was dead. She couldn't say the same for what might be lurking out there, beyond the tree line.

Brooke changed course and stepped into the living room, taking in the details she missed when she first ran inside. A worn, leather couch and matching chairs punctuated the space, with a thick, wooden coffee table in the center that was almost certainly made by hand. A wicker rocking chair sat near the broken window, where the curtain was still ruffling and flowing in the gusts of wind that dared enter this tomb. Matching table lamps adorned the two side tables that flanked the couch, with yellowed shades that made their glow all the more golden. And then there were the books. Every wall was lined with bookshelves, and every shelf sagged with the weight of the books it was forced to carry.

Out of habit, Brooke started scanning the books on the various shelves, keeping her ears perked for any calls that might be coming from outside. There was nothing yet, but the guys shouldn't be too much longer. Or at least she hoped they wouldn't be too much longer.

She went from one shelf to the next, looking at the books without really seeing them. They were organized just as haphazardly as downstairs, although most were much older, with cracked spines and torn covers. Her eye landed on a collection of leather-bound books with nothing written on their spines. She probably wouldn't have even noticed them, if there weren't so many piled together. There were dozens upon dozens, some large and some small.

Brooke picked out one of the smaller ones, quickly flipping through the pages with feigned interest. It was a journal of some kind. The pages were brittle with age, and the ink inside faded. Every page was filled with precise, carefully written script. She returned the journal to its spot on the shelf and picked up the next one. It was more of the same. As was the next one, and the next one.

Brooke pulled out one of the larger books next. Inside were grainy, black-and-white family portraits, dating back to when cameras were probably first invented. The people in the images were dressed in what looked like colonial garb, none smiling and all staring at the camera with blank expressions and vacant eyes. Underneath one picture of a rather severe-looking woman was the name Scarlett Dubois. *The first one, maybe?*

Brooke flipped through the pages, becoming increasingly aware that she hadn't heard the rev of an engine yet or the crunch of gravel beneath tires. *They should be back by now.* The sense of something being wrong expanded inside her chest like a malignancy, threatening to take over the space her vital organs needed to function.

She returned the album to its shelf and grabbed another at random. This one was filled with newspaper clippings, none of the headlines comforting in the slightest. "Search Continues for Missing Hikers", "Third Person Goes Missing in Rural Vermont Town", "Father Begs for Safe Return of Runaway Teen".

Brooke shivered. She shut the album and hastily returned it to its resting place, not wanting to feel the leather against her skin anymore. The dread in her chest was becoming more and more unbearable, like a living thing inside of her. A living thing with teeth and claws. Something was here—some sort of answer to the questions she wasn't even sure to ask yet.

She snatched one of the journals off the shelf and let it fall open to a random page. She squinted, trying to make out the worn script inside.

*"...the sickness has now taken hold of her mind as well. She uses the only strength she has left to say words I have never heard come from her mouth before. Unfathomable filth and grotesque desires to..."*

Brooke heard footsteps outside, rushing toward the front door. She slammed the journal closed and threw it back on the shelf, not wanting the guys to catch her reading it, although she wasn't sure why. *What the fuck did I just read?*

Her head snapped to the front door as Travis hurried inside, quickly followed by Noah. "The keys have to be somewhere," Travis growled.

"No luck?" Brooke asked, although the question clearly wasn't necessary. "What about hot-wiring it or something?"

"Grand theft auto isn't exactly my strong suit, babe. I'm more of a push-the-button kind of guy."

"Me too," Noah lamented. "A phone would sure be nice right about now so we could google it."

Brooke nodded, knowing that wasn't going to happen. She also knew the answer to her next question, but she decided to ask it anyway. "So we're not driving anywhere then?"

Noah and Travis shook their heads in unison. "No," Travis said, "we're not.

# Chapter 22

*Sunday, 12:42 p.m.*

They sat in the living room back down on their own level, the guys discussing what they should do next. Brooke barely heard them, their voices drowned out by the deafening volume of her own thoughts. The strangely timed suicide. The severed phone line. Those creepy-ass journals. Something was wrong here—something that just didn't seem to add up right. Like a puzzle where half the pieces were missing. How could you know what the picture was with so few pieces to play with? If Maurice really did commit suicide by a sudden wave of unexpected guilt, why bother to cut the phone line? There was no explanation for it. At least none that she could think of. Which meant something else was going on here; a puzzle piece that was yet to reveal itself.

*Think, Brooke. Come on and think.* Katelyn's phone. The shed. The notes. That midnight visitor lurking outside. Her mind latched on to the swing, and to the heavy oak branch moving in the clearing. Her body instantly reacted to the memory, her skin tingling under the surge of a hundred thousand goose bumps. Was that another puzzle piece? Or was her mind starting to unravel?

"We have to get moving. Just like we were planning on doing this morning." Noah got to his feet, his mind made up. "I don't know what the hell we're doing just sitting around right now anyway. It's time to leave this freaking place while we still have plenty of light."

Travis stood. "Agreed. Brooke, time to get up and—"

"Maybe he had a partner," she whispered, ignoring Travis. When she looked up at him, he was staring at her with an incredulous expression. They both were.

Travis groaned. "Babe, we don't have time for this." He pulled her up to standing and attempted to lead her toward the sliding door, but Brooke resisted, eventually having to twist her wrist from his grasp to avoid being pulled forward. "I'm serious, Brooke," he snapped. "No more crazy ideas. *Now let's go.*"

Brooke shook her head. "It doesn't add up, Travis. We're missing something. His suicide is… I don't know. Doesn't it seem too convenient? Katelyn disappears, and then Maurice kills himself the next day? Hell, maybe even the same day."

"Yeah, 'cause he felt guilty."

"So guilty he cut the phone line?" When Travis didn't respond, Brooke pressed on. "What if he wasn't doing this alone? What if there were two of them? Killing people. Doing things in that shed of theirs. What if—"

"There is literally no reason to suspect that, babe."

"Except there is," she insisted. "The phone line. And that fucking swing moving last night. That could have been his partner out there, watching us. Waiting to see what we'd do next. Hell, Maurice's suicide might not even be a suicide. It could have been staged—"

Travis's jaw ticked. "Enough! This is freaking ridiculous. No more horror stories, Brooke." He grabbed her wrist again and started walking toward the door. "It's time to go."

Brooke stumbled as she resisted Travis's forward momentum. "No!"

Exasperated, he released her. "Babe, it is my job to keep you safe. We talked about this. I promised I'd protect you. And that means leaving. Right now."

"I think there's someone out there, Travis," she pleaded. Her eyes darted to the tree line, but all she saw was the not-so-gentle sway of the pine trees at the forest's edge. The sun had disappeared behind a thickening layer of clouds, and everything in the clearing looked murky and foreboding. She looked back at Travis. "He's out there," she insisted. "He might be watching us right now, just waiting for us to go outside. Then he can pick us off. One by one."

Travis let out a heavy sigh, the same sigh he always expelled when she asked him to get out of bed in the middle of the night to investigate a mysterious noise or an ominous shadow. "So we just happened to pick an Airbnb, not with one serial killer, but with two? Come on, Brooke. The odds of that are astronomical."

"A guilt-ridden person doesn't cut a phone line!" Brooke exclaimed, slapping her hand against her thigh. She sounded manic, but she couldn't help herself. "There's someone else involved. There has to be!"

"You're sure, Brookey?" Noah asked. He hadn't spoken in so long Brooke had almost forgotten he was there. She looked over at him, her eyes pleading.

"It's possible, isn't it?" she asked. "I *know* someone was out there last night. I'm sure of it."

"Maybe," Noah said, although reluctantly.

Travis shook his head, the muscles in his jaw working. "No, dude. Not you, too."

"At least consider it, Travis." Brooke reached forward and tugged on his hand. He didn't resist her, but his expression didn't change either. "He was on the swing in the middle of the night. And if Maurice was already dead, then it has to be someone else, doesn't it? The same someone else who cut the phone line, and probably killed Maurice and made it *look* like a suicide."

Travis ran his fingers through his hair, then looked at her from beneath hooded eyes. "Except we don't know if Maurice was dead yet or not. Hell, if there really was someone on that swing, it could have been Maurice himself. We already know he likes to sit out there at night. Remember the chair?"

Brooke's jaw clamped shut. The fucking chair. She had forgotten about the chair. "Well…" she trailed off, her mind working. "Maybe that wasn't Maurice at all. Maybe that was his accomplice all along."

Travis's eyes scanned the tree line, his irises just as green as the surrounding forest. At last, he shrugged. "It doesn't matter," he said, his voice flat and defeated.

"How can it not matter?" Brooke stepped between him and the window, forcing him to look at her.

"It doesn't matter if it's two people. And it doesn't matter if I believe you or not." He rested his hands on her shoulders. "Bottom line is, we can't stay here. We can't call out. And we can't drive out. The only thing to do is walk out. If there really is a second person—and I'm not saying there is—then who's to say he won't go after you next? Or any of us, for that matter?" He leaned down so his eyes were level with hers. "It's time for us to leave this place."

"How do you suggest we do that?" Noah asked, his eyes ping-ponging between the two of them. "If the only way out is to walk out, and Brooke says there's some killer out there watching us—"

Travis released her shoulders. "Then I'll go alone," he said simply. "I'll be able to move faster that way anyway."

"Travis. No." Brooke grabbed his hand and gave it a hard tug. "I will not let you go out there alone. Not when—"

"Brooke, I am your husband. I vowed to protect you. And sitting around in a crime scene isn't protecting you. Regardless of our personal opinions about how Katelyn and Maurice died, the fact of the matter is that I'm not protecting you by sitting on my ass and just waiting for something else to happen. Something that could happen to *you*. So I'm going.

And nothing you say is going to stop me from protecting my wife. Got it?"

Noah came up beside him. "I'm going with you," he said. "At least one of us will make it, so we can make sure Brooke gets out okay."

Travis shook his head. "You can't go, bro." Noah opened his mouth to protest, but Travis held up his hand, silencing him. "I need you here. With Brooke. I can't leave her alone in this place, especially if what she said is true. You need to stay and protect her until I come back." He turned and grabbed hold of Brooke again. "And I *will* come back."

"Travis," Brooke said, her voice wavering. "Don't go. Please don't go out there." A tear descended her cheek, hot and biting. He brushed it away with his thumb. "There has to be another way."

Travis leaned forward and kissed her softly on the corner of the mouth. "There isn't. Unless either of you have any better suggestions?" Noah and Brooke exchanged defeated glances. Travis nodded, resolved. "It's settled then."

Brooke and Noah watched in silence as he collected his phone, checked the charge, then shoved it into the pocket of his jeans. He then threw on an extra jacket and came back to Brooke.

"There has to be another way, babe," she whispered. Another tear fell, neither of them bothering to wipe it away.

"There's not." He gave her a wan smile. "But I'm a lot more nervous about bears than I am about serial killers. And more than anything, I'm worried about keeping you safe." He kissed her, long and hard, then followed it with a peck on her forehead. "Try not to worry too much, lovely wife. I can handle myself. And I only have to get to where the phone has a signal. I'll be back in no time. Hopefully in a police cruiser." He winked.

Brooke nodded, although she didn't feel all that hopeful. Maybe he was right, though. Maybe there wasn't a second killer. Maybe there were only animals in the woods. No murderers, no ghosts, no evil spirits. And if they went with him, they'd only slow him down. She would anyway.

Travis and Noah hugged, this time skipping the masculine pounding on each other's backs. "You keep her safe," Travis whispered in Noah's ear. When he pulled away, his expression was deathly serious.

Noah nodded, equally serious. "Of course I will."

Travis strode over to the sliding glass door, pausing to take one more look at the tree line before stepping out onto the deck. He shut the door behind him, pointing his finger at the handle. "Lock this," he said. "And keep it locked. Got it?" They both nodded. "Okay, hang tight. I'll be back before you know it."

Brooke reached out, searching for Noah's hand. He wrapped his fingers around hers and gave her a comforting squeeze. They then watched in silence as Travis walked across the deck and disappeared.

# Chapter 23

*Sunday, 2:52 p.m.*

Brooke sat beside Noah on the couch, watching the second hand on the clock as it spun tirelessly around in an endless circuit. She wasn't sure how much time had gone by, only that the minute hand had also made a full revolution as it tried miserably to catch up to the second hand. A race it was doomed to lose.

Brooke's mind was spinning tirelessly as well. Like the Tilt-A-Whirl at the county fair. Only instead of seeing laughing children and cotton candy stands with each spin of the ride, she was seeing memories of Travis. One spin, and she was at the college bookstore where they met. He approached her after a particularly embarrassing—and unsuccessful—struggle to retrieve a book from the top shelf. After offering her said book, he made a wager that he would be able to guess her major based on the textbooks she was holding. He won the bet, and a date with her to boot.

Another spin, and they were moving in together. She had been very concerned about the available closet space in his modest one-bedroom apartment, so he crammed all of his dress shirts into the drawers to make room for her. Subsequently, he went to a very important job interview in a badly wrinkled shirt.

Another spin, and they were at a lake he took her to in northwestern Vermont, where sightings of a lake monster were so frequent that the monster even had a name. Champ. As they stood on the beach, Travis's eyes widened and he pointed frantically to the middle of the lake, causing Brooke to whirl around in hopes of catching a glimpse of the elusive Champ. She didn't. But when she turned back around, Travis was on one knee.

Another spin, and Brooke was sitting in a darkened room, the only sound being the ominous ticking of a clock mounted on the wall. The ticks were almost deafening in the thick silence, and Travis was nowhere to be seen. Brooke's brow furrowed. This wasn't a memory… this was what was happening right now. She was sitting in a room, useless and afraid, and Travis was gone. He was out there somewhere, alone, on a rarely used road in the middle of the woods. And it was her fault he was alone.

Brooke shuddered and sniffled away the tears that were burning in the corners of her eyes. She needed a distraction. Right now, before she lost herself completely. Travis wasn't gone forever, but she would be if she allowed herself to get sucked into the abyss of what-ifs. She needed something else to think about, something to keep her mind busy until her husband came back to her. And he *would* come back.

The minute hand had made it another half revolution by the time her eyes focused on the numbers. 3:30. *Two hours. He's been gone for two hours.* That doesn't mean anything bad happened, though. It was a long walk, after all—seven miles to cell reception, and then waiting around for however long it took for help to arrive. And then, of course, the drive back to the house. *He's probably on his way back right now. No, not probably. Definitely.*

Brooke looked over at Noah, whose eyes were glazed over with memories just as hers had been. She bit down on her lower lip, trying to decide what to say so she could sneak away. She wanted to—*needed to*—get her mind on something other than just waiting. And finding out what was written inside those journals was just the thing to capture her attention. She didn't want to tell Noah that's where she was going, though, because in all likelihood he would try to stop her. Travis told them to stay put, and Noah would follow his brother's instructions. He always did.

Brooke stood, stretching her arms over her head. It took Noah a full ten seconds to register her movements. When he finally did look up at her, she said "I think I'm gonna go lie down. I—I can't stop thinking about what might happen out there, and I just need to turn my mind off for a little while."

Noah stared at her, still slightly dazed, before his eyes finally cleared. He looked over at the master bedroom, then back at Brooke. An unidentifiable expression passed over his face, and then was gone. He cleared his throat. "Yeah, sure," he said. "Go ahead. I'll stay up and keep watch."

"You sure?" Brooke lingered in the living room, wondering what that weird look was all about, but when Noah looked up at her again, whatever she had seen there was gone.

"Uh huh. You bet. Go ahead." He nodded toward the bedroom. "I'll be right here."

"Okay," she said, already feeling guilty. She didn't like lying to him, or lying at all, really. Maybe she should just cave and ask him to come upstairs with her.

*But if he stops you, you'll never get to find out what's written inside those journals.* And she *had* to know. With each passing second, the urge only grew stronger. Almost like the journals were calling to her, beckoning her as a siren beckons a sailor. Or as a wendigo beckons its next victim.

The truth danced on the tip of her tongue, but ultimately, she swallowed it. Along with her sanity, most likely. "Thank you, Noah," she said, and scurried into the bedroom, closing the door softly behind her.

*Now how the hell are you going to get upstairs without him noticing?*

Brooke's finger ran along the lock to the bedroom's sliding glass door, knowing the second she flipped the latch and stepped outside there would be no going back. She was committed by that point. Truth be told, she already was.

She undid the latch and slid the door open one inch at a time, only opening it wide enough to fit her slender frame through the gap. She then slipped through and slowly pulled the door closed.

Mercifully, the stairs were only a few feet away from where she was standing. She took them one at a time, testing each one for creaks before putting her full weight onto the step. The few stairs that did squeak in protest, she stepped over and avoided completely. After an arduous ascent, Brooke reached the top landing.

The woods surrounding the front of the house felt ominous and oppressing. Were they always pushed up against the driveway like this? Before, the small, gravel-covered parking area felt wide and inviting. Now, it felt like the trees had been creeping closer and closer all this time, their branches reaching for the doors and windows to pull out whoever was inside. Or to let in whatever was outside.

Brooke hurried to the front door and let herself in, locking it behind her with a satisfying clunk of the deadbolt. The curtain bellowed inward from the broken window, causing her to jump. Was that just the wind? Or was something behind the curtain…

Panicked, her eyes searched the room, but nothing was there. No clothes pile monsters. No lurking serial killers. No reanimated corpses of suicidal innkeepers. Only the curtain, settling back into place as the wind died down outside.

Not wanting to waste any more time, she went straight to the bookshelf that housed the leather-bound journals. She grabbed a stack and threw them onto the floor, then returned and collected another stack, letting them land on top of the first. She repeated the process until the shelves were empty of Maurice's secrets.

With shaky hands, she pulled one of the table lamps as close to her book pile as the cord would allow. The room was gloomier than it had been when they were there earlier, and the wind licking at the curtain much more intense. A storm was coming. She had felt the chill in the air as she ascended the stairs, and each gust of wind that infiltrated the living room was colder than the last.

Brooke sat down amongst the black and brown leather-clad books and started going through them systematically. Warm light from the table lamp flooded the pages, feeling like a nightlight in the surrounding gloom. A nightlight to keep the monsters at bay. Unless the monsters were inside these pages, that is.

Two of the larger albums contained nothing but photographs. The oldest were what Brooke saw when she first looked at the albums that morning, dating back to the 1850s. Brooke saw Scarlett Dubois's picture again, taking an extra moment to peer into the expressionless woman's eyes. Based on the dates, she was almost certain this was Scarlett the First.

Midway through the album another Scarlett appeared. She was prettier than the first, but just as plain and devoid of emotion. The third Scarlett, near the end of the book, smiled for the camera, and it wasn't until the fourth, featured in the second album, that Brooke finally got to see one of them in color. All had thick, wavy brown hair, but with each generation, the Scarlett's got more attractive and less emotionless.

The last Scarlett was a pretty thing, with a baby cradled in her arms and what looked like one of the older Scarlett's standing behind her. Written in delicate script next to the picture were the words *Maurice Dubois, 1954*. Brooke brought the picture up to her face and studied it, but she couldn't find any resemblance between that happy baby and the dead man lying in the next room with his wrists slit open.

As the pages went on, she started to recognize the boy as he turned into a teenager, and then a man. With each decade that passed, he looked less happy, and there were less family members flanking his sides. The last picture was of a gravestone, *Scarlett Dubois V* carved into its marble side, with fresh flowers lying on top of even fresher soil. *The last Scarlett. Maurice's mother.*

Brooke set the album down, almost gingerly. The remains of a family were inside those pages, reduced down to nothing but developed film. Something that can burn, turn to ash, and get carried away by the wind. As if on cue, a particularly harsh gust tore at Maurice's curtain, and her skin prickled as the cloth slithered across her back before falling back into place.

Brooke started on the next album, which proved to be much more disconcerting than family photos. This one held the newspaper articles she had glimpsed earlier. She found the article related to the missing hikers and skimmed the lines that followed.

*Search Continues for Missing Hikers*
*November 20, 1972*

The search continues for Susanna Collins and Nicolas Freemont, two experienced hikers that disappeared while traversing the Appalachian Trail earlier this month. The couple was last seen at a campground near the southern Vermont border...

Brooke scanned the rest of the article, saw nothing concrete as to why the couple disappeared, and continued on to the next article.

### Third Person Goes Missing in Rural Vermont Town
### January 31, 1979

Lyndonville, Vermont has experienced its third disappearance in just as many weeks. Alfred Junesport, a local handyman, was reported missing when he failed to arrive at his shop for the fourth day in a row. Junesport, who was known around town as an avid hunter and fisherman, was last seen purchasing tactical equipment in preparation for an upcoming hunting trip...

Brooke jumped down to the next article, and then the next. It was all just more of the same. Hikers, hunters, campers—all gone without a trace. Presumed dead by exposure to the elements, but no bodies were ever recovered. Not one. All different ages, all levels of experience, and all ventured into the woods never to be heard from again.

Brooke sat in silence, listening to the eerie trickle of the wind through the broken glass. What the hell kind of sense did this make? Men, women, old, young, weak, strong—all gone. Maurice couldn't be responsible for this many people. There were dozens upon dozens of missing persons collected in these pages. So why keep the articles? If this wasn't serial killer trophy shit, then what was it? And why did Maurice care about seemingly random disappearances in the woods? What was the link?

She flipped through the articles again, only looking at the dates this time. *1972, 1979, 1979, 1984, 1984, 1985, 1990, 1990, 1990, 1997...*

All the disappearances happened in the winter months, in clusters, and all were spaced out from one another by intervals of five to seven years. Sometimes more disappearances happened in a given cycle, sometimes less. But always with at least five years in between.

Brooke looked at the most recent article. *2016. And it's 2022 now. That's six years.* Fear trickled through her body, just like the wind through the shards of glass behind her.

"But why?" she asked aloud to the room. "And why keep articles about it?" She pushed the albums aside and started going through the journals instead. Maybe there would be some answers in there. Because now she was just more confused than ever. If Maurice wasn't a serial killer, then there was no accomplice—yet another conclusion she jumped to without thinking, like playing a particularly morbid round of hopscotch. *And if there is no accomplice, then who was outside last night? Or what?*

Brooke returned to the journals. Seven or eight were written in the same handwriting, then it transitioned into someone else's handwriting, and so on. She looked for the carefully transcribed script she had seen earlier, finally finding it in one of the dark brown, and much older, journals. Possibly *the* oldest journal, judging by the brittle pages and fading script.

Brooke started reading one of the earlier passages, taking her time to make out the small writing as best she could.

*November 29, 1873*

*Mother tells me not to fuss over the noises, but at times, it is all one can think about. The screaming and the grunting, always in the night and always coming closer to the cabin. At times, I think I can almost hear the footsteps outside, unfathomably heavy and full of girth. I beg Father to let us go to town, away from this place, but he says our name, Dubois, means 'of the forest', and we belong here. But after hearing those noises in the night, I cannot help but feel we are trespassing. Mother insists the noises are only those of typical forest beasts. But I have never heard a beast of the forest make such a horrible noise. At times, I even wonder if it is my name slipping through its fangs, torn from its throat by the freezing wind.*

*December 16, 1873*

*I struggle to keep my spirits high during these difficult times. The storms came on furiously fast and have not yielded since. We expected another expedition to town before the roads became impassable, and our rations for the coming months are less than previous years. Father expects this to be a very trying winter indeed. Most of my* concerns, however, lie with the fate of brother Joseph. He has been missing three days past now. The last I saw him, he was going to collect firewood just beyond the tree line. I warned him not to go past the river, but he laughed at my silliness. I may be young, but even I could see that the laughter did not reach his eyes. A fortnight ago I heard him tell sister Claudia that the available wood was growing sparse around the clearing, and that each venture for firewood forced him to go deeper into the forest. He said when he was in the dense covering of the trees, he sometimes heard voices, calling for him across the river. I wonder if it was the same thing that calls for me in the depths of the night.

*December 29, 1873*

The storms have not let up, and we are still unable to leave the homestead to travel to town for supplies. Even more unbearable than my growling stomach is baby Marie's crying. Not because I don't care for her—she is just a babe and has no knowledge of what terrors her cries might bring down upon us. In the night, as I lie awake as close to the fire as safely possible (not for warmth, but for the safety of the light), I can hear Marie's bellows down in Mother's room. I pray that Mother will be able to silence Marie swiftly, before the baby's cries are overshadowed by the screams of the one beyond the tree line.

My belief that the river kept us safe from the screamer was erroneous, for just two nights past, I saw the branches of the trees bending and swaying under the weight of whatever was down below. Marie's cries had brought it forth, past the river, and right up to the pines that shade our cabin in the warmer months.

Mother's insistence that my fears are unfounded has grown weak. She looks to Father for answers, but all Father can say is to keep the baby quiet before he is forced to silence her himself.

January 21, 1874

Mother has been behaving differently since baby Marie's passing. The snow is unyielding and thick, and the roads impassable. We have been unable to go to town since the storms began, and our food reserves are nearly empty. At supper time, Mother makes what little we have for dinner (bone broth and stale bread) and provides all the sustenance to us. Father eats very little, and mother eats none. She says it is because she does not want us to go hungry, but after thirteen years of life, I know what hunger looks like, and Mother does not appear hungry. I wonder what she must be eating to sustain herself, just so she is able to offer what food is available to her children. Rats maybe, but I have not seen any rats this winter.

January 30, 1874

Mother has fallen ill. At first we thought it was the pox, but as her condition continued to worsen and her flesh remained unmarked, we have surmised it must be *something else that ails her. Father has tried everything we have in our stores as a possible remedy, but nothing yet has proven to ease Mother's suffering. Father says all we can do now is pray for her swift recovery.*

*Mother's screams now rival the screams of the forest. Her wails fill the air and are matched by screeches of what lays beyond the trees. At night I cover my ears with my pillow, anything to stop the incessant cries that drift through the air, but nothing can stop the screams. I fear it will drive me mad. And sometimes, between the groans of Mother and the cries from the forest, I can hear it calling my name, beckoning me to join it amongst the drifts of winter snow.*

*February 22 1874*

*Mother's condition has worsened to the point that every morning I wonder if I shall find her with us or with the Lord. She has become ghostly pale, and her skin is stretched taut over her bones in a way that makes her look more like a skeleton than the mother that birthed me. Father has told me to care for her, saying that I was named after her and I must be there for her until the end. I try to live up to the name she has given me, but many times I feel frightened to be in her presence.*

*Her body wasting away I have grown accustomed to, but it is the things she says that frighten me most. The sickness has now taken hold of her mind as well. She uses the only strength she has left to say words I have never heard come from her mouth before. Unfathomable filth and grotesque desires to consume the very people she once cared for. The profanities I can endure, but it is the eagerness in her voice that I cannot stand, as she expresses her urges to take my flesh and swallow it whole. She tells me in moments of strength that she cannot control what she says and they are only words. But then at other times, like when I lean close to wipe the sweat from her brow, I can see her face inching closer to me, her dry, cracked tongue slipping out from between her blackened teeth as she tries to nibble at my flesh.*

*I always pull away, revolted, practically running to the door and away from her. And when I turn back and look at the woman who created me, she is licking her lips with that cracked tongue, begging me to come closer. Begging me to give her just one taste. Telling me she is so very hungry, and that only my flesh can stop the growling pains that are gnawing at her insides.*

Brooke dropped the journal, her hands shaking too violently to keep hold of it. *"Did she eat that baby? Did the mom eat that freaking baby?"*

She didn't want to read any more. She didn't want to know what transpired on the following pages. Either this young Scarlett was going insane, or there really is something worse out there. Worse than bears, and worse than serial killers and murder sheds. It was something that prowled the woods, and existed not only in campfire legends and ghost stories, but in the real world. In the world she also inhabited.

Brooke's eyes scanned the script, noticing how much it had changed since she first started reading. It was no longer precise, no longer elegant. It was more of a hasty scrawl now, the writing degrading just as the author's mind decayed, as she whispered dark secrets from one century to the next.

Brooke looked down at the other journals scattered across the floor. She grabbed one, then another, then another, flipping ravenously through the pages and gleaning as much information as she could.

Scarlett the Second, the author of the first journal, watched her gaunt, emaciated mother run into the forest just days following the previous journal entry. The screams intensified through the remainder of the winter, and Scarlett could hear her mother's voice in those screams, begging her to come join her among the trees. Scarlett was all but ready to flee the house for good as soon as the first thaw, but when the warmth of summer came, the screams disappeared. It was seven years until they returned—until her *mother* returned, only she wasn't her mother anymore. And once again, Scarlett's mental state began to unravel. Her writing turned chaotic, and her script barely legible. Brooke found one entry where the girl, now a woman, had written "help me" over and over again for the length of eight pages.

Scarlett stayed at the house for the remainder of her life, feeling torn between the urge to escape the horrors that came once or twice each decade, and the family homestead she felt compelled to not let fall into disarray. She married a local blacksmith, and together they had eight children. Five survived, and three disappeared into the woods. Her daughter, Scarlett the Third, had five children. Only one disappeared, along with her husband, one cold February night.

The journals continued, decade after decade, generation after generation, sometimes offering coherent thoughts and daily events, and other times offering nothing but illegible scribbles and broken sentences. *Kill the screams. Flesh gone red. Starving. Breathing ice. Silence the children. Hunger unsatisfied.*

Maurice was the last surviving child of nine. The— *creature? spirit? wendigo?*—that was his great-great-great-grandmother lured four of his siblings into the forest, including the next generation of Scarlett, but Maurice fought the urge to ever answer her—*its*—call. When the last surviving Scarlett, Maurice's mother, passed from natural causes, the remaining siblings moved away, unable to stomach another loss, and refused to ever return to Scarlett Springs. Maurice remained for reasons unknown.

Brooke found one journal that might have belonged to him, however she couldn't be sure because the person who it belonged to never signed their name. A few loose newspaper clippings were tucked inside, all obituaries. Genevieve Dubois, Richard Dubois, François Montpelier, and Carlson Dubois. Brooke briefly looked over the obituary for François, quickly confirming that the woman's maiden name was also Dubois.

Very few handwritten notes were in the journal, and what few entries there were, were written over and over again until the pen carved through the pages and cut down to the ones beneath. Brooke flipped through the pages, seeing the same scrawled phrases and words written repeatedly throughout. Words she recognized from the other journals, as if their thoughts were one just like their blood.

*Drawn to greed. Selfishness. Violence.*
*Hibernation.*
*Always hungry.*
*Greed.*
*Always hungry.*
*Winter.*
*Selfishness.*
*Starving.*
*Always hungry.*
*Violence.*
*Cannibalism.*
*Always hungry.*
*Help me.*
*Always. Hungry.*
*Always.*
*Hungry.*

# Chapter 24

**Sunday, 5:27 p.m.**

Brooke crept down the stairs and snuck back into her bedroom. Once inside, she went to the bed and tousled the sheets, not wanting any evidence of her treachery clearly visible from the living room. Not until she admitted to Noah what she had done. She then looked over her shoulder at the living room door. Had he checked up on her? Did he already know she was a liar, and he was sitting out there with his arms crossed and a scowl on his face?

She went to the door and gently opened it, then peeked out into the living room. He wasn't there. Not on the couch. Not in the kitchen. Not… anywhere. Puzzlement quickly transitioned to worry, and Brooke rushed out of her room and went to the spare bedroom across the way. Nope. Not there either. *What the hell? What the hell, what the hell, what the hell?*

And then she heard it. Running water in the pipes. Not coming from above, but down below. Noah was downstairs, presumably taking a shower. Brooke's eyes went to her own bathroom. *But why not shower up here?* And then she saw the glimpse of red on the wall and looked away. *That's why.*

She went to the window and scanned the clearing, not sure why she felt slighted that Noah left without telling her, even though she had done the same to him. Outside, the approaching storm was showing little mercy on the surrounding pines, and their boughs bent and swayed beneath the force of the powerful winds. And everywhere there was crimson, the oaks' leaves tearing free from their branches and whipping through the air like dancing blood splatter.

Brooke shivered. Before long, night would creep out of the woods and lay claim to the land. And Travis was still out there, somewhere. She never should have let him go. She wouldn't have, if she had known. She should have told them about the journals when she first discovered them. They would have read them together, before he left, and then he never would have gone. He'd still be in here, with her, and not out there with… with whatever the hell was out there.

The fear in her chest steadily grew as she watched the shadows crawling out from the woods. Why wasn't he back yet? Surely he should have been back by now. Brooke went across the living room and into their bedroom. She wanted something of his—a hoodie, maybe. Something she could wrap around herself to make her feel warm and safe. To make her body stop trembling like the oaks outside, and to help the frost in her chest to thaw.

She went over to Travis's side of the bed and started digging through his duffle bag. She tossed out a couple pairs of jeans, some T-shirts, and finally found what she was looking for near the bottom. His favorite hoodie, well-worn and way too baggy for her, but something that would smell like her husband and make her feel safe until she could be in his arms again.

Brooke tossed the hoodie over her head and wrapped her arms around herself, feeling the comforting weight of the heavy material on her shoulders. She piled up the jeans and T-shirts she had flung out of the bag, wanting to keep the area neat. She couldn't control the chaos outside this room, but at least she could keep Travis's side of the bed tidy. Much tidier than her side anyway.

She placed the clothing back into his duffle bag, her fingers brushing against something hard near the bottom corner. She pulled it out, her brows furrowed in confusion. It was a small wooden box. A cigar box, maybe. But neither Travis nor Noah smoked. She slid the lid off, even more confused by the contents inside.

She picked up the first item. *Why would Travis bring an old, number two pencil with him? Who even writes with these things anymore?* She tossed it back into the box and pulled out the next item. A pen. It was gold and glittery, and undoubtedly designed for girls. Only it wasn't hers. A pit formed in the depths of her stomach. *Is he cheating on me?* She dismissed the notion, feeling almost silly for thinking such a thing. It could be a coworker's pen, a friend's, a dentist's.

Brooke grabbed the last item in the box. It was a book of some kind. She paused, suddenly nervous. Was all this a gift for her? And she was ruining it with her snooping? Unable to resist her curiosity, she cracked the book open. Only it wasn't a book, it was a journal. A journal with pink pages and pink ruling, unused except for a single page that was torn out. *Wasn't Katelyn's note written on paper like this?*

She dropped the journal back into the box and grabbed the pen, her hand shaking as she struggled to retrieve it. *It's just a coincidence. The paper being pink is just a coincidence. Besides, Katelyn's note was written with a purple pen. And this pen is...* She dragged the point of the pen across her hand, leaving a line of ink going down the center. She stared at it, her mind struggling to catch up with what she was seeing. The ink wasn't black, or gold. It was...

Her heart teetered, then fell from its cage, immediately sucked down into the growing pit that was once her stomach. Her hand tightened around the pen—the *purple* pen—and frost spread across her chest, hardening and shooting icicles through her lungs. Like daggers. She couldn't breathe. She couldn't—

The sliding glass door slid open and then slammed shut. Brooke jumped up, the pen still clutched in her hand, and whirled around. "Noah—"

Travis stood in the doorway, rubbing his arms up and down as he tried to warm himself up. He brought his hands to his mouth and blew into them, his eyes landing on Brooke. "Babe, I told you to keep the doors locked. It's not safe to have them open like this." He hurried across the room and wrapped his arms around her, pulling her in close. "Are you okay? What's wrong?"

Brooke's arms hung at her sides, feeling too heavy to wrap around her husband, let alone hold him tight. She let the pen slip from her fingers. "You're back," she said, her voice muffled against his chest. He pulled her closer, leaning his head down so it was resting against hers. Her lips grazed the exposed skin of his neck, which felt as cold as her insides.

"Of course I'm back, babe. Like I said, there aren't any killers out there. The monster was in here the whole time."

"Yes," Brooke said, her lips still brushing against his cool skin. "He is."

Travis pulled away from her. He placed one of his hands on each of her shoulders, holding her at arm's length so he could look into her eyes. "Maurice is dead, Brooke. You have nothing to worry about." He scanned her face, a crease appearing between his brows. "What's wrong?"

"Why do you have a purple pen, Travis?" she asked. It was the little-girl voice again.

The crease in his forehead deepened until Brooke thought his face might crack down the center. And what would be left there after it fell away? Once the mask was gone? Who would she be looking at? *The monster was in here the whole time.*

"What do you mean?" he asked, confused. "What purple pen?"

"The one that was in your bag," she whispered. She tried to take a step back, but Travis held her firmly in place. He looked down at his duffle bag, then scanned the floor until his eyes landed on the cigar box, and the purple glitter pen that was lying next to a discarded sock. His grip tightened, bordering on painful.

"Where did those come from?" he asked, his voice no longer sounding concerned. Or loving. Instead, it sounded hard. Cold, even.

"You know where they came from, Travis." Brooke tried again to step away, but he pulled her into him, so close she could feel his breath fanning across her face. The smell of him, one she yearned for only moments ago, now made her want to gag.

"Why were you going through my stuff, *babe*?" The word 'babe' didn't sound endearing anymore, it felt like an insult. Like he could have easily switched it out for another word that was much less loving.

"I wanted your hoodie because I missed you."

"Awe. That's so sweet, *babe*." He leaned down and brought his mouth to hers. Brooke tried to kiss him back, to act normal, but his lips felt cold and rigid. Not like her husband's lips at all. "I love that you worry about me," he whispered, his mouth still pressed against hers. He cupped her cheeks with his hands, his fingers digging in to the point of pain.

Brooke whimpered. When he still didn't retreat, she had to forcibly turn her head away to break the kiss. She brought her arms up and tried to push him away, but he swiftly pulled her into a hug, his arms engulfing her small body. She could feel the air getting squeezed from her lungs by the force of his embrace. She tried to choke back a sob, and was only partially successful. "Travis, why is Katelyn's pen and her journal in your bag?"

"It sounds like you already know why, *babe*. So why don't you tell me?"

"Because they're not Katelyn's," Brooke choked. "They're yours. You wrote that note to Noah, pretending to be her." Travis squeezed down harder, and Brooke cried out from the pain it sent across her rib cage. "Travis, please."

Travis dipped his head down and spoke into her hair, not loosening his grip. "God, I certainly did marry myself a little detective, now didn't I?" He took in a deep breath, smelling her shampoo. "So tell me, Sherlock, what happens next? How does the heroine manage to get away in one of your little books?"

Brooke tried to squirm out of his grasp, and in response, he rolled his shoulder inward and against her face, cutting off her air supply. She froze, panic setting in, and ceased her struggles against him. In turn, he brought his shoulder back so she could breathe again. She sucked in a deep breath of precious oxygen, then slumped against him, defeated. She wasn't going to get out of his hold, not unless he wanted her to. "Where's Katelyn, Travis?" she squeaked.

Travis laughed. It sounded hollow. Humorless. "Not in the fucking shed."

A tear descended her cheek, absorbed by Travis's jacket. This wasn't supposed to happen—her tears were supposed to disappear once she was inside her husband's arms, not get brought on by the same. "What did you do to her, Travis?" she asked as more tears followed the first.

He sighed, and Brooke could feel him shaking his head above her. "Oh, my lovely wife. What's with all the crying? Aren't you having a good time?"

"Where's Katelyn, Travis?"

With one quick motion, he shoved her away. She jerked back violently, her feet tangling in the handle of the duffle bag. She was halfway to the floor when he caught hold of her arm and yanked her forward again, stopping her just an inch away from his face. "Oh, babe," he growled, his fingers digging into her wrist until she could feel the bones begin to shift, "you might not be having a good time right now, but you're about to."

He struck Brooke on the side of the face, the shock of it more painful than the actual blow. It wasn't enough to knock her unconscious, but was enough to cause her to stumble backward. He then scooped his arm around her waist and pulled her against his chest, so his front was molded to her back. His other hand clamped down over mouth, stifling her pitiful attempts to scream.

He lifted her easily with one arm and walked across the room, taking her with him. The glass door slid open, and cold air cut into her body everywhere except where he was pressed against her. He went to the stairs and started their descent, his hand still clamped over her mouth.

Brooke struggled to gain her footing on the stairs, but with how high he was holding her, she couldn't reach the ground. She flailed her legs through the air, kicking at anything she could reach. Her foot connected with the side of the house, but only scraped across the wooden planks as she was carried further down the stairs. Once they reached the clearing, her feet swept through nothing but icy wind.

Her eyes locked on the lowest deck. Noah's door was closed, the light on inside. Was he still in the shower? Could he see them? Hear them? Brooke screamed into Travis's hand, but all that came out was an incoherent, muffled garble of half-words, taken away by the wind. She continued to flail her legs, trying to make as much movement as possible so she could catch Noah's attention.

For all her efforts, no movement came from inside. The house sat silently on the ravine's slope, watching her struggles, the light from its windows almost looking like eyes in the growing gloom.

Brooke gave up on the house and started searching the clearing. If she could just get out of his grasp, maybe there was a weapon of some kind she could grab. But instead of seeing a weapon, all she saw was scarlet. Oak leaves covered the ground, the red so dark it was almost black in the thickening dusk. A frigid breeze rattled the nearly bare trees, and the final traces of autumn rained down, along with tiny, frozen flecks of winter. It had begun to snow.

Brooke let out one more muffled cry as Travis carried her past the tree line and into the woods, where night had already fallen. The lights from the house faded among the trees, and then disappeared completely.

Travis

# Chapter 25

*Sunday, 3:42 p.m.*

Travis Hayden kept his eyes on the center of the road, watching the breaks in the yellow line as they came and went. When traveling in a car, the lines almost blurred together, but on foot each dash went by with agonizing slowness. Four strides to be exact. And then a break. Four strides, then a break. Four strides, break. Strides. Break. Why this road wasn't a no-passing zone was beyond him.

Travis lifted his gaze and scanned the trees on either side of the highway, not that he expected to see anything of interest. It was all just a bunch of green and brown anyway. Branches and trunks. Leaves and bark. It never changed, never got interesting. Just like the yellow line. It was all just a monotonous bore—the kind that would put him to sleep if he was inside the comforting warmth of a vehicle and not shivering his ass off outside.

It had been over two hours since he left the house, the first hour almost completely dedicated to working his way down the long driveway and then the even longer dirt road that led to the highway. The dirt road had been an arduous task, the abundant potholes threatening to twist his ankles every few paces. Not to mention the branches he nearly had to crawl over, and the thorned bushes that scratched at his arms if he ever strayed too close to the shoulder.

The old man really should have done a better job of maintaining the roads. But shit, if he couldn't even keep the house up to snuff, how the hell was he going to be able to keep the roads in tip-top shape either? Not that it mattered anymore. Scarlett Springs wouldn't be having any more guests traversing its paths. And before long, the house would fall into total disrepair. The stairs will wither and give way to the forest floor, and the shingles will get torn from the roof with each passing storm. Eventually, the whole house will crumble and sink into the ravine, nature finally clearing the blemish of humanity from its skin.

Travis looked up at the tempestuous sky. The encroaching clouds had thickened considerably since he departed on this fool's errand, and they were now wrapped around the sun like a heavy winter blanket. Only dull, gloomy light remained, reminding him of what it felt like beneath the forest canopy, where murky shadows enshrouded everything—and everyone—that dared enter its depths.

Travis thought he would at least have some sunlight while out on the highway, away from the forest's clutches, but instead the clouds had rolled in and chased away what little autumn warmth remained and brought what he expected to be snow before the day was up. And possibly a lot of it. The temperature gauge in his mind still said it had a few more degrees to fall before it reached freezing conditions, but with how quickly that particular number was dropping, it wasn't hard to discern that it would be prime snow weather before nightfall.

Rain or snow, Travis thought, those bloated-ass clouds weren't going to keep their bellies full for long. And whether it be frozen water or liquid, this walk was about to get a hell of a lot more shitty. Especially if the clouds opened up sooner rather than later.

Travis had originally hoped that his valiant trek to rescue would be a quick one—he would flag down the first car that passed by, tell them of the horrors inside their rental home, and then get driven to the nearest town. Or at least have the cops meet him on the road so he didn't have to walk so damn far. But after two hours, he hadn't seen the likes of one goddamn motorist on the deserted highway. *Got the incoming storm to thank for that one,* he thought bitterly as he trudged along the yellow line. Nobody wants to navigate a winding mountain road in a snowstorm.

So Travis—the hero that he was—continued onward, checking his phone every few minutes to see if he had regained cell coverage. He forgot how many miles it was from the house to where the signal cut out, but something told him it was around seven. *Too damn long,* he thought, because now it looked like he was going to have to walk the full seven instead of flagging down a Good Samaritan midway through his journey. At least when he made it to cell coverage he could just sit on the side of the road and wait for the authorities to come to him. And hopefully not in a fucking blizzard.

*Must be getting close now,* he thought, and checked his phone again. Nope. Not yet.

His mind drifted to his lovely wife, and to what she must be saying to Noah right about now as they waited for his safe return. A bunch of theories about serial killers that hunt in pacts, or some other crazy-ass shit like that. Moving branches and midnight visitors and murder sheds. What a bunch of bullshit.

He should have known better. He should have known that his lovely wife would latch onto her crazy, fantastical theories and ignore simple logic. That she would ignore all the *facts* he had carefully constructed. *Facts* that would have the cops nodding their heads and sending them on their way, telling them how lucky they were to survive such a tragedy. *Facts* that were now going to get muddled thanks to his lovely wife's insistence that serial killers run in pacts, like fucking wild dogs.

He had set it all up perfectly—both for the girl and the old man. Their deaths canceled each other out. A simple murder-suicide tied up neatly with a bow. *Here ya go, officers. Enjoy the clean up and we'll just be on our way.* 60 Minutes, *here we come.*

But before the signed affidavits, and the TV interviews that would inevitably follow, he first had to call those officers and get them out to the damned house. And that involved walking along a deserted highway only hours before dark while an impending snowstorm circulated overhead.

Travis looked at his phone again. Couldn't be much longer now. Couldn't be much longer at all.

# Chapter 26

*Yesterday*

Travis stood in the bedroom, watching Brooke as she hurried across the clearing to where Noah was standing near the tree line. His brother had been there for nearly twenty minutes, calling for Katelyn and looking around for clues, of which, Travis was quite certain, there were none. A mess? Yes. But clues? No. He had made sure of it.

Travis watched as they talked for a moment, then disappeared into the trees. *Better get this done now,* he thought, and stepped out onto the deck. He hurried up the staircase, throwing one quick glance over his shoulder when he reached the top. They were still in the woods somewhere, where they would hopefully stay for at least the next twenty minutes or so.

Travis rounded the house, the tire impressions from Katelyn's Ford still visible in the scattered gravel out front. He had driven the car out to the main highway after the mess in the forest, and then pushed it over the side of the first embankment he could find. He watched the silvery moonlight bounce off the chrome frame as the SUV tumbled down the steep hill, before finally getting wedged between two pine trees some fifty feet below.

It was out of view from the main road, but he was quite certain the police would still be able to find it eventually. Which was exactly what he wanted. Katelyn could have easily driven the car off a treacherous mountain pass in the middle of the night—especially if she was frightened and had been drinking. And then, dazed and disoriented, she had simply gotten out of the car and wandered off, eventually succumbing to the elements. Tragic. But believable.

The note Travis wrote for Noah said as much—Katelyn left in a hurry, not even taking the time to wake him or pack up her belongings. In such a state of mind, she would have been driving erratically, not thinking straight. All that booze. All that fear. It's bound to rattle a person up. Especially a timid girl like Katelyn.

Travis stopped at Maurice's front door, silently cursing the old man for having to get involved. This wasn't part of the plan. *Maurice* wasn't part of the plan. He wasn't even supposed to be here. What B&B owner stays in the house he's renting out? It's an invasion of privacy, that's for damn sure. And then the creepy bastard doesn't even *try* to make himself scarce. He just sits up on that balcony of his, watching them all the damn time. Listening to their conversations. Staring at his lovely wife. And peeking through the windows to see what they were up to in the clearing. What *Travis* was up to in the clearing.

Travis thought the old man would have been fast asleep when the... *incident*... occurred. I mean, who would be awake at that hour of the night? And why? But as soon as Travis got back into bed after taking care of the girl's car, he could hear Maurice up there. Stomping around. Moving things back and forth. All the commotion had even woken up Brooke. And Travis had really been hoping she would sleep through the whole damn thing. But, of course, like everything else this weekend, he had gotten the shit end of the stick.

The only plausible explanation Travis could think of for Maurice's midnight activities was that the old man had witnessed the *incident* in the clearing. Maurice was up on that balcony, or at least peeking through one of the windows, and was watching when it happened. Which meant he knew too much. None of Travis's carefully constructed pieces were going to fall into place if Maurice was blabbing to the cops about the crazy shit he saw one of his tenants do in the damn backyard. Instead of Katelyn's disappearance being a tragic accident, it would turn into a murder investigation—one with the eccentric old innkeeper pointing his gnarled finger directly at Travis.

So there goes that perfectly believable explanation for Katelyn's sudden and untimely demise. She couldn't have simply left a note and then crashed her car during a hasty getaway—not when there was a nosey Frenchman upstairs.

One that saw too much, and who apparently had a wicked case of insomnia.

*But how?* Travis thought as he lay in bed next to his lovely wife, listening to the bastard upstairs as he clomped around like he was in a goddamn marching band. Morning was too near, and Brooke was in too fitful of a sleep, for Travis to slip away again. He was already pretty damn lucky that he had gotten away with Katelyn *and* dumping the car without Brooke noticing his absence. Now, if he so much as rolled over, she would startle awake and reach for him. And he better have his fucking ass in this bed when she did.

By the time dawn breached the night, Travis had come up with what he thought was a reasonable solution. Something that would pass the blame to the fucker upstairs, as well as silence him for good. Two birds, one stone, and all that bullshit. He just hoped he could get to Maurice before Maurice got to the cops.

This was certainly going to muddle up his hazy, ambiguous statement for the police, though. That's for damn sure. Saying the girl just up and left while they were asleep left a lot open to interpretation. But the guy upstairs turning up dead, too? He needed to tread carefully now. He had already made too many mistakes as it is.

It wouldn't be too hard of a transition to add Maurice's sudden departure from the living into Katelyn's disappearance. Especially now that the old coot could be Suspect Numero Uno for those crime scene investigators. Katelyn's car could still be found on the side of the road (good thing, too, since Travis had no way of getting it back), only now that upturned vehicle was pointing at Maurice, who obviously got rid of the car in an attempt to hide evidence. He murdered Katelyn, *obviously*, but for what sick purpose no one will ever know. He disposed of her body and then got rid of her car. And then… then he got so overwhelmed with guilt that he couldn't stand to go on living. Murder-suicides happen all the time. Travis was certain of it, since Brooke made him watch those *Forensic Files* shows all the time, whether he wanted to or not. The more he watched, the more he realized they were like tutorials—half-hour segments on how *not* to get caught. Thanks, lovely wife.

Travis just needed something to solidify the case against Maurice, and he was pretty sure he already had it: Katelyn's phone. He saw it lying against one of the oak trees when he went down into the clearing that night, and absentmindedly shoved it into his pocket for safekeeping. He had planned to stealthily return it to Noah's room in the morning, but now he had a better idea. That phone was the key to laying the blame on Maurice, and Travis knew just where to put it: inside that creepy-ass shed in the woods. Instead of slipping it back into Noah's room, he'd slip it right into Maurice's padlocked shed. And if he couldn't get it inside, he'd at least toss it somewhere nearby. Either way, it would get the cops looking in Maurice's direction and not his own.

Things weren't working out quite the way Travis had in mind for this weekend, but in the end, he'd still manage to get out of this unscathed. Thanks, *Forensic Files*.

Travis stood at Maurice's front door, readying himself for what came next. He shook out his hands, rubbed hard at his eyes to make them appear red, and then took a few gasping breaths to make himself look distraught. Satisfied, he rapped his knuckles on the weatherworn wood.

Maurice answered on the second knock. The old man had put on a pleasant, if not slightly strained smile when he first opened the door. However, as soon as he saw Travis's face, the smile slipped.

"My wife..." Travis panted, his eyes wide and voice trembling. "She fell in the shower and twisted her ankle." He waited for Maurice to say something, and when he didn't, he went on. "It's swelling up really fast, and we need to call for an ambulance."

Maurice's eyes narrowed, his gaze flicking over Travis's shoulder to the vacant parking area. When they settled back on Travis, a crease had formed between his bushy brows.

*He's wondering why we don't drive to the hospital ourselves,* Travis realized. *That or he knows exactly what I did with her car.*

"One of our companions had to leave for a family emergency last night," Travis stammered, jerking a thumb over his shoulder. "She took the car, and now we have no way to get out of here." When Maurice still didn't respond, he added, "And our phones aren't working."

Travis tried to keep the expression of a concerned husband plastered to his face, but inside, he was already calculating how quickly he could shoulder-ram this guy into the house and slam the door shut before he got a scream out. Maurice obviously saw what happened in the clearing last night. He might have already called the cops even, and was just waiting for them to arrive with their top lights painting the forest trees surreal shades of blue and red.

Only Maurice wasn't looking in the direction of the driveway, where the police would inevitably be approaching from. He wasn't even looking at the parking area, or to the empty spot where Katelyn's car should be. He was looking out at the woods. The old man's eyes kept darting to the forest over Travis's shoulder, scanning the trees every few seconds.

Confusion attempted to overtake Travis's worried expression, but he stubbornly refused to grant it access to his face. He needed to look overcome with concern for his wife, not confused by Maurice's lack of attention span. He had been expecting the old man to be scared, but he thought that fear would be directed toward him. He was fully prepared to force his way into the home—had been planning on it actually—but now all he could do was wonder what the hell this guy was looking at.

Finally, Maurice nodded his head and stepped aside, allowing Travis access to the house. *Huh. Well this is going a lot easier than planned.* Travis stepped inside, turning his head to follow Maurice's gaze, which was still locked on the tree line. Only there was nothing there. *Fucking weirdo.*

"I'm so sorry to hear 'bout your wife's accident," Maurice said, shutting the door quickly behind them.

Travis took a few steps into the house, but stopped when he heard the click of the deadbolt as it slid into place. He turned back and looked at Maurice, wondering why he had bothered to lock the door. The old man now had his back to him, and he was peering out the window.

*What the fuck is this guy looking at?* Puzzled, Travis opened his mouth to speak, but clamped his jaw shut when he realized what was happening. *It is the fucking cops. He must have told them about a way to get through the trees, so they could sneak up on me. And now he just has to keep me distracted until—*

Travis's eyes fell to the front door. To the *locked* front door. *But why lock the door if you're expecting the cops to come rushing in to save you?*

Maurice whirled around, catching him off guard. Travis fumbled for a second, before throwing the concerned expression back in place. "Please..." he begged. "My wife. I really need to use your phone."

Maurice nodded his head up and down, almost too enthusiastically. "Of course, of course. I'm sorry. Right this way." He held his calloused hand out in front of him, gesturing to a hallway directly across from the foyer.

Travis allowed him to pass, then followed him down the hall. His eyes scanned the walls and furniture as he went. Table in the hallway, pictures on the walls, dining room table, door to the balcony, bathroom. He watched Maurice walk over to the kitchen, where a landline telephone was perched on top of a mustard-colored Formica countertop.

"Please," Maurice said, "help yourself. I sure am sorry your wife was injured."

Travis took a step forward, studying the old man. The anxiety coming off of him was palpable. And although Travis was expecting anxiety, and a lot of it, none of it was directed towards him. Either Maurice had quite the poker face, or something else was bothering him.

"Thank you," Travis said, moving closer to the phone.

Maurice gave him a wave of his hand, but didn't spare Travis another glance. His eyes were now locked on one of the back windows, facing the clearing. They swept from side to side, following the tree line.

*What in the living fuck is wrong with this guy? The cops wouldn't be coming from that direction.* Travis scanned the room, looking for anything that might be out of place, but didn't see anything worth noting. He guessed the dining room was where Maurice was stomping around last night, although there was a closed door beyond it, which might be situated right above their bedroom downstairs. The bathroom was also nearby, but nothing looked amiss inside.

Travis picked up the phone and turned to face the kitchen, putting his back to Maurice. He made a show of dialing, although the numbers he hit on the old phone were not 911. After hitting three arbitrary numbers instead, he waited for a few seconds, then spoke into the empty line like he was speaking to a dispatcher. He identified himself, told them the situation about Brooke's impromptu ankle injury, and then asked them to quickly send an ambulance to Scarlett Springs.

While he had his imaginary conversation, he scanned the kitchen for an easily accessible knife. He would have brought one from downstairs, but he wanted it to be Maurice's personal knife—one from a set that he has used for many decades. It was Maurice's suicide; it needed to be Maurice's knife as well. *Obviously.*

Travis saw what he was looking for in a wooden block next to the sink. He threw a quick glance over his shoulder, and saw Maurice was still staring out the window at the clearing. Travis made some more *mmhmm* noises, like he was listening to instructions from the dispatcher, and then quietly set the phone back in its cradle. He then snuck around the counter and gingerly removed what appeared to be the largest knife in the set. He curled his fingers around the handle, feeling the weight of the blade in his hand.

He turned, cocking a brow as he watched the old man. His stiff posture, the minor tremor in his left hand—Maurice was definitely spooked about something. But he sure didn't look like a man who knew he was standing in the same room as a murderer. If so, he wouldn't keep turning his back on the danger at hand. Would he?

No. If you're feeling threatened by something, you keep your eyes on the danger at all times. And the only place Maurice couldn't seem to pull his gaze away from wasn't in his home right now. It was out there.

Travis sighed, then followed it with a shrug. It didn't matter where Maurice was looking. Not really. The risk of allowing him to live was just too great. Simple as that. He had to die.

Travis took one step forward, then another. He was acutely aware of how noisy these floors could be, and he needed the old man to focus on the window until he closed the distance between them.

Slowly, he crept up behind Maurice, his eyes involuntarily following the man's gaze out the window. Still a whole lot of nothing. And from the looks of things, Brooke and Noah were still somewhere in the woods. Thank God for small favors.

Travis reached out and the floor creaked loudly under his weight. Maurice, already on edge, startled at the noise. He jerked away from Travis, then whirled to the side and lurched away from the window.

*Goddamnit, that fucker is fast,* Travis thought, and spun on his heels to give chase. The chase was short-lived, however, when Travis easily outmaneuvered the old man and blocked his only means of escape: the hallway.

Maurice instead lunged for the phone—like that was going to save him—and had the receiver halfway to his ear when Travis severed the cord with a quick flick of his knife. Maurice froze when he saw the blade, the phone falling to the counter with a clatter.

Travis took the opportunity to seize his wrist, then spun him around and curled his arm up behind his back. Maurice fought—albeit poorly—until Travis jerked up on his arm. Hard. *Serves him right for trying to run,* he thought, and gave the arm another harsh tug. Maurice let out an anguished cry, which was cut short when Travis used his free hand to press the kitchen blade against his throat.

"Don't scream or I'll make this worse for you," he hissed into his ear.

The old man gave a half-hearted struggle, let out a garbled curse, and then was still. His shoulders slumped and his posture sagged to the point that Travis had to withdraw the pressure on the blade to not accidentally cut the man's throat. *Huh. For being so quick on his feet, he sure didn't put up much of a fight.*

"Move," Travis snapped, not wanting to let his guard down in case Maurice decided to make some sort of ridiculous effort to save himself. He shoved Maurice toward the ajar door that led to the bathroom. *People always do it in the bathroom, don't they?*

Once inside, Travis caught sight of the old man's expression in the mirror. The fear was gone, replaced by a sorrowful acceptance that Travis didn't quite understand.

Travis's eyes shot up to his own reflection, and the man he saw staring back at him didn't look like himself at all. His eyes seemed darker, and his lips were curled up into a cruel sneer. He looked away. It turns out it was true what they said about looking yourself in the mirror. You could do practically anything it seemed, just as long as you don't have to see yourself doing it.

Travis directed his gaze back to Maurice. He tightened his grip on the old man's arm, causing him to grimace. "What did you see?" he asked, watching Maurice's reaction in the mirror.

"I-I don't know what ya mean. I didn't see yer wife get injured."

"You know that's not what I meant," Travis snapped, and pulled up on Maurice's arm. The man let out a whimper, and Travis loosened his grip. "Well?" he prodded. "Start talking."

"I didn't see it," Maurice stammered. Then added, "Not yet anyway."

"What do you mean *not yet*?" Travis asked. "Were you watching me or not?"

Maurice's eyes found Travis's. He stared at him through the mirror for what felt like an eternity, then slowly shook his head. "You? I was never watchin' you."

"Bullshit." Travis pressed the blade down harder, but not enough to draw blood. "You've been watching us the whole time. Why? What sick shit were you trying to see?"

Maurice shook his head again, only slightly, to avoid cutting himself with the knife. "I only watch to make sure ya don't go into the woods."

Travis snorted. "What the hell does that matter?"

Maurice opened his mouth to speak, then stopped. He averted his eyes, causing Travis to pull up on his arm again. He yelped and returned his gaze to the mirror. "It's not safe to go into the woods," he said simply.

"Yeah, you told us that already. Bears. Poison oak."

Maurice held Travis's stare. "There ain't no poison oak around here. And I haven't seen a bear in years."

Travis laughed, but it sounded more like a growl. "Nice poker face, old man. So why then? You think someone is going to get hurt out there and file a lawsuit or something?"

"No." Maurice cleared his throat, causing the knife to bob up and down with his Adam's apple. "Not exactly."

"What then?" Travis felt his patience wearing thin. Brooke and Noah would be back soon, and he should just get this over with already. But now his curiosity was peaked.

"It's not supposed to wake up this soon," Maurice said softly. "It... I-I don't know why it's already awake. It never wakes up this early. That's why I don't rent the place out in the winter, ya see? It's not safe. Ya folks were gonna be the last group 'til spring. I thought—I thought there would be plenty of time. And I needed the money."

"What the hell are you talking about?"

"When the temperatures go down I start watchin' the woods. Sit out there some nights, just to make sure it's still sleepin'. This cold front comin' through, it was... unexpected. I thought ya folks would be gone before—"

"Jesus Christ. The dementia must be hitting you pretty hard up here. All alone in the woods as your mind slips out your ears."

"You should leave," Maurice said. "Right now. Before it—" He stopped, and clamped his mouth shut.

Travis's eyes narrowed as he watched him through the mirror. "Before it what?" Silence followed, filling the confines of the bathroom. Travis let out a frustrated grunt. Time was running out. "What have you been doing up here?"

Maurice lowered his eyes. "I'll do anything for my family," he whispered.

"You told us you didn't have any family."

"No, not livin', I don't."

"You're fucking crazy, man. Seriously." Travis considered the knife he was holding. Cutting the throat would be easier, but he didn't want it to look like a homicide. *No, it has to be the wrists,* he thought. *That's how they all fucking do it.*

"You won't make it out of here, ya know," Maurice said, not so much pleading, but simply stating a fact. He looked at Travis. "Not without my help."

Travis smirked. "What could I possibly need your help for?"

"My great-great-great-grandmother."

Travis guffawed. This guy was completely off his rocker. He might have committed suicide anyway, even without Travis's help.

"She woke up last night. I heard her screamin'. I spent the rest of the night tryin' to get everythin' ready to—" He paused, considering if he should continue. A look of acceptance flitted across his brown eyes, and he then went on. "If I don't feed her soon, she'll go after you. She probably will anyway. She's been asleep for so long—"

"What do you mean *feed her*?"

"Nothin' crazy. Deer and elk mostly. Anythin' I can hunt down out there without havin' to go too deep inside." His lower lip trembled, and he sucked in a shaky, clogged-sounding breath.

"Too deep inside?"

"The woods. It's damn near suicide to stray too far from the house. That's why I lied 'bout the bears and poison oak. To keep ya from goin' too far."

"And what happens if you go too far?"

"She gets ya," Maurice said. He didn't bother to elaborate.

Travis stared at the old man, his mouth hanging open. "She gets ya?" he parroted. *Fucking loon.*

Maurice swallowed, then reluctantly continued. "They never find 'em, ya know? Search and Rescue and the like. Whoever goes in, never comes out. That's why I got to keep feedin' her. It's why I never left when all my family did. I'm just tryin' to keep the victims to a minimum."

"Victims of your…"—Travis shook his head, feeling silly for even humoring the senile old fucker—"great-great-great-grandmother?"

Maurice nodded. "I hunt as many deer as I can, but it's never enough. And I can't afford to buy it at the store. Meat's too expensive nowadays. Can't spare the cost." He tilted his head in the direction of the closed door beyond the dining table. "I keep my huntin' gear in there. Was plannin' to go out as soon as ya folks left."

"Go out and hunt deer?"

"Ahuh. Whatever I can find. I bring it to the shed after. Butcher the meat there. Then I take it across the stream and leave it lying on the other side."

"Why bother butchering it at all? Why not just leave it where you shot it?"

"She seems to take more kindly to my offerin's if I split 'em open first. It's not like it's what she wants to be eatin', so I try to make 'em as appetizin' to her as possible. "

"Try to make it appetizing because what she really wants to be eating is… people?"

Maurice nodded, his eyes brimming with tears. "I don't wanna do it," he croaked. "I hate killin' animals. And even more, I hate cuttin' them open. But if I don't, she'll go after others. Children. Families. It's better that I keep feedin' her, ain't it? Even then, sometimes I fail. Sometimes she gets others anyways. And it's all my fault. Their blood is on my hands."

Silence reclaimed the small bathroom, broken only by Maurice's quiet sobbing. "Just do it," he choked out. "I can't keep goin' on like this. I don't wanna. I rather it be here in this bathroom with you, than out there in the woods with her."

Travis's lip twitched. This guy was serious. After a moment's hesitation, he released Maurice's arm, ready to overpower him again if necessary. But the old man only dabbed at his eyes with one of his flannel sleeves. He then turned around, facing Travis, and gave him an accepting nod. "I'm ready," he said.

Travis gaped at him. This must be a trick. It had to be. He kept waiting for Maurice to attempt an ill-fated escape, an attack, *something*. But instead, Maurice stood where he was, waiting patiently.

"If you don't do it, I will," he said, resolved. "I can't live like this anymore. In constant fear. Just waitin' for her to turn me into a monster like she is. More than anythin', I don't want that."

Travis rolled his eyes. "You really have gone crazy out here, haven't you?"

"You don't have to believe me. Just get the people ya care for outta here. Fast as ya can."

In the end, Travis wound up doing the deed. Maurice didn't struggle as Katelyn had. In fact, Travis almost thought he saw a look of relief in the old man's eyes as the life faded out of him. Travis wiped off the handle of the knife with a dry portion of Maurice's shirt, briefly pressed it against the man's limp fingers, then tossed the blade on the floor beside him.

He then went to the window and scanned the clearing. He could see movement coming from the trail that led to the shed. He held the curtain aside, his stomach twisting into knots as he watched Noah, and then Brooke, enter the clearing. He had taken too long with the old loon, listening to his crazy talk when he should have just gotten it over with quickly.

When Noah and Brooke stopped walking and looked up at Maurice's balcony, Travis let the curtain fall closed. He only had a minute until they were back at the house. Time to fucking move.

Travis ran through the house, out the front door, and beelined for the stairs. He was about to round the side of the house, when he heard footsteps down below. *Shit!* He jerked to a stop, nearly slipping in the loose gravel underfoot. It was too late… they were going to discover he was gone and put two and two together. *Shit fucking shit!*

He ran back into the house, scurrying from room to room until he found the doorway he was looking for. He yanked it open and saw the indoor staircase, descending into darkness. He ran inside, shutting the door behind him and going down as quickly as he could in the total blackness that surrounded him. *This fucking thing needs a nightlight,* he thought absentmindedly as he reached the bottom. He fumbled in the dark, praying the lock wasn't something he would need keys for. Mercifully, when he found the latch, it was for a single deadbolt.

He undid the lock, hoping they weren't already standing inside the living room, and let the door swing open. The room was empty, thank God, but he could hear voices on the stairs, and close.

Travis shut the stairwell door, giving it a shove until it clicked firmly into place. He then tiptoed across the living room, darting past the sliding glass door mere seconds before Brooke and Noah crossed the deck. He ran into the master bedroom, shut the door as quickly—and quietly—as he could, and stumbled out of his shoes. He then dove into the bed, burrowed under the covers, and tried to slow his breathing to a respectable level before Brooke came inside.

Not that it mattered. Even if he was still breathing erratically when she "woke him up", he could just tell her it was a nightmare. Brooke knew all about those. She had them all the time. And this time, she would be the one to comfort him about the scary things he saw in his head, instead of the other way around.

# Chapter 27

*Today*

The wind tugging at Travis's hair was growing colder with each gust. He had been walking for over three hours now, and his feet were beginning to ache with the effort. Not to mention his teeth started chattering twenty minutes ago, which was a delightful addition to the protests in his lower body. He clamped his jaw down against the incessant clicking and fished his phone out of his pocket.

*"Fuuuck,"* he growled, shoving the phone back into his jeans. He left his hand there, letting it linger in the warmth that resided inside.

How the hell could there still not be a signal? He couldn't keep going much longer like this, not with the weather growing darker and more dreary with each passing minute.

And if he couldn't get ahold of anyone, then he had the entire trek back to think about.

Of all the things Travis thought could potentially harm him on this little outing, the elements weren't high on his list of potential threats. Not when there were hungry black bears stalking about, eager to fatten up before they called it quits on another summer. The same bears the old man had been feeding all this time, whether he believed it or not. Bears that now associated people with food.

"What a fucking shit show," he muttered, shaking his head bitterly. At least it was almost over.

He decided to distract himself from the blistering cold by running through the details of the ill-fated weekend again and again, trying to pull out any loose threads that required attention so he could mend them before the police got involved. To his relief, everything seemed to be tied up perfectly in a neat little bow. Hell, even the note he left in the stacks could be easily explained now, since Maurice apparently had a room full of guns and a laundry list of unexplained disappearances in the area.

Travis had originally left the note for Brooke to find, sticking it in between a couple books where he knew she would stumble upon it. And it was certainly easy enough to do, since he took the first shift that night and knew Brooke would be looking at the books next, trying to stay awake. At the time, Travis needed his lovely, yet predictable, wife to read that note and start pointing her finger at the evil innkeeper. Get that blame where it needed to be before the cops got involved.

He didn't expect Brooke to pull out some ludicrous theory about a pair of serial killers or whatever—but he should have seen something like that coming. Either way, she still did exactly what he wanted her to do: lay blame on Maurice. Whether he murdered Katelyn alone or with a blood-lusting buddy didn't matter, as long as the blame was on him.

And after their little bathroom heart-to-heart, it turns out the old man probably does have quite a bit of blame stacked on his arthritic shoulders. Making a habit of feeding bears only brings them closer to people. How many disappearances could have been avoided if Maurice wasn't out there all the time feeding the damn things? Making them associate people with food? Stupid old coot.

Travis sighed and looked out at the sea of trees, their boughs swaying methodically in the harsh wind. The greens of the forest had deepened with the oncoming storm, and the pines now appeared almost blue. Just like Travis's fingers were becoming. He squeezed his hands into fists, trying to conserve what little warmth he had left, and gazed out at the passing trees with feigned interest. Blues and browns. Branches and trunks. Pine needles and bark—

A shrill screech cut through the blue and brown ocean that was lapping at the sides of the highway. Travis froze in his tracks as the cry grew in volume and sliced through the chaotic wind whirling through the air. It seemed to go on forever, before finally fading back into the trees.

Travis stood in the center of the highway, looking more like a statue than a man. His fear of getting struck by a passing motorist had long since been abandoned, much like the highway itself had become. Abandoned. Forgotten. Desolate.

Wind whooshed and whispered through the pines, sounding like the waves of the ocean pulling in and out along with the tide. His eyes followed the tree line, dipping and swaying with the boughs of the trees, but he saw nothing emerge from inside the wall of bark and needles.

"A loon," he said, barely hearing his own voice. "Just a pissed off loon." He took a step forward, then another, his feet resuming their pursuit of the dashed yellow line.

When the second screech ripped through the forest, his shoulders hiked up to his ears and his hands instinctively came up in front of him. His body had perceived a threat, even if his conscious mind hadn't accepted it yet. "What the…" He tried to swallow, but his mouth had gone dry, his throat feeling like it was coated in coarse sandpaper.

The screech abruptly cut off midway through its gut-wrenching crescendo. *A bear,* he thought. *A bear just attacked a loon. Damn, it must be pretty desperate to go after something so small.*

As if on cue, Travis heard a cracking branch somewhere off to his right. His head jerked in that direction, his eyes searching for movement among the swaying trees. Nothing.

He had already taken several steps backward by the time he realized his body was retreating. Whatever was out there, his sympathetic nervous system wanted no part of it. He continued to back up, step by step, his senses on high alert. His vision felt acutely focused, picking out individual branches in the dense tree line, sometimes individual twigs.

And his hearing was keenly aware of every whisper, every gasp, every breath of wind. Something was hiding out there. He was sure of it. Something lurking just beyond a shroud of undulating foliage.

"Fuck this," he muttered, and pivoted on his heels. He started walking along the broken yellow line, back the way he came. "I'm not getting eaten by a fucking bear." He hurried along, focusing on the yellow dashes that came and went instead of on the unnerving silence inside the trees.

A few minutes later, he heard another branch crack somewhere deep inside the underbrush, and ten minutes later, another. It was keeping pace with him. The bear was following him, lumbering along in the shadows, assessing how much of a challenge he would be to subdue.

*Not much,* Travis thought. *Not for a fucking bear.*

He picked up his pace, the chill in the air no longer keeping his attention. His senses remained on alert, his eyes scanning the trees and his ears attuned to disturbances in the forest where his eyes couldn't see. The minutes ticked by at an excruciatingly slow pace, prompting him to further increase his speed, as if his cadence would accelerate time itself. Faster. Everything needed to go faster. Because that meant he'd be back sooner. He'd be *safe* sooner.

Travis cursed under his breath. *I was supposed to be in a warm-ass car by now. I was supposed to go back in a goddamn police cruiser. Not on foot. Not like this.*

After twenty minutes of silence, Travis was sure the bear had lost interest in him. His shoulders began to relax, the tension draining from his muscles. Still, he kept on at his steady pace, not wanting to slow too much in case the bear would take that as a sign of weakness and resume its pursuit.

He was about to turn his mind to other things—baseball, perhaps—when a heavy snort came out of the trees, only a few paces away from the road. *Jesus fuck. How did it get so close without me noticing?*

Travis stumbled to a stop, his head whipping in the direction of the grunt. He fully expected the bear to emerge triumphantly from the nearby foliage, but there was nothing there. Still, he stood where he was, frozen in place, trying to discern if it was the wind or heavy breathing that he was hearing, when the cracking sounds of breaking wood broke his concentration. The sharp cracks and splintering snaps grew in volume until there was no mistaking it for anything other than a tree falling over.

*That's a big-ass bear,* he thought. *Thing must be fucking huge.*

The tree thudded heavily on the forest floor, somewhere deep inside the pines, and then the whispering resumed. Travis sucked in a frigid breath, startled by the anxious whine that had replaced his own breathing. *What the hell is going on?* He clenched his jaw shut, forcibly stopping the annoying sound from slipping again from his lips. His resolve didn't last long, though, because when the next crack of breaking wood came, a full-on sob escaped his throat.

He broke into a run. This bear had been following him for over half an hour now, and it wasn't giving up. It was knocking trees down, for Christ's sake.

Travis ran hard, the aching in his feet forgotten. This bear was clearly too much of a threat for him to take on by himself. When they leave tomorrow—him, Brooke, and Noah—they will all go together. Safety in numbers, right? God, why had he insisted on coming out here alone? Fucking stupid. Especially after Maurice confessed to feeding the damn things. So fucking stupid.

Travis almost ran past the green sign for Scarlett Springs Road, the dense foliage grasping at the frigid metal with each passing gust. He hesitated for a moment, not wanting to enter the confines of the forest. Out here, there were guardrails, and the trees were kept at a reassuring distance. Now he would have to go *inside* them. Inside the screaming forest, where shadows danced and concealed the threats hiding among the pines. But what choice did he have?

Travis ran onto Scarlett Springs Road, trying to keep his focus on his breathing and maintaining his footing on the treacherous terrain. He didn't want to get winded, and even more so, he didn't want to fall. He was grateful for every day he spent in the gym, keeping his endurance up and his muscles finely tuned. If he had known he would have to outrun a bear, he might have kicked up his efforts even further, hitting the weight room seven days a week instead of just five. Hitting eight miles on the treadmill instead of just six.

He swerved to miss a fallen branch, then lunged himself over a particularly wide pothole. Fifty yards ahead another broken branch, the break so fresh that the bark inside looked like it was bleeding. *From the storm,* he thought. *It has to be from the storm.*

He cringed when an angry screech filled the air, sounding like the loon, but not at the same time. Could a bear make a noise like that? Fuck it. It didn't matter. *Just keep running.* His lungs began to ache as he pushed ahead, feeling pathetically childish for running, but at the same time overtly frightened by the thing keeping pace with him among the trees. *Not the thing—the bear. God, keep it together, Travis. And don't stop running.*

A carved piece of weatherworn wood reached out from the undergrowth, pointing to the overgrown driveway that led to the house. Travis veered to the left and sprinted down the driveway, surprised and relieved by the sudden burst of additional energy. *Almost there. Can't get attacked when I'm almost there. Come on. Push it, motherfucker.*

Something moaned, uncomfortably close to the path, and somehow in front of him instead of behind. Travis didn't slow, and bolted past the spot where he heard the awful sound without so much as looking at the passing trees. He couldn't stop now, couldn't turn and run the other way. A branch snapped directly behind him, some thirty feet back on the path. He didn't bother looking over his shoulder either. One missed pothole and he was down and out for good.

The glow of the house loomed in the distance. *Thank Christ,* he thought, feeling the final reserves of energy leaking from his muscles. His lungs were screaming, but they paled in comparison to the incessant cries in the forest—cries that almost sounded like voices among the trees. His legs quivered, ready to give out on him at any moment. *Not yet, not yet.*

*Almost there. I'm not going to be bear food, goddamnit. No fucking way.*

Travis ran into the parking area, his sneakers crunching in the tire treads from Katelyn's car. He went straight for Maurice's front door, praying for it to still be unlocked. His fingers touched the cold, blissful steel of the door handle, and he threw it open and hurled himself inside in one quick motion. He then whirled on his heels, almost falling from his forward momentum, and slammed the door shut behind him. He threw the deadbolt into place and pressed his hands against the wood, waiting for the impact that would surely follow on the other side.

Seconds ticked by, growing into minutes. Travis kept his hands firmly planted on the door, his eyes watching the living room curtain as it billowed in and out from the broken window pane. Each time the curtain fell back into place, he expected to see the bear's enormous paw reaching through the opening, its claws impossibly long and impossibly sharp as it reached inside almost delicately. Insistently. Expectantly. The curtain billowed in, then fell flat. Nothing. Billowed in. Fell flat. Still nothing.

Travis watched the curtain, almost hypnotized by the moving fabric. Almost like it was a stage curtain, about to be pulled away to reveal the actor on the other side. To reveal the *monster* on the other side.

*Any second now,* he thought, waiting for the paw to emerge. Waiting for dark fur and black paw pads. It billowed in, then fell. Nothing. Waiting for long, ivory claws clacking together. Billowed in, then fell. Nothing.

Travis went to the window, giving the curtain a wide berth as if it was contaminated in some way, and stepped up to the portion of glass that was still intact. He peered out at the small parking area, searching for the bear among the trees. But there was nothing. Still nothing. It couldn't have gone far, though.

He went back to the front door, his hand hovering over the lock. He didn't want to go back out there. Not when his legs felt like melting jello. He couldn't just keep standing here like an idiot, though. He needed to get back downstairs. To Brooke. To Noah. And preferably before the storm hit.

Travis took a deep breath and unlocked the door, pausing to see if he heard the sounds of an animal rushing up to greet him. Greet him or eat him, he thought, the joke offering little humor now that the door had lost its reassurance of safety. But there were no hurrying steps outside, no crunching gravel. Only whispers.

He cracked the door open, then peeked out at the doorstep for signs of black fur or yellow teeth. Still nothing. He opened the door, did a weary survey of the surrounding forest, and then stepped back outside.

He stood there, reluctant to leave the safety of the porch, and waited for the threat to reveal itself. There's no way it would give up so easily. Not when it almost had him. Surely, the second he stepped away from the house it would burst forth from the trees, fully intent on devouring him. Surely, it was still out there somewhere, drool dripping from its jaws and splattering onto the soil beside its outstretched claws, just waiting to make its move. Just waiting…

Travis continued to stand on the porch for what felt like eons, stubbornly refusing to believe he was alone out here. Stubbornly refusing to believe it would give up on a meal so easily. It had followed him all this way, just to turn around and leave because of a shut door and broken window? No, it had to still be out there somewhere.

He decided to give it a few more minutes, standing silently on the porch as the storm continued to intensify overhead. But still, nothing came.

Noah

# Chapter 28

Noah stood in the downstairs living room, his mind replaying the details of the last moments he spent with Katelyn. All the while, his eyes scanned the vacant space, jumping from one belonging of hers to the next. Her carry-on suitcase, the top hanging open and a jumble of pastel clothing overflowing the sides. Her flip-flop lying upturned next to the suitcase. Her phone charger on the nightstand. Her cryptic note on the coffee table.

Noah went to the note, picked it up, and stared at the carefully written words transcribed in purple ink. It felt like eons since he found it, Katelyn's absence having rearranged the concept of time.

Water hummed in the pipes overhead as it surged toward the shower he turned on when he arrived, light pouring from the bathroom as tepid water poured from the faucet. He had no intention of using it. It was merely a decoy, something Brooke would hear when she woke up and found out he was missing. She'd assume he was taking a shower and leave it at that.

He wouldn't have had to create a decoy if he had gone earlier like he should have, right after Brooke went to her room to lie down. Unfortunately, it had taken him nearly two hours to finally work up his nerve for what came next. Two hours to accumulate enough courage for what he was about to see, and for what he was about to discover out there. And anyway, the shower diversion would buy him at least twenty minutes, which was more than enough time to do what he was planning on doing.

Maurice's key ring sat in Noah's pocket, pressed snuggly against his thigh. He had found it during their search of the house, and since the car key wasn't attached, he had pocketed the keys and not told the others. Not because he was fond of lying or sneaking around, but because he was almost certain they would stop him from what he was about to do. Because one of the keys looked different from the others. One of them was small and rectangular, and most likely made for a padlock instead of a door. A padlock that was currently keeping him from the truth. And the truth was out there, alright—in that dank, blood-splattered shed in the woods.

Noah listened to the hum of the water, his eyes vacantly staring at the cloud of steam that was rolling out of the bathroom like an approaching fog. He expected to feel fear, apprehension, or at least nervous excitement about what he was about to do, but instead, some sort of blank resolve had fallen over him. Like a creeping black death inside his chest, the darkness taking over his heart and turning it cold. As cold as a corpse would be. Cold, dead, and *empty*. So empty it was suffocating.

Emptiness was something Noah was used to, a state of being he had grown to accept over the past six years. It was a lonely, painful existence, but there wasn't a damn thing he could do about it, so he had learned to live with it all the same. To live with the emptiness, with the loneliness, with the heartache.

But then Katelyn had come along, and she had filled that void in his chest with her laughter, her warmth, and the sweetness of her smile. She had become the embodiment of hope to him—hope for the future, hope for the comfort of having a loving partner by his side, and most importantly, hope of moving on. And now that glimmer of a better life had been snuffed out. It had been taken from him. And all that was left was her wrinkled clothing, a useless phone charger, and this note.

Noah stared at the words, remembering what Brooke had asked about the handwriting. Was it Katelyn's? It was a good question, and one that he felt like a failure for being unable to answer. He didn't know what Katelyn's handwriting looked like, not in the slightest. He could pick out Brooke's anywhere; it was pretty and bubbly, just like her. But Katelyn's... all he knew was that she liked putting emojis at the end of her text messages. Smiley faces, kissy winks, heart eyes. But her handwriting? No, he had never received a note from her. Not until now.

Noah ran his thumb over the script, feeling the slight indentations of the pen pressed into the pink paper. Did he even know the girl who had written this? If he did, he would have been able to identify this note as hers. And he just... couldn't. The thought hurt more than the emptiness enshrouding his chest cavity. Why did he know so little about the girl he was sleeping next to? The only explanation within reach was that he hadn't given her enough of a chance—hadn't given *them* enough of a chance. He thought he had, he thought he might even love her someday, but now he'd never get to find out. And he'd never know what her handwriting looked like, other than this cryptic note written in the dead of night.

Noah crumpled the paper, the blackness in his chest burning red at the edges. This was all his damn fault. If he had known her better, this never would have happened. He would have noticed the signs of discontent. He would have noticed she was planning on leaving. And he could have stopped it, or hell, at least gone with her. She would have been safe if he was by her side. But once again, he was distracted. Stupid-ass Noah, always getting distracted by things he shouldn't be looking at, and even worse, longing for things he couldn't have.

The crushed note fell from his hand as a disconcerting thought surfaced in his mind. *Is that why she left?* Not because of monsters, but because of *him*. Was that the reason she didn't wake him to go with her, or tell him that she was leaving in the first place? Because she noticed how his eyes strayed to where they shouldn't? Or how he smiled differently when *she* was around?

*Of course that's why.* Women are so perceptive; how could Katelyn *not* have noticed? *Shit.* This really was all his damn fault.

*I shouldn't have brought her along this time,* Noah thought with a bitter shake of his head. It was too soon. He hadn't completely moved on yet. He thought he had, but apparently that was all bullshit. Because Katelyn had picked up on it. And then she left because of it. *And now she might be dead. Because of me.*

Guilt waged war with the blackness clouding his heart. If only they had more time. He could have loved her—*would* have loved her—if only they had more time. He was sure of it. He could have moved on for good and become the boyfriend she deserved. Hell, maybe even more than that. All that was needed was more time. But that was stolen from them. *She* was stolen from him. By the man lurking upstairs.

Noah turned his head and peered out the window, the presence of the surrounding woods heavy upon his shoulders. In the clearing, the oak trees were bleeding leaves. The wind had picked up since he arrived downstairs, and it appeared the storm clouds that had been circling overhead were finally closing in. And, as if this weekend could get any worse, the clouds had brought an arctic chill along with them.

He had to get going. Now. Before the storm wrapped its clutches around this godforsaken house. If he hurried, he could get out to the shed, take a look around, and then get back to the house before the storm really got going. And even if it did start dumping torrents, he'd still go out there. Something of Katelyn's was inside that disgusting shed, and there was no way in hell he was leaving this shithole until he took a look in there himself. Something else of hers might be in there, or *she* might be in there. And even though he screwed up a lot during this damn trip, he wasn't going to screw up so badly that he didn't even bother to look inside the freaking murder shed. He owed her that much. He actually owed her a hell of a lot more than that, but this would have to do.

Noah reached down and felt the keys in his pocket. *God, please let one of these be for that padlock.* He tilted his head and listened, his ear directed toward the ceiling. If Brooke was awake, pacing the living room like she does when she's nervous, he'd be able to hear it. But there was only silence up there, which meant she was still asleep. It was time to go. Hopefully he would be back before she even realized he was gone.

Noah went to the door, gently slid it open, and stepped out onto the deck. He then turned and closed the door as quietly as he could, feeling his chest tightening with unease for the brief moment he had his back to the woods. *Just nerves,* he thought dismissively. Although it felt like something else—more like instinct than nerves. But whatever, he was going to have to ignore that for now. Because nothing was going to stop him from checking inside that shed. Nothing was going to stop him from failing Katelyn yet again.

Noah stood on the deck, listening for footsteps up above, but only heard the harsh whispers of the wind through the trees. That and the nearly bare oak branches crackling together with each gust of wind, sounding like a crude wind chime of skeleton bones.

He shivered, not sure if it was from the frigid air burrowing into his clothing or from the image of femurs and ribs and shin bones clacking together as they dangled from dirty twine. He wouldn't put it past Maurice to have a wind chime like that—the sick bastard certainly did give off a *The Hills Have Eyes* vibe. If only he had noticed it sooner.

Noah sighed, the sound lost among the heavy breaths of oncoming winter. Which was exactly what this storm was bringing—winter, snow, and sheets of ice so cold they'd match the barely beating organ inside his chest. And to think, only two days ago they were all at the lake together, basking in the cool yet pleasant sunshine. But then the weekend had transformed, just as the weather had turned, morphing into an existential nightmare in the span of only one night. He went to bed with a sweet, beautiful girl beside him, his heart hopeful for what the future may bring, and he woke up to a constantly evolving horror show. One that was about to get worse, if the shed's secrets were anywhere near as dark as he expected them to be.

Noah hurried over to the stairs, went down to the clearing, and with one quick glance up at the main deck to confirm that he was alone, ran across the grass until he reached the cover of the woods. He didn't want Brooke following him this time, not when there was who knows how many dangers lurking among the trees. He didn't really believe he'd run into the second half of a serial killer duo, but he sure as hell believed in bears and mountain lions and rattlesnakes. And that dusk was a bad time to go for a stroll through the wilderness.

Noah peered out from the undergrowth, watching the house for signs of movement. Sharp angles of wood and glass stared back at him, any warmth the house once possessed now gone. In its place was an ominous presence, standing over the forest and casting its judgment on those that dare come near. The only warmth that emanated from the structure was the golden light spilling from its windows—and even that was losing its influence. The clearing was now a battleground where silver winter warred against the golden glow of comfort and safety. And the silver was winning. The *cold* was winning, converting anything warm and safe and hopeful into shards of shattered ice.

A glimmer of movement in one of the bedrooms caught his eye. Brooke was inside, throwing a hoodie over her head, probably sensing the oncoming storm as well. Noah's eyes lingered on the window, lingered on *her*, before he forcibly looked away.

He started walking through the trees, heading in the direction of the shed, his hand gripping the keys so hard it hurt. Good. He wanted it to hurt. He *deserved* for it to hurt. And Katelyn deserved for him to do everything in his power to find out what happened to her. So that's what he was going to do. No matter how creepy this freaking woods was, and no matter how violent this storm might become. He was going to find out what happened to her. Starting with the shed.

The trees and bushes surrounding him quivered and sighed as he passed by, fighting a not-so-silent battle against the relentless wind. And they were losing, too, just like the light. He kept his eyes on a constant scan of his perimeter, remembering Brooke's insistence that something was in here, watching her in the night. Something, or someone, big enough to bend branches. Something that was lurking right where he now stood.

*Nope. Don't think about that. You need to be brave right now. You need to be brave for Katelyn.*

Noah kept his senses on alert, but allowed his mind to drift to happier times. To Katelyn sitting in the car beside him as the sunlight danced across her lap. To how her smile made his heart flutter. To how holding her at night made him feel like he might just be able to crawl out of the dark hole he had fallen into ever since Travis introduced him to his new girlfriend. Introduced him to Brooke.

Noah's mind snagged on Brooke, and again he had to forcibly push the thought of her away. It was becoming easier for him to do—almost second nature, actually—but then again, he had had years to practice. Years to hone his don't-think-about-Brooke abilities. Years to master his avoidance strategies so that every time she popped into his head, he was able to convert his thoughts into ones about work, about TV shows, about literally *anything else.*

When Katelyn entered his life four months ago, a pretty, blonde wisp of a woman sitting in a coffee house with some sort of whipped-up sugar frappé thing in front of her, he hadn't had the nerve to speak to her. It wasn't that he lacked charm and flirting skills, but because it was rare that he felt anything for the women that approached him. Not unless they were petite brunettes with a penchant for horror movies—and there was only one of those. One that was not his to think about. And since Noah wasn't the type to use a woman for a one-night fling, he found himself alone much of the time. Alone enough that Travis often made jokes about it, not realizing the reason for Noah's loneliness was in the same room and had a ring on her finger. A ring that Travis picked out, no less, and with Noah by his side at the jewelry store. That night, once Travis dropped him off and went home with that diamond masterpiece in his pocket, Noah made it his mission to discover what was at the bottom of his whiskey bottle. And it turns out it was just a whole lot of depression hiding down there. And a raging headache the next day.

But then along came Katelyn. Beautiful and sweet as the drink she was sipping on. She was the first girl since Brooke came into his life that he had felt anything for. And damn, did that make him nervous.

He started frequenting the coffee house, hoping to get another glimpse of her. Hoping to muster up the courage to speak to her. Apparently, courage doesn't come naturally. You have to fight against your gut instincts when it comes to courage. And when everything in your body is screaming at you to run away, you must stand your ground and face that fear head on. Whether it's a monster in the woods, a gruesome discovery in a hidden shed, or a beautiful girl in a coffee house that has the potential to break your already shattered heart.

It wasn't until the fourth time he saw her that he finally decided to act, having no intention of missing yet another opportunity. *Face your fears, damnit. Move on. Damnit.* He said the cheesiest line of them all, the words tumbling out before he even realized he was speaking, and embarrassment quickly filling their place in his throat. But she didn't roll her eyes or tell him to go away when he said that god-awful pickup line. Instead, she giggled. And damn, was that smile infectious.

The romance that bloomed in the following months was the happiest he had been in years. He was finally moving toward something, instead of running away. He was moving toward the growing feelings he had for Katelyn, and finally leaving behind the love he had for Brooke—and the shame that came along with it. As it turns out, hope was a much stronger emotion than shame. It overpowered it. It made him feel like happiness was something he could still have one day, instead of watching his brother soak it all up for himself.

Not that Noah resented Travis. He loved his brother more than anything. The memories they shared together would always be cherished, from childhood, through adolescence, and well into adulthood. The fact that Travis was just a little bit better at everything—a little stronger, a little smarter, a little richer—never bothered Noah. He enjoyed being an athletic trainer at the university much more than he would ever enjoy being an engineer. And Travis beating him at arm wrestling didn't bother him one bit, since he was still able to beat most everyone else. In fact, it wasn't until Travis brought home the most beautiful woman Noah had ever seen that he first felt a pang of jealousy in regards to his big brother.

When Noah first met Brooke, he had convinced himself no woman that gorgeous would have a personality worth knowing. God does not give with both hands, or some bullshit like that. But as family outings became weekend trips, and Noah got to know her more and more, he realized she was just as beautiful inside as she was out. *Damnit. Damn. It.*

No matter how much he tried to resist those feelings, he couldn't help but fall for her. Fall for his brother's girlfriend. Something that became more and more unbearable with every moment they spent together. Holidays. Weekend visits. Travis's crazy vacations. And there he was, on the sidelines, watching them fall more and more in love. Watching them get engaged. Watching them get married. Someday watching them have kids. *Damn. It.*

Meeting Katelyn was like a breath of fresh air after all that jealousy and shame. Here's a woman he *could* love. A woman he didn't have to feel shame for falling for. And it was starting to happen, too. It really was. This trip was a testament to that. He wasn't looking at Brooke like he had on previous trips— not much anyway—and he wasn't thinking about her when he went to bed. He was looking at Katelyn, holding Katelyn, thinking about Katelyn. It was the most wonderful freedom he had felt in the past six years. A hopeful future, a chance to move on…

And that asshole upstairs had stolen it from him. Stole his hopeful future. Stole Katelyn's life. Or at least Noah suspected that he did. He needed proof, though, and that was here in the woods. The woods where all the red was, the woods where her phone was found, the woods where she died. *Possibly died.*

The shed came into view among the trees, a few shingles on its roof flapping violently in the quickening wind. How they stayed on at all was a mystery. Noah hurried forward, his senses still on alert and feeling like a chaotic symphony in his head—the whispering sounds of the forest, the frigid breeze brushing across his face and tugging at his hair, the smell of pine trees and promised snow. If there was something else in the forest, there was too much chaos around for him to notice. But could he *feel* something? A presence? A sixth sense that he was not alone? Bugs crawled beneath his skin, his body's response to the unperceived threat.

Noah stopped and did a full circle, scanning the trees. Still not seeing anything, he closed the distance between himself and the shed. His hands were shaking by the time he arrived at the locked doors, the keys tinkling together as he fumbled to find the right one for the padlock. His fingers grasped at the smallest key, the blunt one with the squared-off head that he was pretty sure would fit. He grabbed the padlock and attempted to shove the key inside, which took three attempts with how much his hands were trembling. Once inserted, he twisted his wrist and let the lock fall open with a satisfying, if not foreboding, clunk.

He stepped away, staring at the opened padlock, a little surprised that it had actually worked. The lock was still hanging from the metal clasp that secured the doors, and suddenly everything inside of him wanted to leave it there. Relock it. Turn and run. Anything but remove it and allow the doors to fall open.

Because then he would see it. See what, he didn't know. All he knew was that he needed to see it, no matter how much his body was screaming at him not to. *Courage, Noah. This is where the courage comes in. This is where you have to be brave. For Katelyn.* And what if she's in there, bloody and broken and stiff with death? Would he be able to control himself?

No. He wouldn't. Whatever was behind these doors, it had the potential to break him. That much he knew. He could feel it in his bones, along with the chill—after tonight, he would never be the same. His certainty of that fact was as real as the deepening gloom in the forest. Night was coming, brought early by the oncoming storm. Shadows caressed the trees and slithered across the forest floor, waiting to be swallowed by the fading twilight. How did it get dark so quickly? So dark and so cold, like someone had thrown a blanket of dread over the woods and everything inside of it.

Noah reached forward and pulled the padlock out of the clasp, hissing as the coldness of the steel seeped into his fingers. He held the doors closed with his foot, preparing himself for what might be inside. For *who* might be inside. Finally, he sucked in a deep breath, the icy air filling his lungs, and stepped back as the doors of the shed fell open.

# Chapter 29

*Sunday, 5:38 p.m.*

The red hit him first. So much of it in such a small space. An image of Maurice flashed through his head, and of all the red splattered across his small bathroom. But this was different. This was *more*. So much more. Deep puddles of dried, cracked crimson on the concrete floor, splatters of angry scarlet covering the walls, drops of liquid carmine collecting on the ceiling.

The smell came next—one of musk, rot, and decay. One of death. "Holy shit," he mumbled under his breath. He was right; it had been Maurice all along. *That sick bastard.*

Noah stepped inside, the smell causing a sour bile to gurgle up into his throat. He squinted into the gloom, scanning the floor for something else of Katelyn's. But just like the girl herself, nothing was there. No Katelyn. No belongings of hers. Just gallons of maroon gone black.

His eyes panned upward, away from the grimy floor and up to the equally grimy walls. The things hanging there made his stomach churn, and the bile simmering in the depths of his throat crept higher, threatening to spill over into his mouth. It wasn't the items themselves that caused his blood to run cold, but what was caked onto each one. Pliers, a hammer, a shovel, a saw—all normal tools, if it weren't for the thick layer of blood and gore that covered each surface, each blade.

Noah stepped over to the saw and inspected the sharpened edge. Bits of something stringy stuck to the blade, and in the darkness it took him a moment to realize it was hair. Matted hair, glued to the saw by clots of dried blood. His breath hitched. Katelyn's hair? Katelyn's beautiful hair that shimmered in the sunshine coming through the coffee shop's window? He reached out and gently picked at a strand, retching at the raspy sound it made as it pulled free. Brown. The hair was brown. And *short*. So short he doubted it could have come from a woman, not unless she had a buzz cut recently.

Noah dropped the hair, having to flick his nails a few times to rid it from his fingers. He turned toward the doors, his eyes landing on a pile of something white splattered red. *Bones.* A goddamn pile of skeleton bones. *Jesus Christ.*

He stumbled in the near darkness, his blood pulsating in his ears so hard it nearly hurt. *There's a damn pile of skeletons in here. Holy shit.* He sucked in a gasping breath and took a step forward. *Courage, Noah. Don't chickenshit out of this now.*

He stopped just shy of the bloody bones and leaned in, wishing he had brought his phone simply for the flashlight. He tentatively reached a leg forward and kicked a bone free from the pile, then looked down at it, puzzled.

Antlers. Not bones, but antlers. As in deer, or elk. As in *animals*. This wasn't a murder shed for people; it was Maurice's own personal butcher shop. *For fucking venison.*

Stunned, Noah staggered out of the deer-killing shed. It all made sense now. The short hair he found on the tools? Deer hair. The chair they saw pointed toward the woods? Probably where Maurice liked to sit while waiting for a deer to come by. The guy being on the balcony all the damn time? He was looking for deer. And why not? It's free meat, and a lot of it, for a guy who most likely couldn't afford it otherwise.

Noah stood just outside the shed, listening to the wind as it struggled through the trees. Hope was flickering inside his chest, an ember struggling to ignite. If Maurice wasn't a killer—not a serial killer anyway—then Katelyn might still be alive. After all this mayhem, it might turn out that she just got spooked and left on her own, after all. She saw the bloody shed somehow, panicked, dropped her phone in the process, and took off. Maybe she was just too embarrassed to tell him that she was leaving.

Noah shook his head, the muscles in his jaw working. No. Something still didn't add up. Multiple somethings. The other note, for starters, warning them to leave. And what about Maurice committing suicide? It made some sort of sense if he was feeling guilty. But now?

Bits of white confetti began filtering through the trees above. Noah tilted his head up. *Snow.* The storm was here. His eyes followed the swirling flakes through the trees as his mind tumbled through possible explanations, all dismissible and all leading to the same conclusion: he had no freaking clue what was going on here.

Noah absentmindedly rubbed his arms up and down, attempting to soothe away a wave of goose bumps that had just prickled into existence across his flesh. It didn't work. If anything, the unnerving, crawling feeling only intensified. It was then he realized it wasn't the lack of answers that was causing his hair to stand on end—it was something else. His body was already responding to it, even though he wasn't consciously aware of any danger. His heart rate accelerated, and his breathing teetered on the edge of hyperventilation. He was gearing up for fight or flight mode, yet he wasn't even sure why. He hadn't seen anything threatening, hadn't heard anything closing in. Yet...

A soft but distinctive exhale pulled his focus away from the flurry of snowflakes drifting through the air. Somewhere in the trees, directly across from the shed, something was breathing. *A bear,* he thought. *It has to be.* Whether it was drawn to him or to the stench of blood wafting from the open shed, it didn't matter. He needed to get the hell out of here. Right now.

Noah took a step toward the house, then stopped. The breathing was close. So close that the bear would surely get to him before he got to the house. What he needed was a weapon. He changed course, and instead hurried over to the chopping block on the side of the shed. He skidded to a stop by the base of the block, his hand reaching through nothing but air. Where was the ax? It was here three days ago, propped up against the wooden block. They had all seen it. So, where was it now? Not in the shed, or he would have noticed it. So where?

Noah frantically searched the area, glancing around nearby bushes and behind neighboring pines. An unsettling sense of dread was filtering into his gut, just like the snow sifting through the trees. Something—*someone*—had taken the ax. If Maurice had it, they would have found it when they searched the house and garage. But they didn't. So where in the hell was it? And who took it?

Nearing panic, Noah gave up on his search and decided he was going to have to make a break for it. What other choice did he have? Other than trying to lock himself inside a dilapidated shed during a snowstorm, or trying to fight a bear off with a handsaw. Neither sounded promising.

His mind made up, it took him an agonizingly long moment to find the narrow trail that led back to the clearing, the darkness and dancing shadows playing tricks with his vision. Finally, he saw the path cutting through the trees. He hurried along, fighting the almost-uncontrollable urge to run. If he ran, he'd fall. And if he fell—

Noah shook his head. He didn't want to finish that thought. That, and the whispers of the woods were getting louder, causing his head to pound and his ears to ache. And every now and then, it almost sounded like they were saying his name.

Calling to him. Beckoning him to come join them. Just like that freaking ghost story.

The clearing came into view, and Noah's last reserves crumbled. He broke into a run, terror seizing him so completely that it took his breath away. He needed out. Out of the woods. Out of the darkness. Out of view from the eyes he could feel crawling over his skin.

He burst from the trees and stumbled into the clearing, breathing a heavy sigh of relief as the house's glow washed over him. There was just enough light out here to make the shadow monsters of the forest feel less real. And that's what they were. Shadow monsters. He didn't hear any breathing out there; it was just the damn wind. And what he felt on the trail—that was just an overreaction. A trick of light and shadow, of wind and snow. He had let his imagination get the better of him, but that's all it was. Just blind panic, and nothing more.

Noah froze when he heard a muffled cry off to his right. He took a generous step back, returning to the trees he had just fled from. What felt monstrous only seconds ago, now felt like safety. The cry didn't sound like the calls of a loon, or like anything else that prowls the woods. It sounded very much human, and not frightening but frightened.

He peered around the nearest pine tree, being careful to keep himself concealed from view. Snow swirled through the sky, riding the turbulent gusts of wind that whipped through the clearing. They were only small flakes for now, testing the air as one might test a pool with their toe before jumping in.

The bigger flakes would follow, the ones that coated the ground and transformed the world into one of hushed silence.

Through the chaotic flutter of snowflakes, Noah saw Brooke and Travis crossing the clearing. Travis was carrying her, and Noah's muscles immediately tensed at the thought that she might be injured. He stepped out from the trees, ready to run over and join them, but stopped when Brooke let out another muffled cry.

Something didn't feel right. He squinted, trying to make out what was going on through the haphazard flurries of frozen sky. He took a step away, toward the tree line, when he realized Travis was going toward the woods, and not away from it. He took another step when he saw how roughly he was handling Brooke. He wasn't gently cradling her in his arms, but hauling her forcefully as she kicked and flailed her legs. *Struggling.* She was struggling. *To get away.*

Brooke tried to scream, and Noah felt his stomach drop as he watched Travis slam his hand down over her mouth, silencing her. *Jesus Christ, what the fuck is going on?*

Once they disappeared beyond the tree line, Noah stepped out from his hiding place. His eyes darted up to the house, hoping to see the comforting flashes of red and blue salvation—of the rescue that Travis had promised. But there was nothing there. No rescue. No safety. No hope.

Noah crouched down and stealthily hurried across the clearing, stopping where Travis dragged Brooke into the trees. He heard Travis curse somewhere up ahead, some forty, maybe fifty feet away, and then what sounded like more muffled screaming.

*What in the name of fuck is going on?* Noah scanned the ground for a possible weapon, feeling like he had just been transported into another dimension. A dimension where he needed a weapon to use against his own brother. Finding nothing, he sighed in resignation. He was going to have to go back in there unarmed.

With a weary sigh, he reentered the forest—the one he had just fled from so eagerly. He kept his body low to the ground as he navigated the gloomy terrain, moving as quickly as the foliage would allow. Every now and then he heard Brooke cry out or Travis curse, and he then redirected his course to follow them, keeping pace as they moved deeper and deeper into the trees.

A detached feeling overcame him as he trekked through the undergrowth, as if he was merely watching a movie of himself chasing his brother through the woods. This couldn't actually be happening. Travis couldn't possibly have ill intentions towards Brooke. No, he must have misinterpreted things. That's all this was. A mistake. But then Brooke would let out another scream, and Noah knew there was no room to misinterpret that. Brooke was terrified. Which meant this was, indeed, actually happening.

Noah reached the stream they had discovered on their first day inside this hell forest. It bubbled and gurgled as water swept sluggishly along its rocky edges. He was about to step into it—the hell with the cold—when he remembered the stepping stones. They must be just a little further downstream.

He hurried along the water's edge, straining to hear anything other than the threatening storm. The snowflakes were growing thicker, and a fine layer of white dust was beginning to accumulate on the forest floor. It would be beautiful, if it wasn't so damn terrifying.

The stepping stones emerged out of the darkness up ahead, bits of frozen powder already clinging to their slick surfaces. That was going to make crossing them all the more treacherous. Noah stopped in front of the stones, noticing the traces of shoeprints in the thin layer of snow dust. He mounted the first stone, feeling his balance sway as he struggled to remain upright. His tennis shoe slid across the rock, sticking to the rough granite just shy of the stone's edge.

He held his breath and reached out tentatively with his foot, silently praying that the next stone was not as slick as the last. He stepped onto the stone, and then the next, taking his time even though everything inside of him was screaming at him to hurry.

He let out a sigh of relief as his feet crunched down on the gravel edge on the opposite side of the stream. *Now what?* The snow cover on this side wasn't thick enough to allow for any footprints yet. And he couldn't hear them anymore, which was even more unnerving than Brooke's screams.

Noah closed his eyes, focusing all his attention on his hearing. But he couldn't *hear* anything. His heart thudded hard inside his chest, threatening to crack the ribs that contained it. He needed to save her. He *had* to save her. He couldn't save Katelyn, but he still might be able to save Brooke. The girl he loved, even though he shouldn't.

"Fuck!" he cursed beneath his breath. He started walking forward, further into the dense covering of trees. *Where the hell did they go?* He was twenty paces from the stream when he heard the subtle snap of a small branch, coming from directly behind him. He whirled around, coming face to face with his brother. Brooke was nowhere to be seen.

Before Noah could react, Travis grabbed the side of his head and slammed it into a gnarled pine tree that stood just off to their left. Darkness filtered into the edges of his vision, somehow darker than the surrounding woods. With the next blow, the little bit of light that remained among the trees disappeared, along with everything else.

Noah had one last thought before surrendering to the blackness. *But where was Brooke?*

# Chapter 30

**Sunday, 6:52 p.m.**

Brooke groaned. The rough bark of the tree she was leaning against was digging painfully into her shoulder blades, yet she didn't have the strength or focus to shift her position. Not with her head throbbing the way that it was, and not with the queasiness lingering in her stomach. Finally, she made a half-hearted attempt to lift her head from its less-than-comfortable resting place, but a fresh round of dizziness rushed in, like a tsunami surging through her senses and causing her stomach to churn.

Brooke let out another groan and reached up, hoping she could somehow rub the aching from her temples, but her hand didn't come up from where it lay by her side. *What the hell?* She tried again, with both hands this time, but again, they didn't move. *I'm paralyzed. Oh my God. I'm freaking paralyzed.*

Nearing panic, she jerked her body away from the tree, but was unable to make it more than a few inches from the frozen bark before something stopped her. Confused, she looked down.

*Bound.* Her wrists were bound. With some sort of old, worn-out rope. Brooke pulled her arms forward, gritting her teeth as she fought against the taut rope. Nothing. She then tried to move only her right arm forward—*just get this one free, and then you can use it to untie the other one*—and felt the opposite arm jerk back behind her. *Fuck.* She tried with the left arm, and wasn't surprised when she got the same result. *Shit shit shit.* Her wrists were bound with the same piece of rope. And what was the rope tied around? *The goddamn pine tree. That's what.*

*No no no no no.* Brooke bent her knees and dug her heels into the ground, wiggling herself backward toward the tree's trunk. *Just get some slack on the rope and then you can use your teeth or something.* She grimaced, hissing through said teeth as the seasickness in her mind quarreled with her willpower. *Keep. Going.* She continued with her efforts until her hips and spine were flush against the pine. And still, the rope was too taut.

A single sob pierced the air, coming from the confines of her own throat. Panic was closing in, and once it took hold of her, she would be useless. Brooke squeezed her eyes shut, willing herself to remain calm—*ha, calm my ass*—or at least maintain some semblance of control. *Just focus on something else. Anything else. Anything but the panic. And breathe. Don't forget to breathe.*

She forced herself to take in a deep breath, slow and deliberate, her eyes still firmly closed. The air smelled of dampness and pine, and of that nothingness that snow always seemed to smell like. And it was biting cold as it passed through her nostrils and slid down into her lungs, filling her insides with frost. That frost was outside of her body as well, wrapped around her like a possessive lover's embrace. A lover that was caressing her face with light kisses of ice, each a snowflake that happened upon her bare skin.

Behind her, the bark of the tree was rigid with cold. The rope that bound her wrists was scratchy and rough, and the knots uncomfortably tight. The burn of its unforgiving hold stood out in sharp contrast to the aching cold in her exposed fingers.

Brooke clenched her hands into fists, trying to conserve the dwindling heat she still had in her fingers—wishing the burning in her wrists would descend into her fingertips and chase the impending frostbite away. Despite her efforts, it did little to impede the bitter cold that was sinking into her bones, and before long she knew she wouldn't be able to feel her hands at all. A new sense of dread coiled through her insides as she imagined her fingers falling off, one by one, blackened and cracked and seeping congealed blood.

Brooke's eyes popped open. Everything around her was still blurred from the beating she had endured, and panic danced in her periphery as she struggled to decipher her surroundings. *Is that shadow a tree? A person? My loving husband, coming back to finish the job?* After a moment's struggle, she closed her eyes again, preferring total blackness to the blurred shapes creeping among the trees. Just like a kid hiding under the covers, she thought, hiding from the monster as it crawls out of the darkened depths of the closet.

*Only that kid gets to plug his ears so he doesn't have to listen to the monster's ragged breathing as it approaches his bed,* she thought bitterly. Unlike her, whose hearing had kicked into high gear to make up for what her eyes were missing. Unable to stop herself, she listened intently for the sounds of an approaching monster—her husband or otherwise—but nothing came.

She waited, the breath lodged inside her throat feeling like shards of jagged ice, but the forest gave away nothing but a hushed whisper. High above, the trees rustled with the pull and sway of the storm, but down below the canopy, there was barely a breath of wind. Somewhere in the distance, off to her left, she could hear the delicate babble of the steam she was carried across. And off to her right, nothing but cold, hard silence.

Unable to stand the silence for even a second longer, Brooke cracked an eye open. The dizzying vertigo of shifting dark shapes was less than before, although she was still pretty sure Travis had given her a concussion when he knocked her unconscious to tie her up. She waited, willing the spinning of the trees to slow and finally fall into place.

The forest floor came into focus first, an assortment of dirt, fallen pine needles, and bits of brown, crinkled leaves. A very light dusting of snow sat atop the dirt and needles, a powdered sugar atop a crumbling brownie of soil and decaying plant matter.

She was at the edge of a small break in the trees, no more than thirty feet wide in either direction. Frozen pillars in the shapes of tree trunks lined the meager clearing, like sentinels that she wasn't sure were there to protect her or restrict her. Up above, the dense covering of pines was fractured, allowing just enough space for some twirling snowflakes to filter through, along with a hint of hazy, silver moonlight.

*A nightlight*, Brooke thought. *Oh, thank God. I have a nightlight. At least now I won't have to die in the dark.*

Her eyes fell to the blackness of the surrounding woods, her nightlight offering little assistance as she struggled to see past the tree line. From what she could tell, she was alone, but that visual reassurance did little to abate the sickening sense that it wasn't true. She might not be able to see it, or hear it, or smell it… but something else was out here in the woods with her. Was it her darling husband standing watch from the shadows, or was it something else? The same something that a young girl wrote about in her journal over a century ago?

The reels of Brooke's inner movie theater started turning, filtering through scary movies set in the woods. She struggled to push the thoughts away, to focus on how she was going to get away instead of how she was going to die, but that only intensified the frightening images flashing through her head. Don't think about an elephant, and all that bullshit. *Cabin in the Woods. Evil Dead. Deliverance. The Edge. Game of Thrones.* The more she fought the images, the more violent they became. Brooke's eyes scanned the trees, half-expecting a White Walker to emerge, or a snarling bear intent on one last meal. But still, there was nothing.

Her mind surged on unabated, berating her with reels of film and page after page of horror novels she devoured back at home. Back where it was safe, and the only monster she had to fear was that goddamn clothes pile. Only this time the thing lurking in the shadows was real. This time Travis wasn't going to save her. This time *he* was the monster.

And where was he? Where was the man she vowed to spend the rest of her life with? *Until death do us part.* He dragged her into the forest, beat her, tied her up, and then just left her here to die? No. This horror story—*her* horror story—wasn't over yet. It was just getting started.

Images of Travis replaced the endless reel of horror story nightmares. However, this time the thoughts of her husband no longer filled her with warmth and longing. Now they felt just as cold and ominous as the horror monsters they had replaced. Kisses in the rain. Vows on their wedding day. Secrets told underneath the sheets as they held each other close. Dips on the dance floor. Giggles in front of cameras. Winks, and touches, and hugs, and laughter. But now it was all cold. All hollow. Bright memories surrounded by darkness. The husband she knew, the life she had, was nothing but another horror novel.

Brooke sucked in a frigid breath and leaned her head back against the tree. "What the hell is going on?" she whispered, her eyes brimming with unshed tears. "What the *fuck* is going on?" She tugged half-heartedly against the rope, already knowing it was useless. She could feel the familiar burn alight in her wrists as the worn rope cut into her skin, but her fingertips she could barely feel anymore.

"I'm going to die out here," she said softly. The finality of the words, and the truth behind them, made it feel like she had just been stabbed in the gut with a rusty blade. But instead of blood leaking out, it was hope that drained from the wound, seeping into the snow and staining it with despair.

Tears followed, becoming frozen tracks against her cheeks. The cold had only continued to intensify since she awoke in the final scene of her own horror movie—as if something was turning down the temperature on a thermostat. The snowflakes weren't even able to combat the cold anymore, and only a scant few fluttered in the stillness beneath the trees.

*It's causing this,* she thought, clamping her jaw shut to keep her teeth from chattering. *It can't get this cold this fast. It's the thing from the journals. Those stories weren't crazy ramblings or cabin fever delusions. It was all true.* The muscles in her jaw began to ache as she strained to keep her teeth still. *It comes in the winter. It brings the cold with it. It brought this storm to us. And it's getting colder because it's getting closer.*

Bone clattered against bone as Brooke lost the battle against her teeth. *It can mimic voices. Force violence. Control minds. Just like... Travis.*

Brooke gasped, the air like shattered icicles as it descended her throat. Travis went from her loving husband to her captor in a matter of days. Hours even. He *transformed.* Just like the first Scarlett did in the journal. Hers was a slow and agonizing transformation, his was fast and violent. But what did it matter? This place was cursed. And it had sunk its razored teeth into Travis. It had stolen his mind. It was causing him to do horrible things—things to Katelyn, things to his wife. He was a victim just as much as Katelyn was, as much as *she* was.

They had to get him out of here, before it was too late. Before it claimed his mind for good. She couldn't do it alone, though. Noah would have to help her. And then they could find Travis and get him out of here. They'd walk all night if they had to. They'd *drag* him out if they had to. But first she had to free herself from this wretched tree. None of it would work if she couldn't free herself. *So come on, Brookey. Stop fucking around. You can do this.*

A cry cut through the air, slicing through the winter forest like a blade through flesh. It was swift, in and out through the trees before she could register what it was. The following silence was deafening, not even the wind above daring to speak. Brooke strained against the quiet, listening for something else—*anything else*—but nothing came. Just cold, impenetrable silence.

She *felt* it, though. In the darkness, beyond her nightlight. Something was waiting. Watching. She wasn't alone out here. And even if what emerged from the trees had a familiar face, there would still be a monster lurking just beneath its surface.

# Chapter 31

*Sunday, 7:18 p.m.*

Snapping branches punctured the silence, somewhere off to her left. Brooke's head whipped in that direction, desperately searching for the source of the noise, but unlike the branches, the darkness beyond her nightlight was unbreakable.

Heavy grunts followed, moving toward her so quickly and so slowly all at the same time. Brooke sucked in a breath and held it, her heart pounding wildly in her chest. How much terror can a heart take before it collapses like a fallen bird at the bottom of its cage, never to fly again? Footsteps drew closer, crunching on frozen ground and barely audible over the fluttering of the caged bird inside her chest.

And then she could see it. Movement among the trees. It was tall, whatever it was, and it wove through the pines easily as it headed straight toward her pathetic excuse for a nightlight. Shadows became shapes as it neared the break in the trees, and Brooke could see that its chest was broad, and it had something heavy slung over its shoulder. It looked so powerful, so graceful, so—

But then it stumbled and swayed to the side, struggling to steady itself. A curse accompanied the stumble, and Brooke's breath hitched. She knew that sound anywhere. Her body tensed, the terror flooding her system transitioning from fear of an unknown beast to that of a familiar one. One she promised to spend the rest of her life with. One that vowed to protect her.

Travis lumbered the rest of the way through the pine trees, more of his features becoming visible as he closed the distance between them. His feet scraped through snow and forest debris, the only sound present in the woods except for his grunts of effort. Finally, he staggered into the tiny clearing and tossed what he was carrying onto the forest floor.

Noah didn't make so much as a groan as he hit the decaying pine needles and leaves that littered the ground, the frosty dust beneath him clinging to his rumpled clothing. The side of his head was bleeding, and bits of broken bark clung to his disheveled hair. The blood creeping down his face looked almost black in the available light, cold and silver just like the moon.

Brooke's eyes widened, her mouth falling open. *Is he dead? Jesus Christ, is he dead? Did Travis kill him? Oh God oh God oh God.*

A ghost escaped Noah's lips—not of his soul leaving his body, but of his breath leaving his lungs. Brooke nearly wept at the sight. He was breathing. He was alive. There was still a trace of hope inside this godforsaken woods. More ghosts followed, translucent plumes of vapor that matched her own breaths. They almost seemed to glow in the scant light, like little puffs of salvation.

A shadow fell over his body, dampening the glow of his steady breathing. Brooke's eyes slowly traveled from the shadow up to the stranger that was standing over her. The stranger's green eyes were narrowed into slits and just as dark as the forest, his expression as cold as the surrounding snow. Her loving husband, not looking so loving anymore. And not looking so sane anymore either. His brow was furrowed in frustration—or was it hate?—and his lips pressed into a thin line of barely controlled rage.

"Travis—" Brooke began, her voice coming out shakier than she wanted it to be.

"Shut up," he spat out. "Look what you made me do." He threw a hand at his unconscious brother, then curled it into a fist and directed it at her. There was blood smeared across his knuckles; from her or Noah, she wasn't sure.

"You couldn't just leave it alone, could you?" he hissed. "Accept that Maurice was a killer and leave it at that. No, instead you had to go *poking* around. Had to go looking at shit you had no right to look at."

Brooke pulled meagerly at her restraints, more on impulse than actually expecting any results. She didn't receive any either, just another uncomfortable pinch as the knots dug in. "Travis, please," she said levelly. She looked up into a face she barely knew. She recognized every crease, every hair, the sharp curve of his jaw and the prominent arch of his nose—but somehow he was a stranger to her now.

"Please let me help you," she pleaded. "This isn't you, Travis. Something did this to you."

Travis quirked a brow, and then laughed. It carried through the forest, sounding flat, empty, and hollow. "Let me guess," he said, holding up his finger as he attempted to ward off another bout of laughter. He failed, and more maniacal cackles filled the air. When they tapered off, the thick, suffocating silence of the woods returned. A silence that wasn't quiet at all.

Travis was seemingly unaffected by the choked stillness in the air. His composure regained, he asked, "So you think you have a perfectly logical explanation for my behavior, right?" He grinned. "Something to explain all this?" He threw his hands out to his sides, gesturing to the surrounding woods.

Brooke nodded slowly, her husband's humorless giggles setting her teeth on edge. Her stomach churned, her heart the frightened flutter of bird wings inside her chest. A bird that apparently hadn't fallen dead. Yet.

"Yes," she said softly. "This isn't you. If you could just untie—"

"What is it this time?" Travis asked with an exasperated sigh. "What fantastical creature feature have you cooked up inside that tiny little brain of yours this time? Is it a witch's curse? A mind-controlling goblin? The reincarnated spirit of an evil innkeeper? C'mon, babe. Tell me. I'm just *dying* to know."

"You told the story yourself. The night we got here. It's why you chose this place. It's not just a legend. It's real."

"Goddamnit, Brooke!" Travis fumed. "You are so fucking predictable. You couldn't even bother to come up with something original?" He shook his head bitterly, rubbing at the stubble along his jawline. *"The wendigo,"* he said in a spooky, mocking tone. "So I've been possessed by the evil spirit of a cannibalistic forest creature, huh?" He raised his eyebrow again, his lips curling into a smirk. *"Predictable."*

"But… you have been possessed, Travis. This isn't you."

Travis opened his mouth to speak, but before he could respond, Noah groaned. Brooke's eyes jumped to him, and for a horrifying second she wondered if he had also been driven mad by the thing in the woods. If so, then this really was her last night on earth. She wasn't going to be the survivor girl in this horror movie—just another victim to add to the forever growing body count.

Noah reached up with one shaky hand and touched the side of his head, wincing as his fingers grazed the broken skin across his temple. He lowered his hand and opened his eyes, looking more confused than insane as he tried to process what was happening. He stared at Brooke without really seeing her, his eyes drifting past her before snapping back with sudden clarity. "Brookey…" he mumbled.

"Stop calling her that," Travis snapped.

Noah slowly turned his head up, looking almost drunk as he struggled to focus on Travis. "What's going on?" he asked, his words slurring together. "My head…"

"Sorry about that," Travis said with a casual shrug of his shoulders. "Desperate times."

"What does that mean?" Noah asked, his voice evening out as his head cleared. His eyes went back to Brooke, searching for answers. Seeing none on her face, his eyes descended her body until they landed on her wrists. "What the fuck?" He pushed himself up from the ground, looking from Travis to Brooke with new understanding. "Jesus Christ, Travis. Untie her."

"Oh, Noah," Travis sighed. "Just shut the fuck up, will you?"

Noah's jaw ticked as he gave his brother an incredulous glare. He turned away and started crawling toward Brooke, reaching for the knotted rope. Just before he was able to take hold of it, Travis grabbed the hood of his jacket and yanked him backward. Noah fell onto his back with a startled grunt. "Travis! What the hell is wrong with you?"

"Sit your ass down, little brother. I don't want to have to hit you again." Travis waited patiently until Noah repositioned himself on the ground, his expression just as frigid as the winter air. Once Noah was situated, his eyes went back to Brooke. "Why couldn't you just leave my shit alone, *babe*? We wouldn't be out here if you weren't so goddamn nosey."

"I'm sure you would have found another reason," Brooke said flatly, refusing to meet Travis's glare. She didn't want to look into those eyes anymore. The irises might be the same emerald green she remembered, but the darkness behind them was something she had never seen before.

Noah's head was on a swivel, looking from Travis to Brooke and then back to Travis again as he struggled to make sense of the situation. The black trails of blood on his face were beginning to crack in the cold. "Listen guys, I don't know what the hell is going on, but we need to—"

"He killed Katelyn, Noah."

Noah's eyes locked on Brooke, opening wide with surprise. He shook his head slowly. "No, Brookey. There's no way."

"See, Brooke!" Travis exclaimed gleefully. "There's no way! You're the one who's fucking crazy."

"If I'm crazy, then why did you hit me and drag me out here in the first place?"

"You hit her?" Noah asked before Travis could respond. *"You hit her!?"*

Travis sighed, ignoring him. "If you just left my shit alone we wouldn't be out here right now, would we, *sweetheart*?"

"What shit?" Noah shoved himself onto his feet. "Can someone please tell me what the hell is going on?"

"The pen and paper that was used to write Katelyn's goodbye note," Brooke said, her eyes not leaving her husband's icy stare. "They were in Travis's bag. *He* wrote that note."

Noah let out a frustrated grunt. "I don't get it. Christ, you guys. Can we just go back to the house and—"

"We're not going anywhere," Travis said evenly, his eyes still locked on Brooke's. "Go on, *lovely wife*. Go ahead and explain your new batshit monster theory. It's a real hoot. I can't wait to see his reaction." Travis's mouth curled into an animated, enthusiastic grin as he waited for Brooke to respond.

"You have wendigo psychosis, Travis."

A harsh bark of laughter escaped Noah's throat, sounding eerily like Travis's. "No, Brooke. That's crazy. That was just a stupid ghost story."

"Look at me, Noah!" Brooke exclaimed. She wiggled her frozen fingers, drawing his attention down to her bindings. "Look what he's done to me. To you!"

Noah stared at her, his head shaking from side to side. "No—"

"*Travis* killed Katelyn," Brooke insisted, her voice desperate. Behind Noah's shoulder, Travis smirked. "*He* wrote the note to you that was supposed to be from Katelyn. *He* got rid of her car. *He* put her phone in the shed. *Travis did it.*"

"No," Noah muttered, taking a step back toward the trees. Behind him, the darkness watched, waiting. "No way. There's no way."

Brooke glared at Travis, shocked at how quickly love had turned to hate. "He killed Katelyn, Noah. And when I found out, he hit me and dragged me out here. He's going to kill me, too. If you let him."

Noah's lower lip trembled, and he bit down on it so hard Brooke was sure it would draw blood. He continued to shake his head, taking one small step back after another, as if he could outrun the truth. "No. He wouldn't. He couldn't." He looked at Travis, his eyes wide with unconstrained hope. "Tell her, Travis," he begged. "Tell her she's wrong."

Travis stared at him, his expression blank. Something passed briefly over his eyes, the glimmer of an emotion, and then was gone again. He said nothing.

"Look at me, Noah," Brooke demanded. *"Look at me."* Noah slowly turned his head, his jaw slack and eyes glazed. "Look what he's done to me. *His wife.* He's not well, Noah. He's sick. He has—"

*"Oh God, Brooke!"* Travis bellowed, breaking his silence. "Are you serious right now? You actually expect him to believe I have—"

"Wendigo psychosis," Brooke finished, raising her voice to be heard over Travis's protests. "Maurice probably had it, too. That's why he killed himself."

Travis rolled his eyes, his body shaking with agitation. "I don't have wendigo psychosis, Brooke. And neither did Maurice."

"How do you know that, Travis?" Brooke asked, her gaze whipping back to him. "You barely spoke to the man, right?"

Travis's eyes flitted up and to the left. He was hiding something. Brooke felt her stomach sink with the realization. *"Right, Travis?"*

The following silence made her groan. "You killed him, too? Didn't you?"

Travis didn't respond. He watched her with cold eyes, somehow colder than the falling snow. His hateful glare disappeared as Noah stepped between them, his back to Brooke.

Seconds ticked by, no one speaking. Snow sifted down from the trees above, and darkness hovered along the perimeter of Brooke's nightlight, pressing forever closer. And all the while, the silence screamed all around them. Whoever thought silence was quiet was wrong—it's deafening. It seemed even the stream had stopped its babbling.

Brooke leaned to the side, struggling to see what was happening between them, terrified of what would come next. Instead of seeing around Noah's broad shoulders and getting a glimpse of Travis's expression, something beyond them caught her attention. Brooke's eyes fixated on a particular spot deeper inside the woods, sensing movement among the trees but unable to make out what it was. She squinted into the gloom, but saw nothing but a few lazily falling snowflakes drifting down from above. Something was there, though. She could feel it, her skin prickling as eyes in the darkness stared back at her.

"Say she's wrong," Noah said in a low, steely voice. "Say you didn't do it."

"I can't, bro."

"Don't call me that," Noah said in the same low voice. "You have to say it, Travis."

Brooke watched the trees, unable to look away. The lower branches of the pines stopped swaying, the traces of wind vanishing below the canopy. Nothing moved but the snowflakes, yet her eyes refused to look away from the same spot among the trees. And then her skin began to crawl, feeling like tiny bugs burrowing just below the surface as her body responded to the presence she couldn't see but knew was there all the same.

"Maurice?" Noah asked.

In the corner of Brooke's eye, she could just make out the up and down motion of Travis's head.

"Katelyn?" Noah asked next, his voice cracking as the name left his lips.

Travis barely nodded his head before Noah lunged at him. The sudden scuffle pulled Brooke's focus from the trees, and she turned her head just in time to see Noah throw his shoulder into Travis's chest. Travis stumbled backward, almost toppling over before righting himself. He dug his feet into the frozen earth and pushed forward, shoving Noah away.

Travis tried to say something, but Noah swung before he could get a word out. His fist collided with Travis's jaw, his head jerking backward with the blow. Travis twisted his body to the side to avoid another strike, and when he whipped back around, he brought his fist with him. He threw his full weight into the punch, striking Noah in the face and then following it with an uppercut to the gut that left Noah bent over and wheezing. Two more blows and Noah was sprawled on the ground, coughing violently in between heavy, labored breaths.

Brooke watched in horror, the thing in the trees momentarily forgotten. "Noah," she whispered as he dry heaved into the dirt. Another cough came, sending a splattering of blood onto the snow. Brooke looked down at the drops of scarlet on the forest floor, then back at the trees. Whatever was out there had taken the opportunity to retreat. It hadn't gone far, though. She could still feel its presence lurking somewhere nearby.

Travis let out a slew of curses, pulling Brooke's attention back to the small clearing. He was bent forward with his hands on his knees, his chest heaving as he tried to catch his breath. Blood leaked from one of his nostrils, a single trail that led down to his upper lip and coated his teeth red.

*All this blood,* Brooke thought, her eyes going back to the splattered snow. The words Maurice had scribbled into his journal shot through her head in angry flashes. Greed. Selfishness. Violence. *It's enjoying this. Watching us. That's why it's still hiding.*

"Goddamnit, Noah," Travis hissed. "You're making me do this." He stumbled over to a nearby tree and reached around the side of the trunk. "You're just as bad as she is," he grumbled as he leaned over to retrieve something that was resting against the opposite side of the tree. When his hand reemerged, he was holding something that glinted in the faint light of Brooke's nightlight. He walked back over to them, wiping his bloodied knuckles onto his jeans.

*"Why?"* Noah sobbed into the dirt, not noticing what Travis was holding, or how the light danced across its metallic surface. "My God, Travis. Why would you do that? Why would you kill her? Why would you kill either of them?" He pushed himself onto his knees, finally raising his head to look at Travis. When he saw the object in his brother's hands, he froze.

"It was an accident," Travis said through clenched teeth, coming to a stop just a few feet away from Brooke's legs. Her eyes, which had been glued to the ax in her husband's hands since he pulled it out from behind the tree, went up to his face. She was surprised to see what looked like genuine remorse etched into his hard features. "It was an accident," he said again, softer this time.

"Where did that come from, Travis?" Brooke asked in the small, little-girl voice.

"Chopping block by the shed," Noah answered, still on his knees and staring at the blade of the ax dangling from Travis's hands.

Travis raised the ax and pointed the head of it at his brother. "Sit down," he ordered, jerking his chin toward Brooke. "Over by her."

Noah obliged, crawling over to Brooke and sitting down beside her. He wiped at his face with his hoodie sleeve, where pine needles were sticking to the fresh blood that covered his skin. His eyebrow was cut open and glistening, and a trickle of blood slithered down his chin from where his lip was split.

"I swear it was an accident," Travis repeated. The remorse was there again, fleeting but undeniable.

"How could killing my girlfriend be an accident?" Noah asked, his jaw working.

Travis let out a frustrated cry, the cords in his neck taut with strain. "Because that's what it was!" he screamed. *"An accident!"* He tightened his grip on the ax, his whole body shaking.

"That's bullshit," Brooke blurted out, and then instantly regretted it. Travis's crazed eyes locked on hers, and any remorse that had been on his face vanished. The hate that replaced it made her recoil. She pressed herself harder into the tree, drawing her knees as close to her body as she could manage.

Travis stood over her, not speaking, his face contorted with silent rage. When she couldn't stand it anymore, she asked, "How could you accidentally kill someone, Travis? I don't get it."

He dug his fingers into the ax's handle, blanching all color from his skin. He took a step toward her, and then another, until his feet were only inches away from her own. "I didn't accidently kill someone," he said slowly, as if speaking to a child. "I accidently killed the wrong person."

"I don't under—"

*"It was supposed to be you, Brooke!"* he screamed into her face. *"It was fucking supposed to be you!"*

Somewhere in the darkness beyond the clearing, a branch cracked, but following Travis's confession, nobody heard it.

# Chapter 32

*Sunday, 7:56 p.m.*

Travis paced back and forth in front of them, holding the ax at chest level and mumbling to himself. Noah attempted to reach for Brooke's hand, but Travis stopped in his tracks and shot him a deathly serious look, causing Noah to withdraw his hand. After a few tense seconds, Travis resumed his pacing, only his footsteps having the bravery to speak.

Brooke watched him, mouth agape, as bits of fallen snow collected on her lower lip and melted away with her breath. Images flashed through her head, slow at first, and then speeding up until they were a chaotic blur. The proposal at the lake. The Stanley Hotel. Secrets under the sheets. Tender kisses. Spoken vows. A single tear slipped from her eye, caressing her cheek and freezing in place before it could reach her chin.

Noah spoke first, sounding just as bewildered as Brooke felt. "I don't—*what?*" He looked up at Travis, smears of dark blood glistening across his face.

"Listen man," Travis said, approaching Noah with the ax. Noah flinched away, then shifted his body closer to Brooke.

Travis stopped walking, his eyes darting between them. He then lowered the ax into a slightly less menacing position before readdressing his brother. "I didn't mean to kill Katelyn," he said, his voice bordering on actual sincerity.

"But you meant to kill Brooke?" Noah asked. "You're telling me that you meant to kill your own wife?" When Travis didn't respond, Noah tilted his head and whispered to Brooke out of the corner of his mouth. "You're right. He has that psychosis thing."

Travis took a step back, his chest expanding with outrage. "There is no fucking wendigo psychosis!" he bellowed up into the trees. "There never was! All that shit is made up! I've been planning this for *months*, and your goddamn girlfriend ruined *everything*!" Travis kicked at the frozen ground, sending bits of hard soil and shattered leaves flying.

"I was out here in the woods for hours," Travis seethed, his enraged stare landing on Brooke. "Waiting for you to come out looking for me. I had everything set up perfectly. I know you always wake up at least once or twice a night, if not more. And when you did, you'd see I was missing, find the note I left for you in the bathroom saying I needed some fresh air, and then you'd come out looking for me. Only you never came out, Brooke. *She did!*"

Travis turned his crazed glare back on Noah. "*She* came out. But I couldn't tell it was her, man. I swear. One of the porch lights was on and all I could see was a damn silhouette. And the two of them are the exact same fucking size. They're practically carbon copies of each other. The only difference is their fucking hair color, and hers was *pulled back*! She was even wearing Brooke's sweater. *Brooke's* sweater. I recognized it. Hell, I'm the one that bought it for her. I didn't know it was Katelyn until it was too late. I swear to God, bro!"

Travis stopped, his chest heaving as he tried to catch his breath. His eyes ping-ponged between the two of them, and when neither spoke, he resumed his tirade. "She saw the ax I left on the ground. It was supposed to lure Brooke over to the edge of the clearing, 'cause by then she'd be worried about me, you see? But then Katelyn saw it and freaked out and started running away, and it wasn't until I dragged her back into the trees and got a good look at her face that I realized it wasn't Brooke. And by then it was too late. She was bleeding everywhere. I didn't have a choice. I had to... had to..."

"You had to murder my girlfriend with an ax?" Noah finished for him. His body was shaking, the vibrations rippling through his torso brought on by rage instead of the bitter cold. His eyes went from Travis's face to the ax he was holding, then back again, his body tensing.

"Yes. But I didn't mean to, Noah. I didn't." Travis's head dipped down as he searched his brother's face for understanding. Noah turned away.

"Brooke was supposed to go out there," Travis rambled, desperation dripping from his words. "The note we'd find in the morning was supposed to be from *her*, saying she woke up early and wanted to explore the woods a little more. And when she never came back, we'd go out looking for her but never find her. The end!"

Noah kept his head turned away, refusing to make eye contact. Frustrated, Travis let out an angry cry and began pacing again. "After the fuck up, I threw away the note I left for Brooke and wrote one from Katelyn instead. I dumped her car, and then I thought that would be it. But then I heard that asshole upstairs moving around and I just knew he saw something. So I threw her phone into that nasty-ass shed first thing in the morning. That way, it could be him who did it. And then when they found him dead, too, they'd assume it was a suicide because he was overcome with guilt. So you see, Noah, it was all going to work out perfectly."

"Perfect except for the fact that you killed two people, neither of which being the one you intended to kill?" Noah finally raised his eyes to meet Travis's stare. His hands fell to his sides and pressed into the hard ground, his body tensing as he prepared to lunge up from his seated position. Travis picked up on the motion, and quickly brought the ax up and aimed it at his brother's chest. Noah wavered for a moment, his muscles twitching, before finally slumping back down to the ground.

"Who are you?" Brooke asked. The words came out small and pathetic, just like how she felt. The little girl that had been tricked. The little girl that believed all the lies she had been told. Like Santa Claus. Like the boogeyman. Like happily ever after.

Travis turned to face her, cocking his head to the side as he looked down at her. The familiar way he tilted his chin used to make her feel loved, cherished even. But now it felt like he was examining a specimen in a petri dish. A lesser being. An insect. It had always been that way, she realized. She was just too enamored to notice.

"I loved you," she whispered, wishing he would stop looking at her like that. Like she was unworthy. She cleared her throat in an attempt to choke back a sob. "And I know you loved me, too."

Travis grinned and set the head of the ax on the ground, leaning into it like a cane. "Do ya now?" He raised the back of his hand to his mouth and stifled a laugh. "God, Brooke. All those books and you still can't tell fact from fiction."

"You really have lost your mind, haven't you?" she asked, almost pleading. She would rather it be that than knowing she spent the last six years living with a monster. Kissing a monster. Sleeping with a monster.

"Yeah, well, marriage can do that to you." Travis twirled the head of the ax on the ground, the blade sweeping the snow away like the wings of a snow angel.

Brooke watched the ax twirl forward, backward, then forward again. Another tear fell, freezing before it reached her lip. It was still getting colder. Before long, they wouldn't need Travis's ax to die—the elements would do it for him.

"It's the psychosis," she mumbled to herself. "It has to be the psychosis."

The ax stopped twirling, and when she looked up, Travis's eyes were burning into her, the only heat present in the frozen forest. Any trace of the husband she knew and loved was gone, if it had ever been there at all. He walked up to her, and she winced away from his approach.

Travis bent down and grabbed her chin roughly with his free hand, lifting her face until she was forced to look at him. "No, Brooke," he said in a snide tone. "It's not the psychosis. The wendigo is a cannibal, remember? And I don't have any desire to eat you. I just want you gone." With that, he shoved her face away and stood back up.

"But why?" she sobbed, her control slipping. "What the hell did I ever do to you?"

Travis rolled his eyes. "You didn't *do* anything to me. This"—he gestured between them with his free hand—"was just an experiment. To see if I was the marrying kind." He gave her an exaggerated shrug. "Turns out I'm not."

Brooke stared at him blankly, her mind unable to keep up with what he was saying. How could she be this stupid? This blind? Like a fucking rat in a maze, running blindly through her life without stopping to ever really see anything. Like what was right in front of her. How could a person remember all the good times in their life and simply block out all the bad? Just like pain. You forget how much something hurts, and that's how you wind up doing the exact same thing over and over again. It's like sensory amnesia. Or, in this case, emotional amnesia.

Sure, Travis always checked for the serial killer she was certain was lurking in the shadows, but he did bitch about it every single time. And sure, he took her to The Stanley for their honeymoon, but he also made sure to frequently mention how much he'd rather have gone to Cancún. And the reason she was so relieved to have Katelyn along on this trip? It was because of how lonely she often felt, because the second Noah arrived it was like she no longer existed to Travis. That's why she went through two, maybe three books in one vacation. Because she was *alone*. Noah tried to include her, but Travis… sometimes it was like he forgot she even existed. Or that he didn't *want* her to exist.

Looking back, he wasn't even that great at pretending to be a good husband. It was her own blindness that was to blame, or perhaps her unwillingness to admit that his love for her was just a facade. And instead of admitting to something so ugly, she chose to bury herself in her horror stories and scary movies. Because surely her life was better than those unsuspecting teenagers about to meet their grisly fates. And at the hands of a monster in an actual mask, no less. Not a mask of fake love and fake vows and fake protection. Her life was the horror story all along. But instead of the monster hiding in the closet, he hid in plain sight. Not even a nightlight could have shown the truth on her marriage.

What was it that Stephen King said? *We make up horrors to help us cope with the real ones.* Was that what she was doing? Was her love of horror stories just a distraction from the real horror in her life—the one in her bed that she slept next to every night?

Travis was still watching her, like he could see inside her skull as she made every painful, soul-shattering connection. Like he could see inside her chest as her heart cracked, each shard falling to the bottom of her rib cage, the fluttering bird finally dead.

"If you wanted me gone so bad, why didn't you just divorce me?" Brooke asked through frozen tears.

"Why?" Travis asked, leaning into the ax and causing it to scrape further into the ground. He shot back up and threw his hand in Noah's direction. "That's why."

Noah stiffened beside her. Brooke looked over at him, but he refused to meet her eyes. Instead, he stared straight ahead, his jaw working beneath the blood and grime. Confused, she turned back to Travis. "I don't—what?"

Travis arched his back dramatically and groaned, becoming more animated by the second. "*Oh, come on!* You can't possibly expect me to believe that you didn't know!"

Travis went to Noah and slapped him hard on the back. Despite the force of the blow, Noah barely moved under the impact. He continued to stare straight ahead, his body so tense he looked more like a statue than a human being. Like the cold had finally frozen him inside as well as out.

With a maniacal cackle, Travis turned back to Brooke. "He's been in love with you from day one!" he exclaimed. "It's so fucking obvious."

Brooke's mouth fell open, the chill lancing at the exposed confines of throat. Her head slowly rotated in Noah's direction until her eyes were locked on his profile. He still hadn't moved, but she could see his lower lip was trembling. "Noah?" she asked softly.

He let out a shaky breath, then finally turned to look at her. He opened his mouth to speak, although no words came out.

Frustrated, he took in a deep breath and tried again, but was still unable to say anything. Resigned, he clamped his jaw shut and returned his gaze to the trees, his features heavy with shame.

Travis laughed gleefully and gave him another hearty clap on the back. "It's okay, bro. We're cool, we're cool. No need to work yourself up over it. *Geez.*"

Brooke reached for Noah's hand, desperate for him to say something—deny it, confirm it, *anything*—but the rope held her firmly in place. She leaned forward, trying to pull his attention away from the trees, when suddenly her own gaze was diverted elsewhere. Her eyes locked on to a dark pocket of shadows beyond Noah's profile, and the unpleasant feeling of being watched washed over her again.

Whatever it was, it was on the other side of them now, closer to the stream, and still out of reach of her paltry nightlight. The clothing pile monster—turned flesh and blood. And it was circling them.

Brooke squinted into the trees, seeing nothing but knowing without a doubt that something was there, until the harsh click of snapping fingers brought her eyes back to Travis.

"Stop staring at him, *babe*," he spat out.

Ignoring him, Brooke looked out into the trees once more, but the presence she felt was no longer there. If it had even been there at all. Discouraged, she looked at Travis. "Even if that was true, I still don't understand why you couldn't just divorce me. What does Noah have to do with—"

"Because you'd still be here, *babe*. You wouldn't just go away. You'd still be in my life—at family dinners, at holidays, at weekend getaways. I'd have to constantly be reminded of my mistake in marrying you."

"Why would I still be here, Travis? You think I'd refuse to divorce you? Well, I won't. Just untie me and give me the fucking papers. Your wish is granted."

Travis smirked. "That's not why." He lifted the ax with one hand and pointed it at Noah, the blade hovering just inches from his brother's face. "It's because you'd wind up with him. Sooner or later. All it would take was one drunken night commiserating with him about your failed marriage. And then it would be just a hop, skip, and a fuck away from you being my goddamn sister-in-law."

Noah turned his head away from the ax, his breath fogging across the icy metal. His eyes went to Brooke's. *I'm sorry,* he mouthed, and then snapped his lips shut as Travis stepped forward and pressed the flat top of the ax against his temple. Noah squeezed his eyes shut as the steel dug in, his head tilting under the pressure.

"Don't go professing your love to my darling wife just yet, baby brother. She's not gonna be around much longer."

"I fell in love with you, Travis. What makes you think I would ever—"

"The only reason you fell in love with *me* is because you met me first."

Brooke scoffed. "You don't know that."

Travis gave her an exaggerated nod. "Yeah, *Brookey*, I do. That's why you have to fucking die. Divorce isn't final enough." Travis gave the ax a shove, and Noah grunted as his head jerked to the side. Grinning, Travis pulled the ax away and brought it up to his chest, his fingers curling around the thick handle.

Brooke turned away, the lack of sanity on her husband's face making her feel ill. Instead, she looked over at Noah. He was staring out at the woods again, but instead of his eyes being locked on some arbitrary location, he was scanning the sea of trees off to their right. Searching for something. *Can he feel it, too?* she thought. The unsettling sensation of bugs crawling beneath her skin returned.

Above them, Travis had fallen silent. When Brooke looked up, she saw he was also looking out at the trees, roughly in the same spot that Noah had been searching.

"We have to get out of here, Travis," Brooke implored.

"No," he said sharply. His gaze settled back on her, having lost interest in the surrounding woods and what might be lurking inside. "We're not done here."

Brooke sighed, exasperated. "If this is just between you and me, why is Noah even here? Why didn't we just go on this trip alone? Why bring witnesses?"

"Oh, Brooke." Travis waggled the ax at her. "You of all people should know that." He squatted down so he was eye level with her. Behind him, only a dozen yards from the clearing, a shadow shifted. "It's an alibi, you idiot. People always suspect the husband first. *Always.*"

"I wonder why," Brooke said dryly, anger filling the void inside her chest that her love for Travis once occupied.

Travis opened his mouth to speak, but Noah spoke first. "Wendigo psychosis or not," he said in a hushed tone, "you're fucking crazy." His eyes were locked on something behind

Travis, in the same direction where Brooke saw the shadow move.

*"I'm crazy?"* Travis gaped at him, rage quickly contorting the handsome angles of his face until he was something else— a monster, perhaps. "It all would have worked out perfectly if you're fucking girlfriend had just stayed in her damn room. It's her fault this has become such a fucking mess. God!"

"God isn't here, Travis," Brooke said in a flat tone. "Only monsters are in these woods."

"Oh, so now there's more than one wendigo, huh? How many? Two? Five? Ten? Please tell me, lovely wife. I'm just dying to know."

"Only two," Brooke said in the same monotone. "The one that has been circling us. And you." She looked up at him, the hate in her eyes matching his.

"Ooo," Travis teased. *"So dramatic."* He threw Noah a sidelong glance. "You seriously want this in your life forever, dude? I'm telling you right now, it doesn't get any better."

"Just let me untie her," Noah said, "and we can go back to the house. Because she's right, there is something out here right now. I can feel it."

"Is it that stupid bear again?" Travis raised the ax and shook it at the trees triumphantly. "'Cause I got something for ya this time, you motherfucker!"

"It's not a bear, Travis," Brooke insisted, struggling against her restraints. "I read Maurice's journals after you left. That story you told us… it's all true. It happened here in *these* woods. To *his* family."

Travis guffawed. "Maurice was a fucking loony tune," he snapped. "You got that much right, *Brookey*." He shot a heated glare at Noah, then looked back at Brooke. "The bastard actually believed his undead grandma lives out here somewhere, and he spent all his time killing animals to feed to her. He's *senile*. Not a monster hunter, or a victim of your supposed wendigo psychosis. Just a batshit crazy old man with more guns than common sense."

Brooke watched the trees, the stillness in the forest growing more unsettling by the second. If she listened hard enough, she could almost hear breathing. Heavy and deep. Not human. She looked back at Travis. "Where did he feed her?"

Travis groaned. "Who cares, you dumb bitch? Don't tell me you actually believe him. No, wait," Travis shook his head, laughing, "of course you do. I forgot who I was talking to."

"Where did he leave the animals, Travis?" Brooke asked, ignoring his cruel laughter. "The ones he fed to her."

"Fuck if I know." Travis's eyes flitted up and to the left.

Brooke sucked in a frozen breath. *Oh shit.* "Where, Travis?"

"Past the stream," he muttered, shrugging his shoulders. "Around here somewhere."

*Oh fuck.* "And where did you leave Katelyn's body?"

Travis's hardened expression faltered briefly with realization. He covered it up with a cough and looked away.

"You're the reason it's here," Brooke stammered. "You woke it up, Travis. *You.* With your selfishness. And your

violence. You killed her, and then you left her in the woods
for it to eat. Just like Maurice did. It woke up because of you."

"We need to get out of here," Noah said, attempting to
stand. Travis pressed the blunt top of the ax into Noah's chest
and shoved him back down. "Do you want us all to die?"
Noah cried. "It's watching us. Right now!"

"Bullshit," Travis snapped. "Nothing ate her. I guarantee
her body is right where I fucking left it."

"Then prove it." Brooke tugged on the rope, barely feeling
it against her wrists. "If there's no wendigo, she'd still be
where you left her, right? So go get something of hers and
bring it back."

Travis rolled his eyes, then scanned the forest. When
nothing moved, shifted, or screamed, he said, "Fine. I'll
fucking prove it." He whirled around and stalked into the
woods, his tall frame wading through the thick shadows.
"Ready or not, bear, here I come!"

Once he faded from sight, Noah asked, "Is he really that
stupid to go out there all by himself?"

"Who the hell cares?!" Brooke squirmed against the tree,
wiggling her wrists inside the knotted ropes. "Get these
fucking things off of me, Noah. Fast. Before he gets back."

Noah hurried over to the tree and started working on her
left wrist. Brooke could feel tugging, but the persistent
pressure of her binding did not relent.

"Shit, Brooke," he said through gritted teeth, "these things
are really tight. And I can't feel my fingers anymore." He
picked furiously at the knots, his frustration growing. "Fuck! I
can't get it off!"

"Please hurry, Noah," Brooke whined. "He's not messing around. He really is going to kill me with that fucking ax. And if he doesn't kill me, the thing in the woods definitely will. I'm tied up like a goddamn sacrifice."

Brooke watched the forest with growing dread, not knowing which monster would emerge from the shadows first. Her eyes caught on a subtle movement off to her right, and she could almost see a shape moving among the trees.

"I think I might be getting the first knot out," Noah stammered, his teeth chattering. "But there's still like, three more."

Brooke ignored him, watching the trees. "Noah—" she started, but stopped when she heard a branch break. It was coming from straight ahead, instead of to the right. Her head whipped around, her eyes going from side to side as she tried to look everywhere at once. Where the hell was it?

Movement drifted in and out of the darkness directly across from her. "Hurry, Noah," she begged, the little-girl voice having made a reappearance. She watched the shape coming toward them, not sure if she was relieved or disappointed when her nightlight revealed that it was her darling husband. His little expedition hadn't taken nearly as long as she had hoped—which could only mean he dumped Katelyn's body very close to where they now sat.

Travis trudged into the small clearing, his eyes zoning in on Noah where he was stooped next to the tree. Travis quickened his pace, lifting the ax as he approached. Once he reached them, he kicked Noah hard in the side and then shoved him away from the tree. Noah cursed and tumbled to the ground, his body tensing as he prepared to lunge back up. Travis stepped in front of him and pressed the ax against his chest, forcing him back down. Noah let out another curse, then begrudgingly resumed his seated position beside the tree.

Brooke looked at Noah, trying to mask the heartbreak that was tearing at her insides. That was their one shot. That was it. Her heart splintered when Noah met her stare and shook his head. She gave her wrist a tug anyway, not wanting to believe it was over—not wanting to believe they had lost—and sure enough, she was still securely fastened to the tree.

Travis laughed, a shrill sound on the verge of madness. "I knew you wouldn't leave," he said to Noah, a crooked smile splitting his face. "You had the perfect opportunity to escape just now, but instead you decided to stay with your doomed sweetheart. Trying to save her, no less."

Travis turned to Brooke and bent forward, leaning in so close that the vapor from his lungs clouded her vision. "And you expect me to believe he isn't in love with you?" he whispered.

Brooke glared up at him. Her insides churned with liquid rage, her body a battle of fire and ice as her burning insides warred against her frozen exterior. "Well?" she asked, ignoring his question. "I don't see anything that proves Katelyn's body is still there."

"That's because it's not," he said, his voice falling flat.

"She's gone, isn't she?"

"Yeah. She's gone."

# Chapter 33

***Sunday, 8:42 p.m.***

*"Gone?"* Noah's breath hitched beside her.

"Yeah," Travis muttered, seemingly unaffected. "The fucking body's gone."

"But that proves—"

"Nothing," Travis said, cutting him off. "It proves nothing."

"It proves that there is something in the woods, Travis," Brooke insisted. "We aren't alone out here."

Travis went to her and leaned forward, his hand resting on his knee, again behaving as if he were talking to a small child. "I know," he whispered. "But it's not what you think it is." He winked, a disconcerting smile curling his pallid lips.

"Then what the hell is it?"

"Have you not been listening at all?" he groaned. "It's a fucking bear! The damn thing followed me all the way home. Almost got me, too. That's why I brought you out here, lovely wife. I'm gonna give you one good chop in the gut and then leave you for it. In the morning, we can just tell the police you were mauled to death when we were trying to go for help."

"There aren't any bears out here, Travis!" Brooke yelled. "It's too fucking cold!"

"And what do you mean *'we'*?" Noah shot at his brother, his chest heaving.

"Oh, come on, man. You'll find another one. A better one. She's used goods anyway. Just let me get rid of her."

"No fucking way," Noah stood up, ignoring the ax that was once again pressed against his chest. He stepped into the blade, catching Travis off guard and causing him to take an awkward step backward. Noah took the opportunity to position himself between Travis and Brooke. "I'm not going to let that happen," he said. "You'll have to kill me, too."

Travis shook his head, infuriated. "We're blood, Noah! *Blood!* You can't turn your back on your family!"

*Maurice sure didn't,* Brooke thought, wiggling her wrist inside the rope. She could feel eyes caressing her body as she worked, coming from the darkness over her left shoulder. Waiting.

"How could you not think of her as family, Travis?"

"You're family," Travis said, gripping the ax tighter. "She's not."

"She became family when you married her."

"Blood family, Noah! We're connected by blood. Me and her?" He jerked his chin toward Brooke. "Just a piece of paper."

"You can't possibly believe that. What about love?"

"Love?" Travis laughed, near hysterical. "That shit is fake. It's made up, Noah. Just Hallmark movies and Valentine's Day. And anniversaries to mark the stupidest decision you ever made, like that's something you'd want to celebrate." Travis glared at Brooke, but she hardly noticed. The eyes behind her overpowered the ones in front of her.

"That's bullshit and you know it," Noah said, still standing his ground between them.

"No. You thinking some fictitious emotion has bound her and I together for all eternity is bullshit. The only real bond is blood."

"You're wrong."

Travis let out a strangled cry, the ax shaking in his grasp. "God, I should have known you'd pick her over your own brother."

"Travis, I'd pick saving someone over killing them every single time."

Travis snorted. "What a goddamn hero," he said with a sneer. "No wonder you want to fuck him, *Brookey*." He took a step closer to Noah, but Noah refused to back away.

"You've always had it easier, baby brother," Travis went on, taking another step forward. "You're nicer. Funnier. *Sweeter.* You could have had anyone, and you pick my fucking wife."

"I didn't pick her, Travis! I couldn't help it. I swear I couldn't. I fucking tried."

Travis stopped, inches away from Noah's face. The ax's blade was now nestled in the crook of Noah's neck, his hoodie being the only thing protecting the flesh beneath.

"I don't want you gone, baby brother," Travis said. "Only her. And then we can go back to the way things used to be."

"We can't go back to anything, Travis. You killed my girlfriend. You're about to kill your wife. I don't even know who the fuck you are anymore."

A branch broke behind Brooke. She cringed, and a small whimper escaped her lips when another broke, closer than the last. She waited, wondering how much longer it would take for whatever it was to start nibbling on her frozen fingers. Would she even feel it? Or would it have devoured her to the palm before she even knew it was there? Could it be eating her right now? Pain didn't come, but a grunt did, not close enough to taste her, but not particularly far away either.

Travis peered around the tree, squinting into the darkness. "Time to move, little brother," he ordered, returning his attention to Noah. "The bear's here. You'll get over her. I promise." He raised the ax over his shoulder. "Now get out of the way."

Noah dug his feet into the ground, shaking his head. "No, Travis. Fuck your blood. I choose love."

"Noah—"

"Love makes you stronger."

*"Love makes you weaker!"* Travis screamed. "Just look at you! It's fucking pathetic!"

"Dying to protect who you love isn't pathetic." Noah staggered his stance and brought his hands up, waiting for Travis to strike.

Brooke pulled furiously at the rope, feeling the few seconds she had left slipping away like the last grains of sand in an hourglass. A harsh exhale came from directly behind her left shoulder. Something snapped in the woods straight ahead. Branches rustled to the right. How was it everywhere and nowhere all at the same time? Her head swiveled, desperately searching for the source of the sounds. Before she could locate it, the last grain of sand in the hourglass fell to the forest floor—a single white snowflake landing in the silver shaft of her nightlight.

*"Travis,"* a woman called from somewhere among the trees, her voice drifting through the arctic air. The whisper caressed the boughs of the pines and kissed the frost shimmering on their bark as it worked its way through the midnight forest.

*"Travis,"* she said again, clearer this time, sounding more like a girl than a woman. Sounding like… Katelyn.

Travis whirled around. Noah's hands fell to his sides. Brooke ceased tugging on her restraints. They waited, all silently frozen in place, the white vapor from their lungs absent as they held their collective breath.

*"Travis,"* Katelyn's voice called, almost yearning. A soft sigh sifted through the trees, causing a fresh wave of goose bumps to spring up on Brooke's frozen skin. *Gotta go gotta go gotta go.* She reached forward with her foot and nudged Noah's ankle.

Noah didn't move, his eyes locked on the shifting shadows deep within the trees. Brooke nudged him again, and again, before full-on kicking him in the leg. Noah hissed through his teeth and finally turned to look at her. His eyes were glazed, almost hopeful. "Katelyn…"

*Oh shit,* Brooke thought. She urgently shook her head from side to side, as if she could shake the thought from his head. Noah's brows drew together in confusion. He opened his mouth to say something else, but stopped when Travis spoke first.

"She's dead," Travis whispered, more to himself than anyone else. "I killed her. I'm sure I killed her. I…" he trailed off, his eyes not leaving the trees. The ax was now hanging by his side.

*"Travis,"* Katelyn's voice urged, calling out to him from just beyond the nightlight's reach.

Noah turned toward the voice, and Brooke kicked him again, harder this time. He looked down at her, still confused and almost… vacant.

*No,* she mouthed to him. *Stay here.*

Behind him, Travis took a step forward, then another. "I fucking killed her," he murmured to himself. "She can't be alive. She can't."

Noah waited until Travis was at the edge of the trees, then squatted down beside Brooke. "If it's Kate," he whispered, "she needs my help. Before he—"

"It's not Kate," Brooke said, slowly and deliberately. "Noah, look at me. *Look at me.*" Reluctantly, Noah met her gaze. "Katelyn is dead. Travis killed her. What we are hearing is not Katelyn. We need to get out of here. *Right now.*"

Realization finally flickered in Noah's eyes, chasing away the vacant stare. Brooke heaved a sigh of relief. He moved in closer to her, away from the haunting calls. "You think it's—"

"The person who is separated from the tribe is the weakest," she whispered against his ear. Her eyes darted up to Travis, who was now thirty feet away and following the calls into the forest. "You stay with the tribe to survive." Brooke searched Noah's face, desperate for him to understand. "It's here, Noah. We don't have much time."

Noah began to nod, but then turned his head away from her when another call filtered through the trees. His expression softened, his eyes searching. "Kate—"

*"Noah,"* Brooke pleaded. He didn't respond. "Noah!" she nearly shouted, but still he didn't look away from the trees. If anything, he began to drift away from her. One inch, then two. A hypnotized rat following the piper's haunting melody.

*"Noah, please."* Brooke shifted as far forward as she could manage, her shoulders threatening to dislodge from their sockets. She needed him to look at her. She needed to pull his attention away from what was beckoning to him inside the trees.

Brooke brushed her frozen lips against his cheek. She could barely feel his skin beneath her kiss, but when he turned into her and his lips found hers, the heat of his breath she could feel. It was warm, and somehow hopeful. And in a world filled with nothing but death and ice, it felt like he was breathing actual life into her. Brooke leaned in, deepening the kiss. She couldn't feel the cold anymore. Couldn't feel anything but his mouth on hers.

And then, just as quickly as it started, the kiss ended. Noah jerked his head away, his eyes locking on hers. His vacant expression shifted into one of shock—shock, disbelief, and most of all, awareness.

"Oh, thank God," Brooke panted, watching him closely. "Noah? Are you there?"

He stared at her for a moment, his cheeks flushed and mouth parted. And then he nodded. "Yeah, I'm here. Shit, I'm sorry." Without another word, he scurried over to her wrist and started working on the knots. "Jesus, Brooke," he said, picking furiously at the rope. "I don't know what happened. It's like it hooked me or something."

Brooke let her head fall back against the tree. "It's okay," she said. "Just try to hurry, please. I'd love to not die tonight." She felt a slight give as Noah worked out another knot. She pulled at the rope eagerly, unable to stop herself, but still it wouldn't give.

"Hey, try not to do that, okay?" he said from behind her shoulder. "It's making the knots tighter."

"I'm sorry," she whimpered. "I just… how much longer?"

Brooke thought of the empty hourglass. *Out of time.* They were out of time. The haunting calls had stopped, Katelyn's voice having vanished from the air along with all other sound. And Travis was gone, too, no longer visible among the trees. Nothing moved, nothing whispered. It was like they were in a vacuum where everything but terror had been sucked out. The silence was like a ticking bomb, and any second now it would—

A shrill, earth-shattering cry rushed at them like a tidal wave, splintering the silence into a thousand jagged pieces. Brooke cringed and pulled her legs up to her body like a makeshift shield. Noah stumbled and lost his grip on the rope. Travis's scream joined in, accompanying the screech that was anything but human. The horrible volume of it all made Brooke's head throb.

"Noah!" she cried over the cacophony of screams. *"Noah!"* She started pulling at the rope in a blind panic, unable to stop herself.

"No, Brooke!" Noah yelled. "You're tightening the knots back up!"

Brooke screamed, her voice drowned out by the symphony of hell surrounding them. She struggled to keep her body still as she listened to Travis's cries. They punctuated the screeches in some sort of sickening gothic melody. *"Noah!"* she begged, unable to take it anymore. Not Travis, and not the other thing.

Noah began yanking on the ropes desperately. "I'm trying!" he hollered over the mounting screams.

A harsh, violent cracking sound shot through the forest as a tree began to topple over. The surrounding trees cried out in unison as their branches snapped under the weight of the falling pine. And still, above it all, was the deafening screech of the inhuman thing coming toward them.

*"Noa—"* Brooke's cry cut short as something hurtled into the small clearing. It hit the ground with a heavy thud,

tumbled through the dusting of snow, and came to a stop just a few feet from where she sat. Her husband. Brooke opened her mouth to scream, but nothing came out.

Travis lay before her, bloody and broken. His arm was unattached at the shoulder, hanging onto his body by flesh alone. One of his legs was missing below the knee. Claw marks raked down the side of his body, his clothing and flesh equally shredded. Everything was red and wet, saturated in his pulsating blood. His jaw was dislocated, his straight, pearlescent teeth at an awkward angle compared to the ones above. One pupil was blown out, the white of his eye filled with blood and blackness. The other eye stared at her, aware and...

*Alive,* Brooke thought, choking on another scream. *He's still alive.* She looked away, not wanting to see it anymore. Not wanting to see what was approaching them either. Her eyes landed on a glint of silver that gleamed in her overhead nightlight. The ax. Still in Travis's hand somehow. It lay in the snow beside his scalp, most of which was pulled back from the glistening white bone of his exposed skull.

"Noah!" Brooke yelled. "The ax! Get the fucking ax!"

Noah lurched up and stumbled over to Travis's body, his hands shaking so badly he had difficulty getting a good grip on the ax's handle. His eyes landed on the mutilated remains of his brother, and he let out a gut-wrenching sob. "Oh my God. Trav—"

"It's too late for him, Noah. *Get the ax!*"

Noah's hands wrapped around the handle just as the wendigo stepped out from the trees and into the light. Brooke saw its feet first—bare, torn, and hideously long in the drifts of snow. Her eyes panned upward, and upward, and upward. Its head towered twelve feet above them, part of the trees instead of below them. Its ashen, gray flesh was stretched thin over its elongated bones, each joint looking like a gnarled knot of a disfigured tree. It was horribly emaciated, more like a skeleton than an actual person, with each rib jutting out with grotesque definition.

It took a step forward, scanning the occupants of the small clearing with red, sunken eyes. The skin of its face was the same corpse-like gray, its lips hanging in shredded red ribbons around a mouth full of impossibly long, impossibly sharp teeth. Row after row of teeth jutted out from its black gums, already dripping with Travis's blood.

Noah stumbled backward, away from Travis's body, the ax clutched to his chest. He kept stepping backward until he disappeared behind Brooke, leaving her alone in the clearing. "Noah," she whispered in the little-girl voice. No response.

The wendigo reached forward with one gaunt, skeletal arm. Frighteningly long claws extended from its withered hand, looking almost like jagged slivers of bone in the scant moonlight. It carefully wrapped its rotting fingers around Travis's almost-severed arm, all the while watching Brooke with its bloody, scarlet eyes. With one flick of its wrist, Travis's arm broke free, leaving a splattering of warm blood on Brooke's chest and face, so hot against her frozen cheeks that it almost felt like it was burning.

A barely audible whimper crawled out from the depths of her throat, refusing to remain trapped inside her lungs. He left her. He left her here to die. He left her here, all alone, with this… monster. An anguished sob broke free.

The smell of rot and decay permeated the air, coming from the wendigo's paper-thin skin, and the scent of rusted iron mingled with the decay as more of Travis's blood spilled from his steaming body.

"Lovely wife," the thing said in Travis's voice, all the while chewing on a piece of his mangled flesh.

Brooke felt a scream scrambling up her throat, but before it could burst forth, a heavy *thwack!* struck the tree behind her. The impact reverberated through the trunk, and the rope she was violently pulling against gave her an extra centimeter of slack. With another *thwack!*, the rope offered an additional inch of movement. Brooke pulled hard against it, but it wasn't until the third chop of the ax that her hands fell to her sides, taking the severed rope with them.

*Free.* She scrambled to stand, but the burning sensation of eyes boring into her body stopped her. She looked up at the wendigo, trembling. It was holding Travis's severed arm, its teeth sunk deep into the wet flesh that dangled from a mash of blackish-red gore. With a jerk of its head, it tore a chunk free. It swallowed without chewing, its red, hungry eyes locked on hers.

"Lovely wife," it said again, matching the same hateful tone Travis had used only moments ago.

Brooke's body felt like lead, the rope on her wrists replaced by an anvil bound to her feet. She willed herself to move, but her body stayed frozen in place. *This must be how a rabbit feels,* she thought, *just before it's eaten.* Her brain screamed at her to move, but her legs stubbornly refused to obey. She couldn't even move when she felt something grab hold of her arm. Instead, she squeezed her eyes shut and waited for her arm to be torn from her body, just like her husband's was torn from his.

But there was no searing pain, and no wet ripping sounds of flesh tearing from bone. Instead there was an incessant, unrelenting tugging sensation as she was dragged through the snow. Brooke cracked an eye open and saw the wendigo was in the same spot, chewing and watching. She looked away, her eyes going to what was above her. *Noah.* Holding the ax with one hand and dragging her away from the tree with the other.

"Brooke!" Noah's voice filtered in, cutting through the buzzing in her ears that she didn't even realize was there. "Get up!" he demanded. *"Now!"*

Brooke kicked her legs beneath her, searching for purchase. Soil and snow and pine needles slipped beneath her tennis shoes before she finally felt her heels dig in. She shoved herself upward, Noah's arm wrapping around her waist and pulling her the rest of the way to standing. They staggered backward together, clutching at each other, as the wendigo silently watched their retreat. All the while, it tore strips of flesh from Travis's bones and slurped them down, slowly and methodically.

Brooke and Noah wove their way through the trees, moving backward at a slow and steady pace. *Just like any other carnivore,* she thought. *Don't run. Don't turn your back. Just take another step. And then another. And another. Keep going. Just keep going.*

The wendigo tore more flesh from Travis's arm, which came off in a bright red strip, still dripping. It sucked it down, ate more, picking the bones clean. *Like a chicken wing,* she thought, her sense of reality wearing thin. Once the arm was free of flesh, it tossed the bones aside. It then dug its elongated claws into Travis's midsection, scooping out a handful of lumpy organs. It curled its hand around a heavy, purplish mass that must have been his liver, letting the other organs and entrails fall to the snow by its feet. It looked down at the liver it was clutching, and then brought it up to its mouth.

Noah and Brooke turned and ran as soon as the wendigo broke eye contact. They tumbled through the trees, swerving and sliding to miss branches and roots that struggled to halt their escape. Branches cut at her face as they hurtled themselves forward, her own blood mixing with Travis's.

Brooke's foot struck a rock, and she almost fell face first into the stream, but Noah's grip on her arm stopped her. They ran through the partially frozen water, not bothering with the stepping stones. Icy sludge saturated her shoes, but she could barely feel it. Could barely feel anything except the desperate need to break free from the forest. The shed appeared in the distance, growing larger and larger until they ran silently past it, their eyes fixated on the golden light emanating from the house beyond the trees.

A frigid breeze engulfed them as they careened out of the woods and into Maurice's clearing. Heavy snowflakes cascaded through the air, so thick they were difficult to see through. They ran through them, and through the thickening blanket of white underfoot. Past the wooden swing, past the picnic table, past the towering oaks that were now free of all their leaves.

Brooke winced when a final shriek cut through the air, deep in the midnight woods from whence they came. Noah half-pulled, half-carried her up the stairs, stopping at the second landing and leading her across the deck. Her soaked feet slipped and slid on the icy wood, before Noah finally reached the sliding glass door and yanked it open.

Brooke fell to her knees inside the living room, turning just in time to see Noah slam the door closed and lock it. He hit the light switch on the wall, bathing the room in darkness, then collapsed beside her and pulled her in close. His arms were shaking as he wrapped them tightly around her, his breath going in and out in harsh gasps. She curled into him, her hands clinging to the material of the sweatshirt spanning his chest.

They stayed like that until morning, watching the tree line until the sun was well above the horizon. In that time, nothing entered the clearing. Nothing bent the heavy branches of the towering oaks. And nothing left bloody smears in the freshly fallen snow.

By morning, the clearing was nothing but a twinkling wonderland sparkling beneath a rapidly clearing sky, the sun turning the snowdrifts into mounds of shattered diamonds. Looking out the window, it appeared nothing could be amiss in such a beautiful place. Surely, monsters couldn't exist in the midst of such beauty.

Because in the light of day, the monster in the corner always turns out to be just a pile of dirty clothes. And the shadows creeping across the bedroom ceiling are only the trees outside, swaying in a gentle breeze. That tapping on the window is just an innocent branch, tittering against the windowpanes. And the calls coming from the forest are just loved ones, beckoning for someone to come join them.

Scarlett Springs

*Burlington Post*
*October 27, 2022*
*Two Die in Bear Attack, Third Commits Suicide*

Three are dead following a nightmarish weekend at a rural homestead in northern Vermont. Maurice Dubois, age 68, was found dead in his home—an apparent suicide—by travelers who rented out the lower levels of the house as a vacation rental. Of the four guests that rented the space through Airbnb, only two survived the weekend, the others falling victim to a vicious, and unrelated, bear attack.

Noah and Brooke Hayden, of Syracuse, New York, and Boston, Mass. respectively, witnessed the attack that claimed the lives of Travis Hayden, age 32, and Katelyn Chambers, age 24. The four travelers were exploring the property on Scarlett Springs Road when a black bear ambushed the group and mauled Chambers. When the predator attempted to drag Chambers' body into the forest, Travis Hayden, brother to

Noah and husband to Brooke, interceded in an attempt to stop the attack, and was subsequently killed by the bear.

The violence of this predatory attack is unprecedented in the state of Vermont. However, due to the time of year and an unexpected cold front that swept through the area, Charles Sweetwater of Vermont Fish and Wildlife said it is not a complete surprise. "As winter approaches, bears are trying to put on as much weight as possible before they begin hibernation. If an aging or injured bear is unable to successfully hunt its traditional prey, it might turn to a different food source out of desperation. While these attacks are tragic, the bear was doing the only thing it knew to do to survive." Vermont Fish and Wildlife continues to search for the bear in question, but following the heavy snowfall, Sweetwater is not optimistic in their success.

When police searched the home following the report by Noah and Brooke Hayden (who managed to safely leave the property on foot the following day) they found Dubois dead inside his living quarters. The investigators have ruled the death a suicide and believe it is in no way related to the mauling that befell Hayden and Chambers...

*Burlington Post*
*November 12, 2022*
*Search Continues for Missing Hikers on Appalachian Trail*

The search continues for the Bryant family, last seen at the Sycamore Canyon Trailhead in northern Massachusetts. Sarah and Robert Bryant, along with their cousins, Jeffrey and Cassandra Bryant, began their hike on the Appalachian

Trail on November 2, 2022. The group had been planning their trip for months, and all were experienced hikers.

The Appalachian Trail, starting in Georgia and ending in central Maine, is the longest hiking-only trail in the United States. Phone records were able to track the Bryants' progress along the trail until they entered southern Vermont, where all communication was lost. Search and Rescue continues to keep up their efforts to find the missing party, focusing on the section of the trail where the Bryants' location was last known. They remain hopeful…

*Burlington Post*
*November 23, 2022*
*Record Snowfall Continues Throughout New England*

New Englanders continue to suffer harsh winter conditions, which started early in the season and are yet to let up. Record snowfall has been recorded across multiple states, with many roads being shut down and multiple power outages reported across Vermont, New Hampshire, and eastern Maine. Meteorologists are baffled by the intensity of the storms, as well as the seemingly consistent location over the three states mentioned above…

*Burlington Post*
*February 19, 2023*
*Family Devastated Following Death of Teenage Son*

Gerald and Kimberly McBride scattered the ashes of their son, Preston McBride, today in a private ceremony. The family made headlines last month when Preston, age 17, lured his sister, Jennifer McBride, age 14, into the family's guesthouse, where he restrained her and began to consume parts of the girl's flesh. Preston was discovered and apprehended when his father heard his daughter's cries for help. Jennifer was taken to the hospital, where she required more than a hundred stitches and multiple skin grafts to repair the damage inflicted by her brother.

Preston committed suicide while in county lockup, using his teeth to sever arteries in his wrists. Upon autopsy, portions of his own tissues were found inside his stomach cavity...

*Burlington Post*
*June 15, 2023*
*Scarlett Springs House Goes Up for Auction*

1749 Scarlett Springs Road, owned by the Dubois family for over a century, is going up for auction next month following the death of the family's last living descendent...

Brooke Hayden ran her fingers along the edges of the newspaper clipping, making sure all the corners were securely attached to the page, before closing the journal and returning it to the shelf. The journal was newer than the ones it accompanied, its leather still stiff and rich with scent.

The bookcase it sat upon was the original heavy oak that came with the house, although the rest of the surrounding furnishings were new, fresh, and barely used. The hardwood floor was polished, and the area rugs brightly colored and free of wear and stains. The peeling wallpaper that originally covered the walls was gone, replaced by fresh paint in various shades of white and beige. All of the original items in the house had been removed, save for the bookcases and the contents on their shelves.

Not only was the house refreshed with new paint and furnishings, but also with new appliances and a new roof, which was in desperate need of replacing. The mildly offsetting vibe the house once gave off left with the dated furniture, and Brooke thought the home looked much more inviting now, despite its troubled past. The only remnants of that phase of the house's history rested on the oak shelves that lined the study, where dozens upon dozens of journals still waited to be read.

The journals, along with everything else inside the house, had sat untouched for months on end, collecting another layer of dust to add to what it had already accumulated over the years. It wasn't until the auction went through and the house was officially hers that Brooke returned to the journals, just as worn and brittle as she remembered them to be. That had been two summers ago, and still Brooke had not made it through all the pages, finding she could only read one at a time before needing to take a break, the content inside often too vivid and too grotesque to take in all at once. She would get through them all, though—of that much she was certain. What she would do with the knowledge inside their pages was still up for debate.

Brooke left the study and went down the hall, taking a brief moment to glance at the candid photo hung on the freshly painted wall. The way he was looking at her in the photograph, it was a wonder she hadn't noticed it on her own; that she needed a raving lunatic to point it out to her. They looked so happy in the picture—her staring at the camera and him staring at her—that she often liked to gaze at the photo, reminding herself that they could be happy like that again. That it was still possible, despite what they had been through.

She went past the dining room and kitchen, inadvertently giving the bathroom a wide berth as she passed. It still sometimes irked her, despite being completely torn out and remodeled. During the day it held little fear, but at night she sometimes still saw the splashes of red inside, despite the valiant efforts of the nightlight mounted on the wall.

Every room on every level of the house had a nightlight now, the constant warm glow keeping the shadow monsters at bay. There was no room in her life for shadow monsters, not when there was a real one prowling the woods.

Brooke stepped out onto the balcony, also freshly painted, and walked up to the railing. The remodeling was almost complete, except for the lowest level, which was stripped bare and had paint cans sitting in the center of the floor, just waiting to be slathered upon the vacant walls.

The extensive remodeling, along with the purchase of the house altogether, had been made possible by her dear late husband. If it weren't for the generous life insurance policy he had taken out for the both of them—just for her would have been suspicious, after all—she wouldn't have been able to afford such a place, or any of the necessary updates. But thanks to her *lovely* husband, the only reminder of the Dubois family was resting on the oak shelves inside the study. Everything else said Hayden—Brooke Hayden, not Travis.

The oaks in the clearing were heavy with fresh growth, the leaves the brightest of greens as they sprouted from the intricate weaving of interlocking branches. Before long the boughs would sag with their weight, and every breeze would be announced as it rustled the leaves together in a delicate embrace.

The pines that lined the clearing always had secrets to tell, every breath of wind eliciting whispers from the trees. Brooke liked their whispers, though—it was the silence she couldn't stand. The silence that hangs heavy below the pines in the dead night of a winter storm. A silence where ghosts don't even dare to speak, and where the wind doesn't dare to breathe.

The path that led to the shed was still there, but the work shed itself was long since gone. Brooke had it demolished and incinerated before she stepped foot on the property, not liking the constant reminder of that bloody weekend staring out at her from the depths of the forest. Not when there were other things that could be watching her from among the trees.

The stepping stones that dotted the stream were still there, although she had not passed them since that silent, frozen night two and half years ago. It was a stream she would never pass, and that she was determined nobody else would get the opportunity to pass as well.

That's why she had chosen to purchase the house in the first place. To keep others out. Noah thought she was crazy to buy it, and even more crazy when she said she wanted to renovate it and move in, but she had insisted it was the only way to make sure nobody else ventured onto the property. Especially after it became abundantly clear that the local police wanted nothing to do with what actually occurred that blood-drenched night.

After walking to town the following day and telling the police what happened, the officers hadn't even tried to conceal their thoughts that she was crazy. Distraught. Delusional. Probably on drugs. Definitely unstable. It was a lot easier to believe those things than the rantings of a hysterical widow, especially when there was such an easy and logical explanation lurking nearby. One with long teeth, black fur, and that was about to go into hibernation.

Their easy, logical theory was even further solidified when they discovered the scant remains of her heroic husband—clearly the work of an animal, if they had ever seen one. And a hungry one at that. Noah was equally discredited, for a grieving brother is almost as dismissible as a grieving wife. The police declared the case closed, recommended therapy for the both of them, and that was that.

Except for the disappearances, of course. Those kept happening, one after another. Hikers, campers, poor souls with car trouble. That damn bear was evidently at it again, and during the winter months no less. He certainly was a determined son of a gun, that bear.

After Brooke spent the course of that first winter filling one of her own journals with newspaper clippings of lost hikers and suspicious deaths, she decided she had had enough. No more disappearances. No more "bear" attacks. That bitch was going down. Or at least placated with butcher meat until Brooke could figure out a more permanent solution.

Brooke stood on the balcony, her eyes scanning the trees until her attention was drawn to a sizzling crackle down below. A savory scent accompanied the crackle, wafting up enticingly from the main deck. She peered over the balcony and down at the grill, where Noah Hayden was tending to two of the largest burgers she had ever seen.

"Hey you!" Brooke called down.

Noah turned his head up, squinting into the sunshine, and then gave her a smile and a wave of his spatula.

"You know that thing is almost as big as I am, don't you?" Brooke pointed a finger at the gargantuan patties.

Noah shrugged. "Yeah, but I figured whatever you don't eat we'll give to Lara."

"You spoil her too much," Brooke said. "You know that right?"

"What can I say? I like my dogs chunky." Noah grinned and waggled his eyebrows.

"And I like my dogs free of heart disease caused by excessive burger consumption."

Noah winked at her, then returned his attention to the grill. "Why don't you come down here and help me?" he called over his shoulder. "I could use a sous-chef."

"There's not much sous'ing involved with cheeseburgers."

The oak trees fluttered in the warm, spring breeze, and Brooke closed her eyes and took in a deep breath. Deep, earthy pine and the rich aroma of grilled meat filled her nostrils as the sunlight danced across her face.

"Yeah, well," Noah said, flipping over the first burger patty, "come down here anyway and keep me company. Lara is a lousy conversationalist."

Brooke agreed as much and left the balcony, shutting and locking the door behind her, as she did with every door that wasn't in direct use. She went to the stairwell past the kitchen, and descended the stairs into the main living room. The doors that had once blocked the staircase had been removed, and they were now able to move freely between the two levels.

Lara was immediately at her feet, running in from the open sliding glass door. She wagged her tail and licked at Brooke's bare toes, making her giggle. "Yeah, yeah. You're just showing me the love because you want the other half of my burger." She gently nudged the mutt aside and walked out onto the main deck.

"Extra cheese on mine?" she asked Noah, grabbing his can of soda off the table and taking a sip.

"Yes, ma'am." He closed the lid on the grill, set down his spatula, and turned to look at her. Lara darted between them, her tail smacking against their legs as she bounded back and forth. "How's the reading coming?" he asked.

Brooke shrugged. "Tough to read sometimes, but I think I'm making some progress."

"You really think there's gonna be anything in there that will tell you how to stop it?" Noah glanced at the woods, then back at Brooke. "I mean, wouldn't Maurice or one of the other family members have tried that already?"

"Not if they still loved their dear old great-granny. Besides, maybe I'll see something they didn't. Google wasn't around back then, ya know?" Brooke groaned. "Or maybe they just thought living with it was better than killing their family member."

Noah quirked a brow. "Even if their family member kept eating them?"

Brooke lightly shoved Noah's arm. "No cannibal talk before dinner."

Noah nodded somberly. "Yeah, sorry. Forgot about that one."

Lara barked and rose onto her hind legs, pressing her paws gently onto Brooke's stomach. Brooke ruffled the fur behind the dog's ears, cooing affections in her good-doggy voice. Staying in the house was contingent on them getting a dog— something that can bark and alert them to anything that might be prowling the woods. So far, Lara's duties had consisted of snuggling on the couch, playing Frisbee in the clearing, and eating Brooke's burgers.

"You take her down recently?" she asked.

Noah opened the grill and tossed on a few slices of cheese, adding a couple extra to Brooke's, then closed it again. "She had a potty break twenty minutes ago. I just think she wants some more Frisbee time before dark."

"We can take her after dinner."

Noah finished up the burgers and set the plates down on the deck's patio table. Brooke fetched a couple of fresh sodas from the fridge, and a chew toy for Lara, then joined him at the table.

"What if we can't figure out how to kill it?" Noah asked between bites, a question he asked often and of which Brooke still didn't have an answer.

"Then we continue where Maurice left off." Brooke took a bite of her burger, savoring the rich taste which paired perfectly with the spring sunshine. "I'm sure you'd make an excellent deer hunter. I'll get you a super hot camo hat and matching vest."

"Except I'd rather not run around the woods killing and disemboweling animals all the time. I happen to like Bambi."

"Yeah, I know." Brooke sighed and broke off a piece of her burger, offering it to Lara who was sitting patiently alongside her chair. The dog gulped it down, then looked up at her, hopeful for more.

"Maybe a well-stocked butcher shop then," she said, looking back at Noah. "I don't know all the answers yet, but I'll keep reading. We still have more time anyway. From what I've read so far, she always seems to hibernate for at least five years. Sometimes six or seven."

"It," Noah corrected. "Not she."

"Right. It."

They ate in silence for a while, listening to the pines as they spilled their secrets. Unfortunately, the secret of how to kill the first Mrs. Dubois wasn't one they were willing to divulge just yet. Brooke was determined to figure it out, though. It was just going to take time. And not too much, hopefully.

Noah finished off his burger and stretched his arms over his head. "Ugh. I ate too much."

Brooke's eyes lingered on his toned stomach, his shirt having slipped up as he stretched. She quirked a brow. "Doesn't look like it to me."

He eyed her suspiciously from across the table, the corner of his mouth curling into a mischievous smile. "Let's take Lara down for a while before you get any ideas. It's gonna be sunset before long."

"Good idea." Brooke shoved herself up from her chair. She offered the remains of her burger to the patiently waiting Lara, marveling in how quickly it vanished from her hand.

They crossed the deck and stepped out onto the stairs, Lara darting ahead of them and bolting down into the clearing. Brooke started, and Noah grabbed her hand and stopped her from running after the dog. "It's okay," he said. "She knows not to go into the woods."

"She knows that we don't like it," Brooke corrected. "But she doesn't know that it's not safe in there." Despite the urge to rush down the remaining stairs, she forced herself to continue down at a normal pace alongside Noah.

As if to prove his point, Lara appeared at the foot of the stairs, tail wagging energetically as she waited from them to join her.

"See." Noah raised his hand and gestured to the rescue dog. "She's a good girl. Besides, it's spring. We have nothing to worry about until the end of fall."

Brooke nodded, giving Lara a pat as they entered the clearing. She leaned down and grabbed the nearest Frisbee, already dented with chew marks despite them having purchased it only a few weeks ago when they went into town. She tossed it across the yard, watching it sail through the pleasantly warm air and land in the grass just past the oak trees. Lara bounded after it, barking gleefully.

"What if this is the winter it comes back?" Brooke asked, her eyes scanning the woods as they always did when she went down into the clearing. She thought the nervousness would pass as time went on, but as it turned out, the horrors of that night were able to penetrate the daylight, after all. Even in the warmth and safety of the summer months.

"I think if we keep our greed and selfishness to a minimum, we might be able to make it another winter," Noah said. "Hell, possibly a lot of winters. And by then, we'll have a plan. Hopefully to kill it, but if not, to appease it until it starts hibernating again."

"Pretty optimistic thinking, Mr. Hayden," Brooke said, pulling the slippery, drool-covered Frisbee from Lara's mouth and tossing it back across the clearing.

"Yeah, that's me." Noah slipped his arm around her growing waist, pulling her body against his. "And optimism and contentment are the things we need to focus on, right?"

Brooke nodded, watching Lara bound through the grass as she proudly carried the Frisbee in her jaws. Birds sang overhead, rejoicing in the departure of winter and the arrival of spring.

Brooke felt like rejoicing as well. They had made it through another winter—one without death and violence and monsters in the trees. And if they kept being grateful for what they had, and what they were about to have, perhaps she would never return. *It*, she corrected herself. Perhaps *it* would never return.

Lara raced around them, still clutching the Frisbee, apparently forgetting the premise of how to play fetch. Brooke smiled, watching her. "I think that's a good plan," she said, leaning into Noah and resting her head against his shoulder.

"Have you decided on a name yet?" Noah asked, his hand resting on the curved rise of her stomach.

Brooke placed her hand on top of his, guiding it to where he'd be able to feel the kicking inside. "Yes, I have."

Noah laughed. "And you're sure about that one?"

Brooke nodded. "Absolutely." The name hadn't even been a question. As soon as they found out it was a girl, she knew. "Scarlett Hayden," she said, and felt Noah nod his head in agreement as he held her close.

They stood that way for a long time, watching Lara dart about in the late afternoon sunshine. The birds continued to sing their songs, playing in the branches up above as Lara played down below. The forest around them was quiet and serene, the clearing warm and inviting. And, maybe, if they could just continue to be grateful for moments like this, and for the love in their lives and the simple joys in life, the deathly silence that accompanied their dark, insatiable winter visitor would never come. And the only calls they would ever hear in the night would be from the loons of the forest and the whispering of the wind.

**THANK YOU FOR READING!**

♥

If you enjoyed *Scarlett Springs*, please consider leaving a review. I read every single one of them, and they mean so much!

# *Acknowledgement*

As always, I would first like to thank my wonderful husband, Ryan McCrory. This book, along with my others, would not have been possible without his love, encouragement, and never-ending support as I follow my dreams. When I first started typing away three years ago (on an old, dusty laptop that Ryan had to get running again, by the way), I never thought it would lead to three completed novels. And it probably wouldn't have, if it weren't for Ryan's unwavering support along the way. It was his faith in my abilities that got me through those times of stress, frustration, and suffocating self-doubt that go hand in hand with following a dream, and I cannot thank him enough for his belief in me as a writer. And also, for always pushing me to keep going, to keep moving forward, and most of all, to keep typing.

In addition to being my husband and constant supporter, Ryan is also about to become a father. *Scarlett Springs* is unique in the fact that the entire editing process was completed while I was pregnant with our first child, and I'm sure Ryan can attest that nothing makes editing sessions and typo patrol more delightful than morning sickness and pregnancy hormones. And yet, he's been there through it all, cheering me on in more ways than one. I think it is safe to say that not only is he a devoted husband, skilled cover artist, and insightful developmental editor, but he's also about to be one hell of a dad. So, thank you, dear husband, for all that you do for me, and for all that you're about to do for our son. There's no one else on this earth I would rather go on this journey with other than you.

I would also like to thank my family, whose support has meant so much to me along the way. Thank you to my mother, Nancy Dufour, to my father-in-law and mother-in-law, Mike and Betty McCrory, and to my brothers-in-law, Michael McCrory and Randy Ballesteros. I truly appreciate your unyielding encouragement while I pursue my dreams.

Thank you to my father, Larry Dufour, for passing his love of reading on to me. It was that passion for reading that led me down the path of becoming an author, and this book wouldn't be here without it. He will forever be missed, and I hope, wherever he may be, that he gets a chance to read this story. I think he would have liked it.

And finally, I would like to thank you—yes, you—dear reader. Thank you for giving my humble book a try. This is my third novel, but I don't think it will ever stop amazing me that you not only found this book, but also enjoyed it enough to make it this far. Writing is something I do because I have stories I want to tell, but to tell a story you need to have someone to listen. *You.* You may not always be thinking of me, but believe me, I am thinking of you—in every character, in every word, in every comma. Someday I would like to dedicate all of my time to writing stories for you to enjoy, but that can't be possible without your help. So, if you enjoyed this book, please don't keep it a secret. Leave a rating on Amazon or Goodreads. Let your friends and family know about the time we've shared. Only with your continued support will we get to share more time together. Time where I can tell you another story. I'm already working on it. So thank you, dear reader, for reading this book. I hope you enjoyed reading it as much as I enjoyed writing it!

Until next time,
Danielle McCrory

# WASP CANYON

## A NOVEL

**WHEN THE DARKNESS COMES, THE TEETH AND THE CLAWS COME WITH IT.**

Jessica Cleary took up running the Arizona hiking trails as a way to cope with the recent loss of her father. While out on a run in Wasp Canyon, Jessica stumbles upon a gruesome scene and finds herself injured and running for her life.

There is something lurking inside Wasp Canyon—something vicious, cunning, and with an insatiable appetite. When people in town start falling victim to a mysterious predator and the police are unable to offer any explanation, Jessica decides it's time to stop running—it's time to stop running and fight.

*Also by Danielle McCrory*

# FOSTER

*A Love Story*

Skyler Seabrooke lives for helping animals. Those in need of saving, she saves. Those in need of fostering, she fosters. Skyler is a hard-working employee at the local animal shelter, and has dedicated more than half her life to rescuing and caring for animals in need.

When Skyler gets a call about an abandoned animal on the outskirts of town, she doesn't hesitate to go out and rescue it before the animal succumbs to the elements. This infant is different, though, and as it begins to grow under Skyler's foster care, she realizes she is caring for something that doesn't belong in her home. It's something big— something dangerous. Skyler knows allowing it to stay with her isn't safe, but the love she has for her foster pet is overpowering her sense of right and wrong.

As the repercussions for keeping such a dangerous animal become horrifically apparent to Skyler, she is forced to make a difficult decision. Just how far is she willing to go to protect the foster pet she has come to love? She needs to decide quickly, though, because unbeknownst to Skyler, time is running out for the both of them.

# About the Author

Danielle McCrory was born and raised in Tucson, Arizona. She has degrees in Graphic Design and Physical Therapy. Danielle started writing because she believes there are still so many scary stories left untold. Danielle loves horror movies, animals, rainy days, and Halloween. She lives in Tucson with her husband, Ryan McCrory.